# THE FLAME TREE

## SIOBHAN DAIKO

Published by ASOLANDO BOOKS

First Edition 2023

The English used in this publication follows the spelling and idiomatic conventions of the United Kingdom.

The moral right of the author has been asserted.

No part of this publication may be reproduced, stored in a retrieval system, or transmitted in any form or by any means without the prior permission in writing of the publisher, except in the case of brief quotations embodied in critical reviews and certain other non-commercial uses permitted by the copyright law. For permission requests, write to the publisher at the email address below.

This is a work of fiction. All characters in this publication, other than those clearly in the public domain, are fictitious and any resemblance to real persons, living or dead, is purely coincidental.

Copyright © 2023 Siobhan Daiko

All rights reserved.

All enquiries to asolandobooks@gmail.com

Developmental editing by John Hudspith

Content editing by Trenda Lundin

Cover design by JD Smith

*For Diarmuid*

# MAIN LOCATIONS

# CHAPTER ONE

## LONDON, 17TH APRIL 1939

Will pulled his jacket collar up around his ears as he stood on the promenade deck of the P&O liner *RMS Carthage*. A chill wind whipped around him and the purr of the ship's engines vibrated under his feet. The other passengers were leaning over the railings and holding onto multi-coloured paper streamers linking them to their loved ones on the dock below. But no one was there to see Will off before he left to start a new life in Hong Kong. He didn't mind; he'd said goodbye to Mama, Papa and his little brother, Jeremy, earlier that day at Temple Meads in Bristol. Too much of a palaver for them to journey to London with him, Papa had said. He'd added that, at twenty-three years of age, Will was independent enough to cope with getting himself and his luggage to Tilbury on his own.

Four deep blasts resounded from the ship's horn and a thrill coursed through Will. Two sailors were casting off the ropes, and a pair of tugs, their dirty smokestacks caked with brine, began to nudge the *Carthage* out into the middle of the Thames. The streamers linking his fellow-passengers to the people on the quay below snapped, and Will gazed at the docks receding into the distance while the liner headed into the estuary.

He breathed in the fresh sea air. The subtle whisper of an exotic perfume—with hints of jasmine if he wasn't mistaken—wafted towards him. He glanced around for the source of the scent. A lone young woman was turning away from the railings. Bundled up in a navy woollen coat with a bright red scarf around her neck, her long, dark brown hair lashed by the wind, she brushed past him and strode in the direction of the doors to the first-class lounge.

Will stepped into the salon to look for her. He took a step back; the room was just like the dining hall of a baronial lodge in Scotland—fireplace, panelled roof, leather armchairs, crossed tapers on the wall, and mounted stag's head. But it was empty apart from a man in a tweed suit, who was sitting reading a newspaper. Will shrugged and went down to his cabin.

Later, after unpacking, Will slipped on his dinner jacket, and checked his reflection in the mirror above the basin in his private bathroom—simply fitted with a shower and a WC. He adjusted his black tie and made sure his cufflinks were in place. How lucky he was to have fallen on his feet like this. He'd been recruited as a cadet in the colonial service after his graduation last summer in Classics at University College, Oxford. He'd subsequently taken a training course in London. At his interview, he'd said he'd grown up reading Kipling and had been inspired by Robert Louis Stevenson's poem about a young boy who'd wanted to travel to China. *There I'll come when I'm a man, with a camel caravan.* Will remembered the words he'd memorised when he was a ten-year-old, words that still resonated with him—although lately he'd been enjoying the more adult Far Eastern tales and travelogues of Somerset Maugham, which had whetted his appetite for life in the orient even more. His interviewer, a brittle middle-aged man from the Colonial Office, had pointed out that the British Empire stretched around the globe. Besides India, the largest colonies were in Africa and, in the east, the most important outposts were in Ceylon, Malaya, Sarawak and North Borneo, and wouldn't Will have preferred to have gone there? But Will had declined. China called to him and that's where he was heading.

He stepped back into his well-appointed single cabin, furnished with an actual bed, not a bunk, and boasting a chest-of-drawers and a desk. He was travelling in the height of luxury to his dream job. One qualm niggled, however—he'd struggled with the speaking skills element of the initial Cantonese course he'd been required to take during his training.

He'd never imagined it would be so difficult for someone of his acclaimed linguistic abilities. But Chinese didn't use an alphabetical writing system like Latin, in which he'd excelled. Instead, Chinese used characters that were composed of parts that depicted physical objects or abstract ideas. And there were no concrete rules for how a character should be pronounced based on its appearance. He'd had to turn everything he thought he knew about language learning on its head. What made Chinese even more different was the fact that it was a tonal language. The meaning of a word could change, depending on the pitch that was used, even if the pronunciation was the same. To make matters even worse, there were six tones in the Cantonese spoken in Hong Kong, compared with four in Mandarin. It had made him almost want to tear his hair out. But he was determined to get to grips with it and he hoped that, once he was in the colony, where he would be immersed in the language, he'd find it easier to learn.

Adjusting his cufflinks again, Will peered out of the porthole of his cabin at the dark sea below. The wind had dropped, and the Channel, reflecting the moonlight, was as calm as a millpond. No doubt the *Carthage* would encounter rougher conditions as it made its way through the Bay of Biscay and onwards. He turned away. The ship was much smaller than he'd expected—he'd imagined a floating castle like the more glamorous *Queen Mary*. Instead, the *Carthage* was much lower in the water; she would probably roll about a lot in big seas. But Will wasn't concerned; he was a good sailor and had never been seasick when he'd taken part in sailing events at school.

The brassy sound of the dinner gong echoed through his door, and his stomach rumbled with sudden hunger. He left his cabin and stepped into the passageway leading to the dining room. The carpet felt soft beneath the soles of his dress shoes as he breathed in the aroma of fresh paint and polish. He remembered the subtle perfume of the woman he'd noticed earlier. The look of her small yet perfect form had made him wish he'd seen her face, and he hoped he would bump into her again. The trip to Hong Kong would take over a month and it might be amusing to pass the time in the company of a woman. Will chuckled to himself...fat chance of a shipboard romance. He was no Romeo and had a poor track record as far as girls were concerned. As soon as they found out his ambitions lay on the other side of the world, they ran a mile.

At the entrance to the spacious dining room, a waiter assigned him to a round table with twelve chairs, and Will introduced himself to the nine people already present. He took his seat and regarded his fellow-guests. On his left sat the Hendersons, a quiet young couple who were heading as far as Bombay, where the husband would take up a post in the Indian Civil Service. They were chatting to an Australian called Carter, who'd spent four years at Cambridge and was going home to his family in Melbourne, catching an onward connection from Hong Kong. To Will's right sat two chaps of about his age, Atkinson and Webb, who were joining the Hong Kong and Shanghai Banking Corporation. To their right was another couple, the Bakers, also travelling to the Hong Kong, Mr Baker would work for Jardine

# THE FLAME TREE

Matheson. The final couple were older—Harry Wyn-Jones and his red-headed wife, Margaret. Harry was Director of Medical Services in Hong Kong, he explained, and they were returning to the colony after a period of leave in England.

Their waiter arrived with a tureen of soup and began ladling out portions, so Will presumed the final two seats would be taken by passengers joining the ship from a later port. He lowered his head and took a spoonful of the chicken broth. The unmistakable scent he'd encountered earlier made him glance up. The girl who'd walked past him that afternoon had pulled out a chair. She was dressed in a stunning pale grey silk cheongsam, but she wasn't Chinese. Her beautiful almond shaped oriental eyes shone brightly in a face with delicate European features, bearing witness to a mixed heritage. 'Good evening,' she said politely. 'Sorry to be late to dinner. My name is Constance Han, Connie for short.' She indicated a buxom woman with frizzy grey hair, who'd come up from behind. 'This is Gloria, my old governess, who's travelling back to Hong Kong with me.'

'Not so much of the "old", young lady,' the woman said, laughing. She shook hands around the table. 'There's plenty of spark in me yet, or I wouldn't have the energy to look after Connie's nieces and nephews.'

'I know your father,' Harry said to Connie. 'Delighted to make the acquaintance of his daughter.'

'His youngest daughter,' Connie clarified. 'I've missed my family so much and can't wait to return. Three years studying in England has seemed like a lifetime...'

'Were you up at university?' Harry asked.

'I read English at King's in London.' She spooned soup into her mouth, then dabbed it with a starched napkin.

'Connie has just graduated with a First,' Gloria chipped in. 'We're so proud of her.'

'All thanks to you teaching me such good speaking and listening skills,' Connie said.

Will had already noticed she spoke without any trace of a Chinese accent. He longed to ask her more about herself, but that would have been impolite.

Conversation soon turned to the Spanish Civil war ending, and Adolf Hitler's latest shenanigans in Europe. Margaret expressed her worry about Chamberlain offering a "guarantee" of the independence of Poland. She added that she hoped there wouldn't be another war. 'The last one was meant to be the war that ended all wars,' she said.

'Not going to come that, dear girl.' Harry patted her hand. 'No more doom and gloom. Let's talk of more pleasant things.'

Which is what they did, in solid British fashion, discussing the weather, the King and the two young princesses, and then the film, *Marco Polo*, which Mrs Baker had thought "spectacular". She was quickly disabused of her opinion by the rest of the table.

'Hollywoodian make-believe,' Gloria declared, and everyone else agreed with her.

Will had seen the movie and thought it was lacking in action.

After coffee, the ladies went to their cabins while the men retired to the smoking lounge.

Nursing a glass of port and a cigar, Will sat back in a leather armchair, and shot Harry Wyn-Jones a glance. 'Connie Han seems like an interesting person,' he said with deliberate casualness. 'You said you know her father?'

'She's the daughter of Sir Albert Han Fung, a multimillionaire Eurasian businessman. They live on the Peak.' Harry blew out cigar smoke. 'The only non-European family allowed to live up there.'

'What do you mean by allowed to live up there?' Will leant forward in his chair.

# THE FLAME TREE

'It's strictly for whites, dear boy. Not that I agree with the ruling. Far from it. Margaret and I consider ourselves reformers and would like to see places like the Peak opened up to everyone.' He shook his head. 'Sir Albert was already living there when the law was introduced. His co-wife thought it would be healthier for their children.'

'His co-wife?' Will couldn't help his jaw dropping. 'He has more than one wife?'

Harry nodded. 'Albert Han Fung's first wife, Ada, was unable to have children, but he loved her and decided not to divorce her. Instead he proposed to adopt the firstborn child of his Chinese concubine instead. After years of trying for a baby, the concubine gave birth to a daughter. Knowing how much Albert wanted a son, Ada persuaded her maternal cousin, Grace, to accept him as co-wife. Grace later gave birth to two sons and four daughters— Connie is the youngest.' Harry smirked, taking in Will's expression. 'You look shocked.'

'Isn't that bigamous?'

'Bigamy is perfectly legal in Chinese society and tradition. Despite being of mixed ethnicity, Sir Albert considers himself fully Chinese, which is also reflected in his way of dressing in traditional long robes. He was knighted after representing Hong Kong at an exhibition in London, an occasion in which he was able to meet Queen Mary, but his allegiances are all with China.'

'Ah,' Will responded, not knowing what else to say. There was much he'd have to learn about Hong Kong's peculiarities, that was for sure. He knocked back the rest of his port and put out his cigar. 'I'll bid you good night, then,' he said.

'Good night, dear boy.' Harry waved him off.

In his cabin, Will changed into pyjamas, used the bathroom, then climbed into bed. But sleep eluded him. His mind was in too much of a whirl. Words chased each other through his head and the only way to settle them would be to get them down on paper. Writing poetry was his way of making sense of the world. A pastime he kept to himself. Will didn't consider his efforts worthy of public scrutiny, but they were as essential to him as breathing. He went to the desk and retrieved his writing case from the drawer where he'd stowed it earlier. He took out a sheet of paper and wrote.

> *I met a girl*
> *With eastern eyes under western skies*
> *But soon it will be*
> *My western eyes under her eastern skies*
> *What lies before me*
> *I ask myself.*

Absolute rubbish, he thought, screwing up the piece of paper. He returned to bed, staring at the darkness through the porthole, and saw Connie Han's beautiful eyes shining back at him, her delicate smile as she dabbed at her lips with her napkin.

He couldn't help smiling now. Perhaps he'd have another try at that poem tomorrow.

# CHAPTER TWO

Connie lay in the luxurious two-bedded cabin she shared with Gloria, the rumble of her old governess's snores keeping her awake. She thought about the passengers she'd met that evening. While they were getting ready for bed, Gloria had told her that a friend of hers was a nurse at the Queen Mary Hospital on Hong Kong Island, and this friend had gossiped about Margaret Wyn-Jones. Apparently, the Director of Medical Services' wife was known as "Red Margaret". Connie responded that Margaret's hair was the reddest she'd ever seen, but Gloria had laughed and said the nickname wasn't because of the colour of Margaret's hair but because of her left-wing sympathies. Connie had expressed surprise—her first impressions of the redhead were of a "do-gooder" rather than a "left winger".

Connie sighed to herself—she'd encountered left wingers while at university. A fellow student had tried to persuade her to join a communist group. At the time, she'd made the excuse she wasn't interested in politics, which wasn't true as she'd been following developments in mainland China since she was old enough to understand them. Father had donated generously to Dr Sun Yat-sen's campaigns to establish the Republic of China well before she was born, and was now an ardent supporter of his successor, the nationalist Generalissimo Chiang Kai

Shek—who was fervently anti-communist and whose troops were fighting them. In fact, Connie's brother, Matthew, was a commander in the nationalist army and fought against both the communists and the Japanese. Connie supported the Chinese nationalists as well, so she kept out of left-wing politics in London and took a first-aid course instead, spending her free time doing volunteer work with the St John's Ambulance Association.

The thrum of the *Carthage's* engines vibrating through her mattress, Connie rolled over in bed and turned her thoughts to Will Burton, the young man she'd met at dinner. Dashingly handsome, with light brown wavy hair and vibrant indigo blue eyes. She'd found out in conversation that he was a cadet in the colonial service. Connie remembered Father telling her about the cadets when she'd asked him how Hong Kong was governed. He'd said they were cardboard cut-outs of each other. All came from solid, though not rich, upper middle-class families, and had studied at public schools, though not the most prestigious. They generally attended one of the older universities, where they read classics or history and stood out for their application to study and for their interest in sport. Cadets came into the colonial service with many shared beliefs about attitudes towards the communities they were to govern, a stance they'd learned from their backgrounds and public-school education. They were groomed to rule "the people" and protect them from local and foreign injustice while living apart from them, whether at home or abroad.

Connie fully expected Will to conform to that archetype. She would have nothing in common with him, which was perfectly all right as far as she was concerned. Connie had kept herself to herself in London and she would do the same on the voyage home. She couldn't wait to return to her own environment and to catch up with her extended family. With a self-deprecating sigh, the thought occurred to her that she wasn't unlike the British cadets she'd been so quick to disparage. Everyone felt more comfortable with what was familiar to them. It was only natural.

The *Carthage* gave a sudden roll, jolting her into awareness of a different reality. Oh, God, she thought, the sea had turned rough. She'd suffered from terrible seasickness on the journey out to England. Nausea swelled in her stomach and filled her throat. She leapt out of bed and ran to the bathroom, only making it just in time before she was violently sick.

'How are you feeling this morning?' Gloria asked Connie a week or so later, pouring her a cup of tea in their cabin. 'You're looking a little brighter.'

'A lot better, thanks.' Connie sipped her drink and glanced out of the porthole at the sandy banks of the Suez Canal. 'Perhaps I've got my sea legs at last.'

'You should go up on deck and get some fresh air. You've been closeted far too long.'

'I couldn't keep much down, you know.' Connie shook her head. 'It was the same on the outward voyage four years ago. My tummy took ages before it could manage anything other than toast.'

Gloria patted her arm. 'Shame you missed experiencing Port Said…'

'Oh, I was well enough to do that on the way out. I'll never forget the Gully Gully Man.' The Egyptian magician had come on board dressed in a long robe, a red tarboosh with a tassel on his head. She'd travelled with Mother that time—Gloria had started looking after Connie's sister Mary's children in Hong Kong and wasn't due any leave yet. The magician's special trick, relying solely on sleight of hand, had been to produce baby chicks from behind passengers' ears, their mouths, and the back of their knees, all the while intoning, *Gully, gully.*

'He was very entertaining.' Gloria placed her teacup on the table. 'Well, I'm off to the lounge to meet the ladies from our dinner table for a bridge rubber. I hope I'll see you in the dining room at lunchtime, my dear.'

'I hope so too.'

After Gloria had bustled off, Connie dressed herself in shorts and a blouse. She slipped on a pair of espadrilles, grabbed her sun hat, and made her way up the companionway to the promenade deck.

Hot wind hit her like a slap in the face. On shaky legs, she went to the railings and clung onto them, taking in deep breaths. The light was almost blinding after spending so long in the gloom of her cabin, and she wished she'd brought her dark glasses. She shaded her eyes with a hand and squinted at the scenery. Empty desert surrounded the banks of the canal—the manmade waterway connecting the Mediterranean with the Red Sea. She turned to look towards where the *Carthage* was heading, but a sudden gust lifted her hat from her head and sent it tumbling along the deck.

Her head spinning, Connie chased after it. A man was lounging on a deckchair. He rose, grabbed hold of the hat, and held it out as she approached him. She recognised Will Burton and smiled. 'Thank you so much. I'm so sorry to disturb you.' She glanced at the notebook he'd left on his chair. 'Were you working?'

# THE FLAME TREE

'Just doing a bit of writing.' He gave her a warm smile. 'It's good to see you up and about. Gloria told us you'd been suffering from seasickness.'

'It's terribly annoying to be a bad sailor.' She wobbled on her feet. 'Sorry, but I need to sit down. The strength has gone from my legs.'

Concern flashed in his vivid blue eyes. He indicated the deck chair next to his. 'Lower yourself gently.'

She did as he'd suggested, gratefully accepting the pillow he handed her to place behind her head.

'I'll go and fetch you a glass of water.' He set off for the first-class lounge.

She glanced at the open page of the notebook and couldn't help reading the words.

> *There, beneath the waves she sleeps*
> *Who would dare to raise her from the deep?*
> *Neptune's bride*
> *A mermaid from the east*

Was Will a poet? She didn't want to appear nosey, so she couldn't ask him outright. She kept her gaze averted from the page as he returned with the water.

'Here you are.' Will gave her the glass. 'Sip it slowly, or you might feel sick again.' He shut the notebook and perched on his deckchair while she drank.

The sandy banks of the canal were giving way to the higher, more rugged ground of the Sinai Peninsula, and the small, white-washed town of Suez glistened in the searing desert heat. She inhaled the scent borne on the wind. 'I love the smell.'

'The smell?' Will quirked a brow.

'It's the smell of the orient. People, exotic foods, spices. In Hong Kong it's mixed with the scent of joss sticks.' She took a big breath then released it. 'I've missed this smell so much.'

'It must have been hard for you to be away from your home.' He looked her in the eye. 'Why did you go to university in England if you don't mind my asking?'

'I wanted to go to the University of Hong Kong, but as I was considered a Chinese, I needed to have taken the Chinese entrance exam. My mother had sent me to an English-speaking school, so I gained entrance to a British university instead.'

'Don't you speak Chinese?'

'Oh, yes. I'm bi-lingual. I grew up speaking it with the servants at home and I can read and write it fluently. But, if I'd wanted to stay in Hong Kong it would have meant me going to a Chinese school for a couple of more years to prepare for the test. I persuaded my parents to let me study in England instead.' She put down her glass. 'Where did *you* go to school, Will?'

He told her he'd attended Clifton College in Bristol before going up to Oxford, where he'd read classics. She couldn't resist a wry smile that he conformed to the archetype. Except, perhaps there was something about him. Something different. Might it be the poetry? She itched to ask him about it but didn't want to confess to having read what he'd written. If, indeed, it had been he who had written it. 'I read English at King's,' she said. 'I love the Romantic poets. Especially Wordsworth.'

'*We poets in our youth begin in gladness; But thereof comes in the end despondency and madness,*' he quoted. 'They certainly took themselves extremely seriously...'

'What made you join the colonial service?' She'd given him the chance to admit to being a poet, but he hadn't taken it. He must have had a good reason for that, so she'd decided not to probe and had changed the subject instead.

'I couldn't envisage a life spent commuting to and from a job in England. China has always fascinated me.' His brow furrowed. 'Except now I have to learn Chinese and, to be honest, I'm finding the speaking element extremely difficult.'

'Are you musical? I mean, can you perceive differences in musical pitch?'

'I can sing a tune accurately, I think. I was in the choir at school. But why? Is it because of the tones?'

'So, you know about them?'

He nodded. 'I was given a taster course in London. Once in Hong Kong, I will need to master speaking Cantonese completely before I can start in my first posting. It's a little daunting, to say the least.'

'I can give you some lessons if you like.'

'Why would you want to do that? I don't mean to come across as ungrateful...' He sounded incredulous.

She'd made the offer spontaneously, without thinking about it. Will had revealed something about himself, a vulnerability that had touched her, and she wanted to help. 'It would be a way for me to pass time on the journey and might give you more confidence,' she said.

'Thank you, Connie.' A smile brushed his lips. 'I'm happy to accept.'

She glanced away from him, suddenly shy. The call of seagulls rippled through the air, and she rose to her feet. She made her way to the railings and he followed her. There, they stood and gazed at the sea.

A manatee broke the smooth surface, making kissing sounds with its bearded mouth, and a flamboyance of pink flamingos flapped past.

'How beautiful,' Will said.

The word "enchanting" popped into Connie's head and she wondered if he would write a poem about the birds.

# CHAPTER THREE

After dinner, Will waltzed Margaret across the polished parquet floor to the tune of *Blue Danube*, played by the ship's band. Dancing on board the *Carthage* took place in a separate area to the dining room. The folding double doors, opening onto the forward sports deck, let in the cool night air, and he caught the scent of Connie's jasmine perfume as she glided past, partnered by Harry.

Will was glad she'd stayed to dance. Earlier, after lunch, she'd retired to her cabin, pleading tiredness when Will had suggested a game of deck quoits. 'I'm not very good at it,' she'd added. 'But I'd love to play when I'm feeling stronger.'

'I'll look forward to it,' he'd said. Of course she was tired; she'd only just recovered from seasickness and needed to regain her strength.

He'd played and beaten both the Hong Kong bank boys, Atkinson and Webb, in separate matches. Then he'd gone for a dip in the plunge pool and had dried off on the sun deck before heading down to his cabin to dress for dinner.

The meal had seemed interminable while he'd waited for the dancing to start. He'd hoped Connie would linger; he couldn't wait to twirl her around the floor. Until that night, he'd partnered Gloria and the married women at his table. Atkinson and

# THE FLAME TREE

Webb, together with Carter the Australian, had danced with the single ladies at other tables who Harry had described as being part of the ubiquitous "fishing fleet"—girls who travelled to India, Singapore, or Hong Kong and stayed with friends or relatives while they "fished" for a husband. But Will hadn't been able to summon up any interest in the unmarried Englishwomen on board the *Carthage*. All he'd thought about had been Connie's beautiful eyes and her captivating smile. He wanted to get to know her, wanted to find out if her personality was as attractive as her looks. And, that morning, when she'd offered to help him practise speaking Cantonese, she'd revealed herself to be as lovely as he'd hoped she would be.

The singer switched to *The Way You Look Tonight*, and Margaret said she'd sit the dance out. Harry and Connie were heading back to their table and Will seized his chance. 'Would you do me the honour, Connie?' he asked with a bow.

The lyrics could have been written to describe how *she* looked that night, she was so beautiful, Will thought as he led her into a foxtrot. She placed one hand on his shoulder and the other in *his* hand, the short sleeves of her pale blue silk cheongsam revealing her slender upper arms. And it occurred to him that her warm smile and tinkling laugh had touched *his* foolish heart, just like the words of the song.

Soon, he was dancing her through the open doors onto the deck. Above them, the moon cut a sliver of silver in a sky that billowed with stars. She faltered and he asked if she needed a rest.

'Just a short one,' she said. 'While I get my breath back.'

They found a deckchair and shared it, sitting next to each other on the footrest while the soft night air soothed them.

He offered her a cigarette, a Player's, which she accepted. She cupped his hand while he lit it, so the breeze wouldn't blow out the match. 'I don't usually smoke,' she admitted with a slight cough.

Will found an ashtray, then lit his own cigarette and took a deep draw. He was about to ask her about his first Cantonese lesson, when Gloria bustled out onto the deck.

'Oh, there you are, Connie,' she huffed. 'You shouldn't be staying up so late. You've only just got better.'

Connie put out her cigarette. She bent her head to Will's while her old governess went back inside. 'Meet me in the library after breakfast for your first lesson,' she whispered. 'Gloria will be playing bridge then.'

'Must you go?'

'I'd better. Father asked Gloria to keep an eye on me...'

Alone on the sports deck, Will tapped the ash from his cigarette. Connie clearly followed the three-thousand-year-old Chinese philosophy of filial duty, or *Xiao*. Will remembered learning about China's arguably most important moral tenet. Children were required to defer to their parents and other elders in the family, even when they themselves became adults. And, given that the family was considered the building block of society, the hierarchical system of respect also applied by extension to the country and rulers of China. It was vital that Will understood the concept of *Xiao*, he was told on his course in London, as it would be paramount in his dealings with the Chinese.

He took a final drag from his cigarette, exhaled a puff of smoke, and stubbed it out. With a sigh of resignation he rose from the deckchair and returned to the entertainment centre for a nightcap before he went to bed.


'In Chinese we have no big words,' Connie said to Will the next morning at the table they'd purloined in the ship's library. 'And all our words are composed of only one syllable. Do you know how many words can be made that are no longer than a syllable?'

Will thought for a moment. 'A couple of hundred, I suppose...'

'Correct. About four hundred. That doesn't seem enough to make a whole language, does it?'

'Um... no, I wouldn't have thought so.'

'In Chinese, because we use only monosyllables, we use tones to add to the syllables and create more words. Foreigners trying to learn our language often find the tones intimidating, but they need not be so. You also use tones in English, by the way.'

'We do?'

'Of course.' Her laugh tinkled and Will couldn't help smiling. 'Think about the words, "you came". The significance is not the same as "You came?" One is a statement, the other is a question. The difference is the tone.'

'How enlightening!'

'In Chinese we use tones in a structured way,' she went on. 'The meaning of a word is conveyed by the monosyllable and its tone together.'

He nodded slowly that he understood... more or less.

'Every word pronounced in Cantonese has six tones. So four hundred monosyllables times six tones make two thousand four hundred. Extremely easy compared to English.' She smiled. 'Do you know how many words there are in your language?'

He shook his head sheepishly. He was a poet, perhaps this was something he should know...

'Over one hundred and seventy thousand.'

'Gosh! So many. I would never have guessed. Although maybe it's easier to remember separate words than to memorise six tones for every word.'

A frown creased her brow. 'You are putting obstacles in your way before you've started. You said you are musical. So, you will have no problem. For instance, 'Go go go go.'

'Come again?'

'It means "that big brother". *Go go* and *go go*. Can you hear the difference? *Go go* means "that one" and *go go* means "big brother".'

'Ah...'

'There are nine sounds and six tones in Cantonese. You must raise, maintain, or lower the pitch of your voice to "sing" each word. "Si", for example, can mean "poem", "history", "try", "time", "market" or "to be", depending on the tone. Listen to me and repeat.'

Connie's tone of voice and pitch varied for each word. They carried on with the lesson for about an hour, Will practicing and making copious notes in his pad. As soon as he'd mastered one word, Connie moved on to the next.

'I think I've pushed you hard enough for now,' she said finally. 'Let's take a break.'

'I thought you'd never ask.' He chuckled. 'My brain feels as if it's about to explode.'

She laughed again. 'How about we go up on deck for some fresh air?'

'Perfect.'

Standing at the ship's railings, Connie gazed down at the sea. 'Are you a good swimmer, Will?'

'I like to think that I am. I swam for my school in Bristol and then for University College, Oxford. How about you?'

'I'm all right in a pool, but I'm terrified of swimming in the sea.'

'Why is that?'

'We used to motor to one of Hong Kong's outlying islands on Father's launch when I was little to we could swim off the quieter beaches. One time, when I was ten, I was swimming back to the launch when I saw a shark's fin surface right next to me. It was terrifying, and since then I haven't been able to bring myself to go back into the sea. Every summer there are shark attacks in Hong Kong...'

He caught the fear in her eyes. She abruptly turned away. 'It's nearly lunchtime. Let's go and have a drink in the bar. We can wait for the others there before going through to the dining room.'

'Sounds like an excellent plan,' he said.

Will met Connie every morning in the library while Gloria played bridge. He hadn't been surprised when Connie had told him she'd confessed to Gloria she was teaching him Cantonese. Connie's sense of filial duty would have prompted her to be straightforward and, evidently, Gloria had wished her well with the task. Will couldn't help thinking that was because they were in full view of everyone. Their moments alone were few and far between, and Will had to resign himself to the fact that Gloria took her responsibilities seriously, keeping an eye on Connie as instructed by Sir Albert. Perhaps, once he and Connie were in Hong Kong, there would be opportunities for him to see her alone. She was enchanting and he wanted to take things further provided she felt the same way.

In the meantime, he had to content himself with her being his teacher. Connie made vocabulary cards for him—the English word on one side, the Chinese word, spelt out phonetically, on the other. Sometimes, she gave him on-the-spot tests to ensure he remembered what she'd taught him, which could be quite daunting. But he was eager to learn and enjoyed the lessons immensely. Not only was he gradually getting to grips with the language, but his sessions with Connie allowed him to spend time in her charming company.

Soon, Connie said she was feeling up to playing deck quoits in the afternoons. She was right about not being that good at the game, but Will was delighted to partner her in a tournament and didn't mind at all when they lost to Webb and Atkinson. Just the sight of her determined expression as she lobbed the rope rings at the target gladdened his heart.

They docked in Bombay to let off and take on new passengers. There, they said goodbye to the Hendersons. After the peace of the long days at sea, the city appeared overcrowded and dirty. There wasn't time to go ashore and Will was relieved when they set sail again; he couldn't wait to resume his morning lessons, afternoon deck quoits, and evenings spent dancing under the stars.

As they sailed further south, the heat increased exponentially and the fierce sun became ever more relentless. At night, Will opened the porthole of his cabin to cool down his sweat-drenched body. All par for the course, he thought. It would be even hotter in Hong Kong and at least he was getting somewhat acclimatised. He and his fellow first-class male passengers switched from black dinner jackets to white in the evenings and the ladies put on flimsier gowns. Connie wore sleeveless cheongsams, made of soft linen instead of silk brocade. They were shorter than those she'd worn at the start of the voyage; the slits at the sides presumably made them cooler and he liked the fact that they revealed more of her long, slender legs.

In Singapore, Connie and Gloria were whisked off by one of Sir Albert's friends, who took them out for lunch at Raffles Hotel. Will had to content himself with exploring on his own. He went to the Chinese quarter and tested his spoken Cantonese in a herbalist's shop, where he bought a jar of Tiger Balm ointment. It was gratifying to have been able to communicate and to have understood what the shopkeeper said to him. Back on board, during his lesson the following morning, he told Connie about the sense of achievement he'd felt, and she said she was proud of him.

Now they were only a day away from arriving in Hong Kong and Will still hadn't kissed her. There'd been many occasions when he'd wanted to, but Gloria watched Connie like an overbearing hawk. Tonight, however, Gloria had stayed down in the cabin she shared with Connie. She'd eaten something at lunchtime that had upset her stomach, apparently. So, Will hoped he'd get his chance.

After partnering the other ladies at the table, he quickstepped Connie around the floor to the tune of *Puttin' On the Ritz*, then led her out onto the sports deck to cool off. They sat next to each other on the footstool of a deck chair.

'I'll miss dancing with you, Will,' she said, staring into the distance.

'Why? I'm hoping I'll be able to take you dancing in Hong Kong.'

She turned to face him, her expression serious. 'Hasn't anyone told you about how life is there?'

'What do you mean?'

'I cannot be seen with you.'

'Why ever not?' He couldn't keep the surprise from his voice.

'I cannot be seen with a European man on my own. It would ruin my chances of making a good Chinese marriage.'

Will's heart sank. 'What if you decided not to marry a Chinese? What if you decided to marry an Englishman?'

'I'm afraid that could never happen. Girls from my background don't marry Europeans. Only girls from the lower classes...'

A sinking feeling came over him. 'Let me get this right. You're telling me this is it? That we won't be able to see each other once we've arrived in Hong Kong?'

'I'm sorry.' She placed her hand on his arm. 'You'll soon find out how things are done. I expect one of the first things you'll be told is not to get involved with a local girl. I'm sure you'll be invited to parties where you'll meet many highly suitable women.'

'But I don't want to meet anyone else, Connie, now I've met you.' He sounded devastated, and he was.

She gazed at him, her beautiful eyes deep pools of regret.

He lifted his hand and stroked her soft cheek. He couldn't help himself—so warm and lovely. He leant in and kissed her gently on the mouth. She pulled back with a gasp.

'Sorry,' he murmured, horrified with himself for acting so rashly.

But then, she lifted her face and pressed her lips to his, and he kissed her properly and she kissed him back.

She broke off and looked intensely into his eyes, her hands on the sides of his face. 'I'd better go down to my cabin.'

'You can't not see me in Hong Kong. Not after kissing me like that, Connie.' He returned her gaze.

'It will be very difficult. Are you sure this is what you want? We'd only be able to meet in secret. I cannot openly defy my parents. It would go against everything I believe in...'

'I understand.' He breathed a heavy sigh. 'But I can't envisage my life without you in it, however limited. Besides, you're my teacher, aren't you? I need you to keep teaching me Cantonese.'

'You will have excellent teachers provided by the Colonial Service.'

'Ah, but they won't be as good as you.'

She gazed into the distance again, then turned back to him. 'There is one place where we could meet, maybe, from time to time. The Botanical Gardens behind Government House. It isn't far from the Peak Tram station, which I use when I come down to the central district.'

'But how will I know when to meet you?' It struck him that Connie was being deliberately vague.

'I will find a way to get in touch with you somehow.'

'Can't I telephone you even?'

She chewed on her lip. 'Better not. I'll phone the Colonial Secretariat and leave a message for you. Would that be alright?'

'I suppose so...'

She brushed a quick kiss to his cheek. 'Goodnight, Will.'

Without another word, she got to her feet and made her way back indoors, the subtle scent of her perfume lingering in her wake.

Will lit a cigarette and took a draw. How could this have happened? He'd fallen for a girl who was seemingly beyond his reach. He should have known better, should have found out more about the social norms in Hong Kong. Connie was the daughter of Sir Albert Han Fung. A powerful man, by all accounts. He would have to tread very carefully once he arrived in the colony. He wouldn't give up on her, though. Her kiss had spoken more than words ever could.

## Chapter Four

Connie was standing on the foredeck with Will beside her. They'd come up straight after breakfast to take in the sights as the *Carthage* entered the western approaches to Hong Kong. She'd been a little awkward with him at the table; she'd spent practically the entire night tossing and turning and thinking about him. It had come as a shock when he'd asked if he could take her out dancing—she'd thought he knew about the colony's social norms—and she'd felt terrible about having to turn him down. His face, a picture of dejection, had made her want to weep. When he'd kissed her, she hadn't wanted him to stop, and so she'd recklessly kissed him back. What had got into her? She'd never behaved in such an uncontrolled fashion before in her life. And now she'd promised to carry on seeing him. In the Botanical Gardens, of all places. The location had popped into her head on the spur of the moment. How very irresponsible of her.

    She wiped perspiration from her brow with a handkerchief. The day had turned hot and sticky already. While they were sipping their morning coffee, Harry had conveyed the information that the temperature was 92° with 93 percent humidity. Typical of Hong Kong in May. Connie's dress clung to her and her nipples swelled uncomfortably against the rayon satin of her brassiere. Sweat gathered not only between her breasts, but also in the place between her thighs she always thought of as "down there". She'd never known such intense awareness of her body before this voyage; she'd become profoundly conscious of being a woman. *A woman basking in the admiration of a man.*

'Connie, there it is, just over the horizon. You can see a shape below the clouds,' the voice of said man exclaimed.

'Oh yes, indeed, Will.'

In the distance a plume of smoke rose, and the dark shapes of what she could barely make out as small craft bobbed beneath the elongated, vertical shadows of their sails. She smiled, breathing in familiar odours mixed with the clean tang of the sea: wood-smoke, incense, cooking spices and condiments.

Islands then appeared—some barren grey, others richly green—rising from the depths as the wind dispersed the early morning mist.

The *Carthage* was gliding through a narrow channel. On the left, a cliff loomed at the edge of a big land mass.

'Is that Hong Kong Island?' Will asked. 'Or is it mainland China?'

'Neither,' she answered. 'That's *Lantao*, which means Rocky Mount. Bigger than Hong Kong, it's our biggest island. The Portuguese, who settled Macao over four hundred years ago, called all these islands the *Ladrones*—Thieves. They were home to pirates until the British began clearing them out. The big thieves driving out the little thieves.' She gave an ironic laugh. 'Disorganised Chinese thieving gave way to organised English thieving.'

'It sounds as if you're anti-British, Connie. Is that so?'

'Not at all.' She shook her head. 'I was born in Hong Kong and consequently I have a British passport. But the British have done dreadful deeds here, despite having also done magnificent things.'

'Dreadful deeds and magnificent things?'

'Yes, both. Hong Kong was a barren, fever-ridden island of a few hundred fishermen and pirates. The British turned it into a great port. But the mansions you'll see aren't built on rock...they're built on the addictive juice of the opium poppy.' She shuddered.

'Ah, yes. I learnt about the Opium Wars on my course in London. It must have been a bitter pill for China to swallow, having to cede the territory of Hong Kong to British control and open treaty ports on the mainland for foreigners to trade from.'

'The Chinese government was forced to stand by while the British turned their people into opium addicts. They did this in the name of free trade and without any thought of the consequences.' Connie frowned. She didn't want to mention that her father and men like him had taken full advantage of the trading opportunities. It was a topic she would explore with Will later...if at all.

'Not everyone in Britain supported the opium trade,' he said.

'Let's not speak of this now. We are approaching Hong Kong Harbour. I'll point out the landmarks to you,' she said, quickly changing the subject. This wasn't the time nor the place for such a heavy discussion.

The grey shape on the horizon had turned into an island studded with irregular hills around a summit. 'That's Victoria Peak,' she indicated. 'Where I live.'

'It's beautiful.'

The *Carthage* was sailing past a tiny scrub-covered isle now, with a whitewashed lighthouse on top and two small houses clinging to its slopes. 'And that's Green Island,' Connie said.

'Very pretty.'

She pointed to where, on Hong Kong Island itself, rows of tenements built of bamboo, wood, and woven reeds descended in tiers like ramshackle steps to the harbour's edge. 'That's the Western District, *Sai Wan*. It's mostly inhabited by poor Chinese.'

'Fascinating,' Will exclaimed. 'Oh, my goodness. Look!'

Ahead, the harbour was forested with masts: the blunt masts of steamers, light-grey tripod mini-Eiffel Tower-shaped masts of naval ships, and the masts of a multitude of wooden Chinese junks. The latter always reminded Connie of high-pooped galleons skittering between the other vessels under their tattered patchwork sails—quilts of stained yellow, rusty brown, and faded purple stretched on frail bamboo ribs. She couldn't help marvelling that such fragile-looking sails remained intact and managed to drive the clumsy boats through the waves. The sight of the junks surging purposefully across the harbour, trailing twisted white wakes behind their square sterns, brought home to her that she was truly back in Hong Kong. And her heart lifted with joy.

Soon the *Carthage* was steaming past the Central District, which shimmered in the heat rising from its stone pavements. 'This is a wealthier part of the city', she said to Will as she pointed out buildings with crenelated façades, which offered shelter from the harsh sun beneath porticoes supported by ornate pillars. A narrow road wound up the Peak, still half obscured by a veil of morning mist. Connie pointed out St John's Cathedral on the lower slopes, austere in its whitewashed simplicity. Behind the cathedral stood a four-square mansion set amid broad grounds. 'That's Government House.' She caught Will's eye. 'The Botanical Gardens are right behind it.'

Gloria came to stand next to Connie as tugboats started guiding the *Carthage* towards Kowloon Wharf, narrowly avoiding the ferries battling their way from one side of the harbour to the other. Connie squinted in the bright sunshine. Where were Mother and Father? She felt a nudge from Will and gave him a smile. He pressed a folded piece of paper into her hand. 'Read this when you are alone,' he whispered.

'What is it?'

'Something I wrote for you.' He paused. 'I'll go now, but I hope to see you soon.'

The *Carthage*'s propellors spun, churning the murky water. Connie secreted Will's note into her pocket and jumped up and down on the spot, waving when she spotted her parents on the quay below.

'Come along, dear.' Gloria exhaled a loud breath. 'We mustn't keep Sir Albert and Lady Grace waiting.'

Two hours or so later, Connie's father's chauffeur-driven Rolls Royce motored under the arch festooned with a carved wooden dragon guarding the gated entrance to the Han Fung estate—three villas where Mamma—Father's first wife—Mother, and Father's concubine, Zhang Mei Lan, kept separate residences, and Father's own mansion, where he lived apart from his mistress, spouses, and offspring. Connie gazed at the familiar carving. Each of the dragon's feet displayed four claws, since only an emperor's dragon could display five. Its hue was indistinguishable from imperial yellow, however, and the object was as beautiful as any inside the Forbidden City in Peking, she knew for a fact.

'Out you get,' Father said as the car came to a stop in front of his residence. 'Your sisters and their children have all come for lunch.'

'Have I got time to freshen up?' Connie was desperate to go to her room and read what Will had written.

'You can use the facilities here,' Father responded. 'Everyone will be anxious to greet you.'

# THE FLAME TREE

Father's decrees were never questioned. Authoritarian to a tee, he was still the same imposing figure that she remembered. He was dressed—as he'd always dressed—in a long blue Chinese gown. Father's features were so European he could have passed for an Englishman if he didn't dress otherwise. And Father had decided years ago that he wanted to be thought of as Chinese rather than British. He'd even allowed his white beard and moustache to grow down like a venerable Mandarin—which gave his handsome face an even more distinguished look. Father was in his late sixties but exuded the energy of a much younger man. Connie loved and hero-worshipped him, but she was also a little bit afraid of him for his somewhat controlling nature.

'Yes, Father,' she acquiesced. 'I can't wait to see everyone too.'

Gloria had clambered out of the car with Mother. They were making their way up the marble steps to The Manor—the family's name for Father's house—when Connie's sisters, Mary, Veronica, Dorothy, and her half-sister, Edith, all four married to wealthy Chinese-Eurasian businessmen, came rushing out of the front door with their children to enfold Connie in their warm embraces.

'I'm so happy to see you,' Connie said. And she was. She'd missed them dreadfully.

After she'd freshened up, she went through to the dining room. The round ornately carved rosewood table had been set for nine—the children would eat with Gloria separately at Mamma's. Connie smiled warmly and greeted Mamma and Father's concubine, Mei Lan, kissing them on both cheeks. The aroma of her favourite dishes had made Connie's mouth water, and she found herself looking forward to picking up her chopsticks and eating Cantonese food once more. It was rare for them all to eat together with Father—he usually preferred to take his meals on his own—and Connie felt profoundly honoured by the occasion.

They waited until Father had helped himself from the dishes on the lazy Susan in the centre of the table—chicken and cashew nuts, choy sum cabbage in oyster sauce, stewed beef brisket with bamboo shoots, and sweet and sour pork—then they all tucked in, chatting about Matthew, the first-born of her parents, who'd been promoted to lieutenant-colonel in Chiang Kai Shek's army. After being sent to the frontline and engaging in battle against the Japanese as they were advancing in the north of China, Matthew had just been assigned to carry out military intelligence duties in the south. Mother was worried about him, given that the Japanese now occupied Kwangtung province, the closest to Hong Kong.

'He'll be fine,' Father said, and Connie surmised he knew more than what he was saying.

'How is Esther?' she asked. Matthew's wife was an American Chinese he'd met when he'd attended graduate training at the US Army Command and General Staff College at Fort Leavenworth in Kansas.

'She's in Chungking,' Mother chipped in. 'I hope she's safe...'

Connie sighed to herself. Japan had started a full-scale invasion of China nearly two years ago. After the Japanese had occupied Peking, the nationalist Kuomintang government had set up their provisional capital in Chungking. The Japanese were bombing it relentlessly, by all accounts, but had not yet tried to take the city. 'Why doesn't she come to Hong Kong?' Connie inquired. Esther and Matthew had a son, James. Surely it would be safer for Esther and him to be here?

'She has many friends in Chungking and is reluctant to leave,' Father harrumphed. Connie knew that he chaffed at Esther's lack of deference towards him—she was far more American than Chinese in her attitudes.

'Jonathan is due to visit soon,' Mamma said brightly.

# THE FLAME TREE

Connie smiled at her other mother. Older than Connie's birth mother by five years, Mamma was still a beautiful woman. She had the hazel eyes of a Eurasian and had been betrothed to Father when he was fifteen and she was thirteen. They'd married three years later as arranged, and he grew to love her deeply, despite her childlessness. Connie loved her too, as did all her siblings for her kindness and the affection she showed towards them.

Connie's sisters, who had been chatting among themselves, expressed their pleasure that their younger brother, who'd been born after Veronica, the eldest of Mother and Father's daughters, would be visiting Hong Kong. Jonathan lived in Macau, where he'd recently built a casino after being granted a concession by the Portuguese government. He was married to Carolina, second cousin of Paulo Rodrigues, who ran the Macau Consortium—a gold trading monopoly. Jonathan had converted to Catholicism and wasn't in Mother's good books as she was a devout Buddhist. But Connie couldn't wait to see him. Jonathan had an irrepressible personality—loud, cheery, questioning, persistent, and gregarious—and he always made her laugh.

She glanced at Mei Lan, whose inability to provide Father with a son had led to her being replaced by Mother, whom Father had married in a Buddhist ceremony. It was a condition of her agreeing to be his "co-wife". Connie had grown up with three mothers and, for her, it was normal. She loved each of them in the same way, as did her sisters, having been brought up to respect and honour them in equal measure. Mei Lan came from a humbler background than Mother and Mamma, and she was pure Chinese. Connie suspected that was the reason why Father hadn't married her as well, but she'd never given voice to that suspicion.

Discussion turned to whether the Japanese would try to invade Hong Kong, a fear expressed by Edith then seconded by Veronica.

'Take on the might of the British Empire?' Father barked out a laugh that put an end to the argument. 'They wouldn't dare.'

Reassured, Connie rested her chopsticks and took a sip of jasmine tea. She'd eaten enough and couldn't wait to go to her room.

Finally, after lychees for dessert, the meal was over. 'I'd like to unpack now if that's alright,' she said.

'Your trunk and suitcases should have been delivered, so you are excused, daughter.' Father beamed his trademark smile. Despite his firmness, he was polite to everyone. He would say good morning to all and sundry, even to beggars in the streets, Connie reflected, and for this, he was held in high esteem.

She kissed his proffered hand and made good her escape. Will's note was burning a hole in her pocket. She raced down the pathway to Mother's villa, built of timber and simply designed with a wide enclosed veranda. Ah Lai, her trusted servant, opened the door. Connie gave her a quick hug and, speaking Cantonese, said she would catch up with her later. 'I already unpack for you,' Ah Lai said.

'M goi,' Connie said. *Thank you.*

'M Sai Haak Hei.' *You're welcome.* Ah Lai beamed a smile, showing a row of gold teeth.

Connie ran up the stairs to her room and went to stand at the window. The Han Fung estate overlooked the south side of Hong Kong Island, and she gazed down at Aberdeen, the fishing village named after the Foreign Secretary at the time Britain gained possession of the colony. She'd longed for the view so much while she'd been away, but how could she have forgotten how beautiful it was?

# THE FLAME TREE

Taking a deep breath, she retrieved Will's piece of paper from her pocket.

> *My vision blurred with salt tonight*
> *That I might never see you again*
> *Oh, that we could be the same*
> *Yet it is our differences that brought us together*
> *A double-edged sword*
> *Has cleaved us apart*
> *Do not forget me, sweet girl from the east*
> *I will forever be your William*

Connie caught her lip between her teeth. The raw honesty and vulnerability of his words touched her to the core, and she knew without a shadow of a doubt that her fate was sealed. Come what may, she would always be linked to Will. In what context, she didn't yet know. Friendship first and foremost—she couldn't imagine her life without him. But a shipboard fling was almost a cliché, she reminded herself. The romance of sultry evenings spent dancing under the stars couldn't ever be perpetuated in real life, could it?

## Chapter Five

Will was sitting in the living room of the house in La Salle Road he was sharing with another cadet, Reggie Stewart, as well as a policeman, Mike Middleton, and a commercial adviser to the government, Nigel Bridges. A ceiling fan whirred above Will's head, stirring the humidity that hung like a wet blanket around him. His fellow housemates had gone to their rooms for an afternoon snooze, but Will had felt too hot to sleep in the sweltering heat of his bedroom and had come into the lounge instead.

He thought about earlier, when ginger-haired Reggie had met him at Kowloon Wharf after the *Carthage* had docked. 'I arrived in the colony at the end of last year,' Reggie had said, leading him to where he'd parked his Austin-7 motorcar. 'You know we would have done our language studies in Canton, don't you? But when the city fell to the Japs last October, the cadets who were there were sent to Macau. Those of us who arrived afterwards are being taught in Hong Kong.'

'I hadn't realised,' Will had said. He was glad he wasn't expected to study in Macau. Forty miles distant by sea, it would have made seeing Connie even more difficult.

He'd clambered into the car with Reggie and they'd set off down a broad thoroughfare lined with porticoed two-storey

# THE FLAME TREE

buildings on one side, and banyan trees growing along wide pavements on the other. Reggie had mentioned it was called Nathan Road after a colonial administrator in the early part of the century. He'd driven with his hand on the horn, hooting at jaywalking pedestrians, suicidal-seeming rickshaw pullers, and bicyclists apparently hellbent on ending up under the Austin's wheels.

Will had expected Hong Kong to be different from England, but he'd never expected it to be quite so fascinating. When he'd climbed down the gangplank of the *Carthage* earlier, he'd been astonished at the sight of the bare-chested coolies on the pier, heavy loads bending the poles slung across their shoulders. Women in dusky trousers and tunics carried lighter burdens, working alongside the men, their faces half-hidden by grimy pennants hanging from crownless circular hats of woven bamboo at least a couple of feet across. The fetid smell of unwashed bodies had made Will's head reel, and the damp air had drenched his cotton shirt and slacks.

'In late spring and summer we wear khaki shorts. And open-necked shirts,' Reggie had said once he'd started the car.

Will had glanced at Reggie's knobbly knees and the long white socks encasing his calves, which looked slightly incongruous worn with black lace-up shoes. 'I'll take a shower and get changed as soon as the lorry with my luggage arrives,' Will had said, turning his gaze towards the street scene unfolding before him.

Chinese gentlemen in long blue gowns were strolling past the slow-moving car, their fans fluttering like captive butterflies to cool faces glistening with perspiration. Hawkers lined the pavement, calling out raucously to draw attention to wares spread on grass mats: gold jewellery and bright porcelain bowls, black iron pots and gaudy fabrics, dried fish, and heaps of multi-coloured spices. The pungent aroma of piquant food came from an assortment of roadside kitchens and mingled with the swampy stench of open drains.

Passers-by, their golden-hued faces strangely aloof, were wearing the most extraordinary clothing. Black-trousered women in white jackets secured with diagonal frog fastenings, their hair scraped back from their foreheads, carrying rattan baskets filled with fruit and vegetables. Could they be the domestic servants Connie had told him about? Other women dressed in similar garb strolled past holding brightly coloured waxy paper umbrellas, shading the heads of elegant Chinese ladies in cheongsams with the ubiquitous splits up the sides, who must be their employers—or *tai-tais* as they were known.

A woman with a baby in a sling on her back had stopped to examine jade bracelets spread out on one of the stalls. The baby's head lolled backwards, but it appeared to be quite comfortable and fast asleep. All the while, through the open windows, the clack of mah-jong tiles clashed with the hubbub of music and voices shouting in Cantonese.

'This is incredible,' Will had said.

'Isn't it just?' Reggie chuckled, making a right turn off Nathan Road. 'Have you got one of these, by the way?' He indicated the white topee helmet on his head.

'Do I really need one?'

'Oh, yes, or you might get sunstroke. Just go to Whiteaway's department store on Hong Kong side. They'll be able to fit you out.'

'Hong Kong side?'

'Across the harbour,' Reggie had clarified.

'I see. What's this road we're on now called?'

'Boundary Street. Previously marked the border between China and the Kowloon peninsula, which was ceded to us in 1860. We leased The New Territories in 1898 for 99 years.

That's when the boundary was moved north to between the Sham Chun River and Mirs Bay.'

Will had learnt about the circumstances of the lease, which Britain had obtained from China after it had been weakened by the first Sino-Japanese war. Other European powers—Germany, Russia, and France—were scrambling to carve up the country, so the British took full advantage of the situation to grab more land to add to the island and tip of the peninsula, ceded in 1842.

'I'm looking forward to exploring the New Territories,' Will had said. 'I've heard the countryside is beautiful.' A range of hills separated Kowloon from the hinterland. Will pointed towards the tallest crag in the centre, which was shaped like a crouching lion. 'Might be nice to hike up there...'

'It's known as *Shi Zi Shan*,' Reggie translated *Lion Rock* into Cantonese. 'I'm game for a climb if you are.'

'I remember learning that Kowloon, *Gau Lung*, means "nine dragons" and the hills are named after them. Except there're only eight as the emperor himself was considered a dragon, the ninth one.'

'Well, you've done your homework. I'm impressed.' Reggie smiled.

A sign showed they'd arrived at La Salle Road. Reggie brought his Austin to a halt and honked the horn again until a Chinese man came running down the drive to open the gates.

Will soon began to realise he was to live like a lord, surrounded by a bevy of domestic helpers. They'd lined up on the driveway and Reggie introduced them: two amahs—Ah Jun and Ah Luk who would do the washing and cleaning—a manservant, Ah King, and his assistant the No. 2 boy. There was also a cook boy and a gardener. Connie had told him about the use of the word, "Ah", in front of Chinese surnames. It meant "Miss" or

"Mister" and was a polite way of addressing one's servants, she'd said.

Will wondered if Connie had read his poem yet, but there hadn't been time to dwell on her reaction as Reggie had bustled him into a big, white-painted house with a green tiled roof. 'You'll have time to unpack before you meet the others. Everyone comes home for tiffin at this time of the year,' Reggie had said. 'They leave for work at first light. It's too hot to do much in the afternoons.'

Later, Will blinked his eyes open with a jolt and realised he must, indeed, have fallen asleep. From the dimming of the light outside, it was already early evening, he surmised.

The door to the sitting room swung open, and Nigel Bridges stepped across the parquet, followed by Ah King bearing a silver tray with a bottle of Plymouth Gin, a handful of squashed limes, an ice bucket, and a pint glass.

Nigel slumped down in the armchair opposite Will while Ah King filled one third of the glass with gin, added the fresh limes and topped it to the brim with the ice before stirring it gently.

'Thank you, Ah King.' Nigel took a swig and released a satisfied sigh.

*Clearly it was a daily ritual.*

'You want drink, Master?' Ah King asked Will.

*Master? Am I to be referred to as Master?* He blinked his eyes in disbelief. But if this was the way things were done, he'd have to go along with it. 'I'll have a gin and tonic, please,' he said. He'd heard that the quinine in the tonic might protect him from malaria, which was prevalent in the colony, and necessitated sleeping shrouded in a mosquito net at night.

# THE FLAME TREE

Reggie and Mike Middleton breezed into the room for their sundowners—a brandy soda for Reggie and a gin gimlet for Mike. 'Let's go out on the town after supper,' Mike suggested, clinking the ice in his glass. 'Introduce Will to Hong Kong's bachelor life.'

'Great idea.' Reggie quaffed his drink. 'How about it, Will?'

'Wonderful, thanks,' he said, torn between the desire to experience everything and the wish that he could be spending the evening with Connie instead.

After a dinner of chicken in mushroom sauce served with steamed rice and a vegetable called *bok choy*, Will and his three housemates got into a taxi which took them to the Star Ferry pier. They went through the turnstiles and made their way to seats in the canvas covered central section of the top deck. The sides of the ferry were open to the elements, and Will relished the fresh breeze cooling his heated body as they crossed the harbour. Hong Kong Island loomed ahead, dominated by the Peak—which was festooned with strings of lights like pearls around the neck of a dowager. Connie had said that she lived on the other side of the summit. Was she thinking of him like he was thinking of her?

Red-painted rickshaws lined the kerb in front of the ferry pier on Hong Kong side, their green oilcloth hoods pulled back. Some of the rickshaw pullers were in the middle of snatching a quick meal, scooping rice into their mouths from small bowls with their chopsticks, but the majority crouched between the shafts of their rickshaws like trap ponies awaiting the crack of the driver's whip. Will and his new friends walked past them and strolled along the Central Praya edging the waterfront to arrive at one of those palatial buildings with a crenelated façade and a portico supported by ornate pillars. Will had spotted it that morning from the *Carthage*. A sign above the entrance identified it as *The Hong Kong Hotel*. 'It's the best in the colony,'

Reggie had said while they were crossing the harbour and discussing where they were headed. 'Everyone calls it The Gripps, which is the name of its excellent rooftop restaurant.'

Inside, potted palms lined the foyer and it could have been any luxury hotel in London, Will thought, the only difference being the Chinese staff. They went to the bar and knocked back a concoction known as "ox's blood", made by mixing champagne with sparkling burgundy and a little brandy. A pianist was playing Duke Ellington jazz songs and the drinkers were all men. Nigel suggested they go to the Toi Chung in the Western District. 'It's an exclusive Chinese millionaires' club,' Reggie whispered to Will. 'Invitation only, but Nigel went to boarding school at Cheltenham with the son of a founder member, who gave him a permanent invite.'

They left the hotel by the back entrance, which opened onto Queen's Road, where they hopped onto a tram. Reggie explained that the tramway system had been introduced at the start of the century and had become an ever more popular means of transport with both locals and expatriates—much faster than rickshaws or, indeed, sedan chairs, and cheaper than taxis. 'Are sedan chairs still used?' Will asked, surprised.

'Oh, yes. Especially up on the Peak.'

A vision of Connie being carried in a chair by coolies came into Will's head.

The tram followed the waterfront from Central into the Western District. Streetlights lit ramshackle buildings, their flimsy wooden balconies festooned with washing strung on bamboo poles. This was certainly a poorer part of Hong Kong, Will realised, as the stink of rotten fruit and decaying vegetables came through the tram window from the rubbish-strewn streets. Strident Cantonese voices filled the air and he felt the same thrill he'd felt that morning to be in a place he'd dreamed of visiting most of his life.

# THE FLAME TREE

They got off the tram at the end of the line in Kennedy Town, named after one of Hong Kong's late nineteenth century governors. 'This used to be a red-light district,' Mike said. 'It was full of brothels, but they disappeared when prostitution was criminalised. Instead, Hong Kong has what are known as "escort girls" who frequent clubs like the one Nigel is taking us to.'

'But isn't that illegal as well?' Will asked, lengthening his stride to keep up with the policeman.

'We turn a blind eye to it. I expect because the powers that be are paid enough squeeze by the club owners.'

'Squeeze?'

'Sorry. Hong Kong word for bribes.' Mike smirked. 'Not to be confused with *cumshaw*, meaning a tip.'

'Ah,' Will said, intrigued. But there was no time to pursue the topic. They'd started climbing a narrow, dimly lit stairway to a bright, garishly painted door. Nigel rang the bell, the peephole opened a crack, and someone barked a question Will couldn't understand. Nigel responded in equally incomprehensible Cantonese, and they were immediately granted access.

Will grabbed Mike's arm in surprise. The interior was so unexpected—a room beautifully furnished with intricately carved blackwood furniture. Wooden ceiling fans cooled the air, and silk screen paintings of rivers and mountains adorned the walls. A manservant came up and handed each of them a hot towel with which to clean their hands before ushering them further into the room.

A group of oriental men sat playing poker. Some wore long gowns, others were dressed in smart European suits. Chinese hostesses in cheongsams fluttered like hummingbirds around the male clientele, serving them with balloons of brandy and collecting tips from their winnings. It was blatantly obvious that the girls would serve them with more than drinks by the time the evening was through.

Other Chinese men were standing around watching the game, smoking cigars and cigarettes and drinking. One of them approached. 'Nigel,' he said in an upper-class English accent. 'How nice to see you. Let me get you and your friends a drink.'

Nigel introduced Will, Reggie and Mike to his school pal, Joseph Woo. 'Call me Joe,' the slender, good-looking man said. On being told Will had just arrived in the colony, he added, 'Welcome to Hong Kong.'

The proprietorial tone of voice used by Joseph Woo brought home to Will that it was only right that it should be a Chinese to welcome him to Hong Kong. The British might have grabbed the territory, but it would never be theirs in perpetuity despite what the treaties stipulated. *The treaties had been forced on China under duress.*

'Don't expect any of the girls to show an interest in you,' Reggie whispered to Will, interrupting his thoughts as Nigel and Mike wandered over to the bar with Joe. 'They would be finished if they consorted with a *gwailo*.'

'*Gwailo?*'

'"Ghost boy" or "foreign devil" depending on the context.'

Will had a hangover the next morning, not the best way for him to start a new job. They hadn't stayed long at the Toi Chung—they weren't rich enough to play poker with millionaires, and they were untouchables as far as the women were concerned. Obviously the barriers mentioned by Connie were prevalent in all walks of life in Hong Kong. The sinking feeling he'd felt on the *Carthage* had returned one hundred-fold. He'd drowned his sorrows in several brandy sodas.

## THE FLAME TREE

Back at home, he'd fallen asleep as soon as his head had hit the pillow. But now his forehead ached, and his mouth was dry. He'd drunk all the boiled water Ah King had left in a bottle on his bedside table; he'd been warned not to drink tap water as it could give him cholera. So, he took a quick shower, dressed in khaki shorts and an open-neck shirt, knee length socks and slip-on shoes, then went downstairs.

In the dining room, Ah King handed Will a glass of freshly squeezed orange juice, which he downed in seconds. 'You want tea or coffee, master?'

'Coffee, please.' It would clear his head.

'Good morning,' Reggie looked up from a plate of bacon and eggs. 'All set to meet the boss?'

Will groaned. 'Wish I'd held back on the booze last night.'

'It's the heat. Makes us all very thirsty. You'll learn to pace yourself. Get some food down you...you'll feel better for it.'

Mike and Nigel had left for work an hour ago, apparently, and Reggie was waiting for his Chinese teacher. Will ate the scrambled eggs he'd requested for breakfast, then phoned for a taxi. Before too long, he was on the Star Ferry traversing the harbour then crossing Royal Square and walking up the path overlooking the back of the Hong Kong & Shanghai Bank building.

By the time he'd arrived at the Central Government Offices, perched on porticoes like a stately old lady lifting her petticoats, sweat was dripping down his face and his beige cotton shirt was soaked. Perhaps he should have taken a rickshaw, but he'd been reticent about a fellow human being pulling him along in a pony-trap like contraption and had decided to walk instead.

A white-uniformed Sikh guard, a turban on his head and rifle on his shoulder, stood to attention at the entrance to the Colonial Secretariat. Will's Caucasian credentials were enough to let him pass, and soon he was sitting in a high-ceilinged office waiting to be seen by Gordon Hartley Smith, the Colonial Secretary himself, no less.

A sun-tanned dark-haired man with a Clark Gable moustache strode into the room. 'Glad to have you join us, dear boy,' he said as Will jumped to his feet.

Smith took a seat behind his mahogany desk and indicated that Will should sit opposite him. The Colonial Secretary picked up what looked like a glass of whiskey water and took a swig. Will stared down at his hands to hide his surprise. An office boy appeared and handed Will an identical glass. He took a tentative sip and breathed out a sigh of relief. *Warm black tea and extremely thirst-quenching.*

'How are you settling in so far?' Smith asked.

'Very well, thank you, Sir.'

'Good. Good.' The Colonial Secretary steepled his fingers and stared at Will like a predatory eagle down his long beaky nose. 'Your top priority will be to sign the Visitors' Books and leave your card at the Governor's, the Police Commissioner's, the Chief Justice's, and the GOC British Forces. Got that?'

'Absolutely, Sir. Erm, where are they situated?'

'Here's a list.' He handed Will a sheet of paper with names and addresses of senior government officials, most of whom lived on the Peak. 'You do have cards, I presume?'

'Yes, Sir.' Will had made sure he'd had embossed visiting cards printed before leaving England and had even brought the printing plate with him.

Smith then went on to issue a warning that chilled Will's heart. 'The cadets we've sent to Macau were rather too fond of having Chinese girlfriends in Canton. They call it having a "sleeping dictionary" to learn the language. Of course, they will never marry the poor women. If any cadet were foolish enough to marry a Chinese, they'd be called on to resign.' He took a sip of tea. 'Never be seen on your own with a local girl, dear boy. It would be a black mark against you and lessen your chances of going out with the European girls who are much in demand...'

Will's jaw dropped. He couldn't think of a response, so he stayed silent.

Then, as if he'd suddenly remembered, Smith went on to talk about the arrangements for Will's study of Cantonese. 'A teacher will come to your house on weekdays. There will be an examination every six months on which your promotion will depend. Your lessons will start next week. That will give you time to leave your cards, open a bank account, replenish your wardrobe with tropical gear, and do anything else needed to settle in.'

'Yes, Sir.'

The Colonial Secretary pointedly glanced at his watch.

Will pushed back his chair and stood. 'Thank you, Sir.'

He turned and left the room, dejection dogging his steps. What a bloody racially divided place Hong Kong was turning out to be. Defiantly, he made his way down the corridor to the telephone exchange. There, he left the phone number of the house in La Salle Road. 'If anyone asks for Will Burton, would you give them this number, please,' he said.

# Chapter Six

Two days after her return to Hong Kong, Connie was perched in the small pavilion at the edge of the lowest of the manicured terraced gardens at home. A book of poetry, which she'd kept from the time when she'd been taught elementary Chinese classics by an old mater who came to tutor her at home, lay open on her lap. She'd been thinking about Will, wondering how she could help him practise speaking Cantonese like she'd promised, and she'd stumbled upon the idea that it might improve his pronunciation if he learnt to recite a poem. How she longed to see him; she hadn't even called him yet. After breakfast that morning, she'd gone to the telephone in the hallway to dial the number of the Colonial Secretariat, but Ah Lai had been hovering and, although she couldn't understand English, Connie hadn't wanted to arouse her curiosity.

A sigh caught in her throat. The trusted servants she'd lived with all her life were part of the family, people she'd been brought up in the Confucian tradition to call "elder brother" or "elder sister"—not "amah" or "boy". They, in turn, referred to her as "Number Five Miss", given that she was the youngest of her father's daughters. There existed a parent-child relationship between Father and his staff, which demanded loyalty from both sides. Ah Lai, or "Number One Elder Sister" as she was known, had been around for as long as Connie could remember. It would be as difficult to keep a secret from her as it would be to hide anything from her father.

Connie found herself longing to see Will and she hoped against hope she might find a way to meet with him and keep within the traditional boundaries established by Father. She'd often wondered why her father had aligned himself with the Chinese Community instead of the British, though. It would have been so much easier for her if, like many Eurasians, he'd decided to follow English customs. But, before setting up his own businesses, Father had worked for Jardine Matheson as an intermediary between the British and Chinese. He'd used his "Chineseness" to become the acceptable voice of eastern "difference" for westerners, and he'd resolutely stuck to that stance.

Mother had once told her that Father's English father had abandoned his Chinese mother and his younger brothers when Father was eight years old. That despicable Englishman had returned to Britain leaving his Hong Kong family to cope on their own. Could such a bitter betrayal have influenced Father's decision to separate himself from his British heritage? He'd endured great hardship as a child but had received a good education having won a scholarship to a school where he'd excelled. Connie's mother had said that Father had been so poor he would go out on the streets to pick up metal—from nails to scrap—which he would sell to a dealer to earn money to buy food. He was almost certainly a product of his upbringing. Even nowadays, despite being a multimillionaire from his newspaper, trading, property, and shipping businesses, he still exercised frugality and had become a generous philanthropist. His motto was, "You must learn how to give before you receive". He would dwell on that Confucian philosophy when reminiscing about how he'd made his money, but he would never, ever talk about his own father.

Movement caught Connie's eye—an egret was flying past, probably on its way down to the coast for a spot of fishing. From her vantage point under the emerald-tiled roof of the pavilion, the view was truly breath-taking. The scent of fresh vegetation, wet soil and decaying plants and wood, wafted from the sub-tropical forest below—where dense clumps of foliage hung like braided ropes in the dank caverns. It had rained the night before, and the burble of rushing water from gushing streams feeding the catchments of the reservoir, competed with the chirping of tree sparrows, the slightly annoying "Uwu Uwu Uwu," of koels, and the melodious "ter-du-koor" of spotted doves.

Further down, protected by hills on all sides, Aberdeen had sheltered sea-going craft since Hong Kong's earliest days. This was the fragrant harbour that had given Hong Kong, *Heung Kong*, its name. The fragrance came from the joss sticks once traded there. It was home to thousands of the so-called "water people", who spent their entire lives on board their fishing vessels. When she was little, Connie enjoyed hiking down from the Peak to Aberdeen with her governess. She loved the sight of the hundreds of junks moored next to each other in a forest of masts and banners, their decks stepped up by planked levels to high poops, where whole families liked to squat under canvas awnings to enjoy a meal together. Long, thin sampans wove between their ranks selling vegetables and other supplies, each boat poled with one long oar by a single standing figure in a black shiny tunic and a hat like a huge bamboo lampshade. Connie used to imagine walking across the mass of junks to explore Ap Lei Chau. Uninhabited except for a small village at its northern tip, the hilly isle was known as Duck's Tongue Island because of its shape. She squinted her eyes and gazed at the South China Sea shining in the distance and gave an involuntary shudder as she imagined how many sharks lurked beneath its surface.

## THE FLAME TREE

She carried on flipping through her poetry book. The egret had returned, its beak empty, to alight on the feathery frond of a wild banana tree and stare at her with its beady eye. Connie stopped turning the pages; she'd found a poem, written by Du Fu, a poet in the Tang Dynasty in around 764 AD. The egret had pointed her to it.

*Two magpies flutter in the Ming green willows as egrets fly up into the clear blue sky.*

She recited the rest of the quatrain to herself. The poem was simple—surely Will would have no difficulty in learning it?

That afternoon, while Mother was resting, Connie was sent to see her father. She'd expected the summons—he'd intimated soon after her arrival that he'd wanted to discuss plans for her future. Still dressed in the shorts and blouse she'd put on first thing in the morning, she made her way along the pine tree-edged path. Fah Wong, the gardener, looked up from his weeding and she gave him a cheery wave. After strolling past the small pagoda-like Buddhist temple Mother had ordered to be built in the grounds some years ago, Connie arrived at The Manor.

When Father had bought the land on which Han Fung Estate stood, the three Victorian-style villas, where his spouses and concubine lived, were already in existence. After consultation with geomancers, Father decided to commission the construction of his own residence according to the ancient Chinese tradition of Feng Shui, placing it where "chi"—the invisible energy that flows through everything—would have a good impact on the family both physically and mentally, its positive force weaving through the building to bring prosperity, harmony, and—most importantly—good luck.

Despite his children's name for it, Father's mansion was nothing like a manor. He'd requested that the roof be identical to those adorning ancient Buddhist monasteries on the mainland, jade green tiles sloping downwards to the red brick walls, and the rooftop curved at its ends to ward off evil spirits—who everyone believed could only travel in straight lines. Wide stone steps led to the colonnaded porticoed entrance, above which presided a grandiose balcony boasting bamboo-shaped porcelain pillars mirroring those on the porch below. Connie pushed open the ornately carved teak front door and stepped into the coolness of the darkened hallway—shuttered to keep out the heat.

Father's study was on the ground floor, overlooking the gardens gracing The Manor's inner courtyard, which featured a lotus-filled goldfish pond and myriad hibiscus, peony, and chrysanthemum plants. A haven of tranquillity filled with birdsong and the echo of wind chimes, it was there that Connie found him, seated on a granite bench under the shady branches of a bauhinia tree.

'Ah, Constance.' He patted the space next to him. 'Sit.'

She did as he'd commanded, then asked, 'Why did you want to see me, Father?'

'Now you have finished your education, the time has come to think about your future. Woo Man Li's son, Joseph, would make a good husband for you.' Father gave her a look that brooked no argument.

Except argue she would, despite being somewhat afraid of him. She wasn't ready to get married so, heart thumping, she gathered her courage and said, 'I've only just graduated. I'd like to take a secretarial course then find a job. Marriage can wait.' She might owe him her filial obedience, and of course she would obey him if he insisted, but she'd got her own way when she'd badgered him about studying in London, and she prayed she would get her own way now.

Father eyed her shorts and blouse. 'You've become very Westernised while you were in England. I trust you haven't forgotten your duty towards me, my girl.'

'No, Father. Of course not.' Connie met his eye. She was her father's youngest, and he'd spoilt her more than the others, so Mother had always maintained. Would he be prepared to indulge her now? Connie twisted her hands in her lap.

'What kind of job would interest you?' he grunted.

She bestowed him with her best smile. 'Perhaps I could work for you?'

'Ha,' he chortled. 'You know how to twist me around your little finger, don't you?' He chucked her under the chin. 'Fair enough. Learn shorthand and typing. Then we'll see...' He breathed a sigh. 'You're nothing like your sisters. They couldn't wait to be married and start their families. But *you* mustn't wait too long or you'll be left on the shelf.'

'I won't. You have my word.'

'Good.' He grinned, then waved his hand. 'Run along, Constance. I have work to do.'

'Yes, Father.' She kissed his bearded cheek.

Father's indulgent laughter followed her all the way across the courtyard and into the hallway. Connie smiled to herself as she headed towards the front door.

'What did your father want?' Mother asked Connie while they were enjoying a cup of tea together later.

Connie told her about his putting forward Joseph Woo as a prospective husband, and quickly added that she didn't want to get married until she'd worked in a job.

'Job?!' Mother's voice shrilled. 'Whatever for? You don't need to work...'

'True, but I'd like to contribute to society, if I can.'

Mother huffed. 'Joseph Woo is a good match for you. He studied law in England before being called to the bar in Hong Kong. It is said that he has a brilliant future ahead of him. And his family has lots of money.'

'I don't want to become a *tai-tai* spending my days gossiping and playing mah-jong. I'd like to be like you and devote myself to helping others.'

Connie had said the right thing. Mother reached across the table and patted her hand. 'Perhaps you could help out in one of my charities...' Being a devout Buddhist, Mother advocated the humane treatment of all living creatures, so she was an ardent supporter of the Society for the Protection of Animals. And, inspired by visits to Dr Barnardo's Homes when she took Connie to England, Mother had also established a college for girls born into poverty on her return to Hong Kong.

'Oh, by the way, Mamma has requested that you dine with her this evening.' Mother eyed Connie's shorts and cotton blouse. 'Might I suggest you dress appropriately?'

'Yes, Mother.' Connie bowed her head. 'I'll go to my room and get changed.'


'Sit up straight and don't slouch, Constance,' Mamma admonished as if she was still a child.

The old lady was a stickler for etiquette, always had been. It was she who'd taught Connie the proper way to hold her chopsticks and bowl when she was little. 'Yes, Mamma,' Connie concurred before asking, 'How is your health?'

It was a way to divert her second mother from harping on about manners and Connie let her mind drift while Mamma launched into a litany about her aches and pains. She suffered from asthma and rheumatism, which had rendered her practically housebound, and Connie's heart went out to her. Mamma then mentioned the celebration of hers and Father's Golden Wedding Anniversary to take place next year. Connie knew about it already, as Mother had told her at breakfast. All the Hong Kong élite would be invited—Chinese, Eurasian and European—to a big party at the Peninsula Hotel.

Connie bit into a piece of steamed grouper fish and chewed thoughtfully. Another day was almost at an end and she still hadn't phoned the Colonial Secretariat. It would be too late now; the telephone exchange would be closed. She would just have to try again tomorrow.

After supper, she helped Mamma walk through to her sitting room, Connie's hand under the old lady's plump arm as she hobbled on her tiny lotus feet. Connie winced, she couldn't help herself. Mamma must have suffered terribly when her toes had been broken and bound in her childhood. Little more than three inches in length, encased in miniature shoes that would have fitted a doll, her feet caused Mamma to totter with a gait that relied on the thigh and buttock muscles for support. A small foot in China, no different from a tiny waist in Victorian England, Connie reflected, represented the height of female refinement. For families with marriageable daughters, foot size translated into its own form of currency and a means of achieving upward mobility. Thankfully, the practice had been banned in time for Mother to escape from such barbarity.

'Take a seat, daughter,' Mamma said after Connie had helped her to an armchair. 'And turn on the radio.'

Connie walked across the Tientsin carpet, decorated with a yellow floral medallion surrounded by blue and purple birds and animals, that covered the centre of the room. It was as if she had never been away, she thought, as she turned on the wireless and a Cantonese opera came over the airwaves. She remembered watching exciting performances "live" and settled back in her chair to listen to the high-pitched singing. The painted faces of the characters, dressed in colourful robes with water sleeves—white silk extensions to their cuffs to produce movements reflecting elegance and tenderness—could only been seen in her mind's eye, but the clashing cymbals, beating drums and the tunes played on two stringed bow fiddles—known as Chinese violins in the west—enthralled her, and she sat raptly until the performance came to an end.

'You can go now, Constance.' Mamma's round face looked tired, and her number three sister had come into the room to help her to bed.

Connie bent and kissed the old lady's chubby cheek. 'Good night, Mamma. Sleep well.'

'Sleep?' Mamma repeated. 'I'll only manage a couple of hours, but it's better than nothing I suppose.'

Connie headed next door. Everyone had gone to bed, so she went to her room. There, she unbuttoned her cotton dress and put on a pair of pyjamas. The wooden ceiling fan cooling her, she stood at the window. Moonlight lit the outlines of the bays and islands below and the distant lights of the fishing junks shone like earthly stars. What has Will been doing today, she asked herself. She couldn't wait to speak to him, to find out about his first impressions of Hong Kong. Come hell or high water, tomorrow she would get in touch with him.

*She couldn't let him think she didn't care...*

# Chapter Seven

The first Friday morning after his arrival in the colony, Will was crossing the harbour on his way to meet Connie in the Botanical Gardens. Finally, she'd called him the day before, apologising profusely that it had taken so long and mumbling about how she'd needed to make the phone call in secret. Will slowly exhaled a deep breath. Was he doing the right thing? He didn't want to get Connie into any trouble with her family. As for himself, he didn't care a fig for what Hong Kong society might think. The Colonial Secretary's warning had fallen on deaf ears. There was only one girl who interested him, so if his being seen with her ruined his chances of going out with European women then so be it. But Connie's reputation was paramount, and guilt formed an ache at the back of Will's throat at the thought he might be placing her in a compromising situation.

While waiting for her to phone him, he'd kept himself busy settling in. He'd gone to Whiteaways and had purchased his tropical gear; he'd dropped off his visiting cards; Nigel Bridges had put him forward for membership of the Hong Kong Club, the Yacht Club, the United Services Recreation Club, and the Jockey Club. Will had been staggered to learn that Chinese were only admitted to the Jockey Club, and that this all-pervasive sense of hierarchy was reflected in the "zoning" of residential areas according to status and race. After an exciting ride up on the funicular railway, he'd walked around the Peak, enjoying the cooler air and magnificent views while posting his cards through letter boxes, and the only local people he'd seen had obviously been servants. Curious about where Connie lived, he'd strolled past the dragon crested gateway to the Han Fung Estate, but the buildings were obscured by trees and there'd been no sign of her.

To keep himself occupied, he'd joined the United Services Recreation Club's rugger team. Reggie had been delighted when Will had told him that he'd been the Captain of Clifton's 1st XV 1933/34, which had been unbeaten by any school that year, and had subsequently played for University College Oxford's 1st XV. The USRC would be competing against the Hong Kong Royal Navy Volunteer Reserve next week and playing one of the army squads the following one. Reggie had informed him that the colony was defended by a garrison made up of battalions from the Royal Scots, Rajput, Punjab, and Middlesex Regiments. 'We all play against each other,' Reggie had gone on to say. 'It will be good to have someone of your calibre on our team.'

Sport had always been an important part of Will's life and when Reggie had clarified that Cantonese lessons would only happen in the mornings, Will's mood had brightened at the thought he'd be able to spend his afternoons at the USRC, swimming in the outdoor pool after a game of rugger. As for the evenings, he'd soon learnt that, following a morning of work and an afternoon of sport, the typical colonial day ended by going out for cocktails, dinner, and dancing. Will had been dragged along with his housemates a couple of times and had enjoyed himself superficially. If only he'd been able to take Connie out instead, his life would have been perfect, he'd thought.

The ferry moored at the pier on Hong Kong Island and Will disembarked. He went to the rickshaw stand and negotiated a

## THE FLAME TREE

fare to the Botanical Gardens. It wouldn't do to arrive covered in sweat, so he swallowed his reticence about being pulled in a type of pony trap by a fellow human. His puller set off at a jog—his trotting legs, bare beneath short trousers, were corded with taut muscles over knobby bones. Mike Middleton had told Will that many of the rickshaw men were opium addicts, and he'd been surprised to learn that the drug was legal for personal use in Hong Kong.

Will's puller took him to Upper Albert Road before dropping him off at the granite arched entrance to the Gardens. Will paid the agreed fare plus a handsome tip—which would most likely be spent on opiates—and made his way towards the pavilion at the far end, where Connie had said she would be waiting for him.

He sauntered along a gravel path past tall palms and thickly branched magnolia, their white flowers swollen with citrus-lemon fragrance, to arrive at a flat central plaza with a lily-leaf shaped pond and a fountain. From there, it was only a short walk to the pavilion. Connie had mentioned on the phone that it was quite secluded and surrounded by flame of the forest trees—he wouldn't miss it as they would be in full bloom.

Will feasted his eyes on the vivid orange-red blossoms—resembling brightly lit torches covering the spreading canopy under which nestled a gazebo—and he drank in the sight of Connie, sitting on a stone bench with a book in her lap. He quickened his stride and went up to her. How he longed to hold her in his arms and kiss her. But instead, he smiled and said, 'Hello. Nei Hou Maa?' *How are you?*

'Ngo Hou Hou.' *I'm fine.* A beautiful smile lit her almond eyes. 'Nei na?' *And you?*

'Ngo do gei hou.' *I'm fine too.* He lowered himself next to her, enjoying the sweet scent of her perfume that he'd missed so much. 'What are you reading?'

She told him it was classical Chinese poetry, and about her idea of getting him to recite poems. 'Would you like that?' She gave him a questioning look.

'Sounds like a wonderful idea.' He paused to collect his thoughts, then blurted, 'I've missed you, Connie.'

A blush pinked her cheeks, and she cooled herself with a fan. 'I've missed you too. And I really like the poem you wrote for me.' She lowered the fan and glanced around. 'But no one can see me alone with you or...'

'...or no Chinese would want to marry you.' He finished her sentence. 'So you said on the *Carthage*. I don't want to place you in a difficult situation. Except, selfishly, I can't help myself. I know we've only known each other a short while but it doesn't feel like that...' He heard the hopelessness in his voice and shook his head. This was so unlike him—he wasn't the type to wear his heart on his sleeve.

She sighed. 'My father has put forward a prospective husband for me.'

'I think one should marry for love,' he said in a flat tone of voice.

'It's the way things are done in my culture. Marriage is not just between two people, it's between two families. For Chinese people, the ideal is "to marry matching doors"...arranged weddings take place among families of equal status. And because Father has aligned himself with China, I must obey.' She fanned herself again. 'Have you ever been in love, Will?'

'Never,' he admitted, floored by her directness.

Connie's mouth twitched. 'I will grow to love my husband when the time comes. But, for now, I've managed to put Father off.'

'How did you do that?' Will couldn't help smiling.

# THE FLAME TREE

'I said I wanted to do something useful before getting married. He agreed that I could take a secretarial course then look for a job.'

'Good for you!'

'I'll start lessons at the College of Commerce after the summer holidays.'

'Wonderful!'

'How about you? What have you been up to? Have you begun your Cantonese classes yet?'

He filled her in on everything except the part where the Colonial Secretary had warned him off local girls. 'A tutor will come to my shared house on Monday. I'm looking forward to making a start.'

'Excellent!' Her silky eyelashes fluttered. *How he wished he could kiss them.* 'I'm sure you'll make quick progress,' she added.

'Especially with you helping me.'

She nodded and glanced around again. This section of the Botanical Gardens seemed quiet. But perhaps it was the hour of day—mid-morning—and most people were at work or at school. 'Next time we should meet even earlier and it will have to be on Sundays. Saturdays I go to the races with my family and on weekdays you'll be with your tutor or playing sport, won't you?'

It was his turn to nod. 'If anyone approaches us, Connie, I can get up and walk away. I really don't want to put you in a difficult situation.'

'Good idea. And while you are practising speaking with me, we must sit with our backs to each other so it won't look as if we are conversing.'

So much secrecy, but the alternative—not seeing her—didn't bear thinking about. 'That's fine by me. How's Gloria, by the way?' He'd never forget how Connie's old governess always appeared to be spying on her.

'She's working for my sister, Dorothy, now. They live in Broadwood Road above Happy Valley.'

'Ah. I have yet to visit that neighbourhood.'

'It was where the early British settlers built their homes. But the area was swampy before it was drained for the racecourse and it was infested with mosquitoes, which gave them malaria although in those days they called it "springtime fever".'

'Fascinating. Is that why the majority moved up to the Peak?'

'Yes. It wasn't as "pestilential"...but it can be extremely foggy at certain times of the year.'

'So I've been told. I was up there the other day, dropping off my visiting cards. I even walked past your place but couldn't see anything.'

'We like to stay hidden.'

Her curt response made him squirm. It must have been difficult for her, a Chinese Eurasian, growing up in a segregated area for whites only. 'Shall we start my lesson?' he suggested, not wishing to pry.

'Yes, let's.' She opened the book on her lap. 'The poems are in Chinese, but I've written down in Roman script the first one I'd like you to learn. It's by Do Fu, one of our most beloved poets.' She retrieved a piece of paper that was acting as a bookmark and handed it to him.

*Leong go wong lai ming ceoi lau jat hong bak lou soeng cing tin*, he read the first line to himself.

'I know "leong go" means two. What does the rest mean?'

She spoke about magpies, Ming green willows and egrets flying up into the clear blue sky, and then turned her back on him while he repeated the words of the entire poem over and over again until he'd got the tones right. She handed him a pen, so he could make notes. Eventually, she said she was satisfied, then got to her feet. 'See you here the Sunday after next at seven in the morning, Will.' She hesitated, glancing around before adding, 'Have a good week!'

'You too, Connie. And thank you.'

With a slight bow of her head and an adorable pink in her cheeks, she was gone.

It was over all too quickly for Will, and a flush of longing spread through him as he watched her walk away.

'Fancy a day at the races?' Reggie asked Will at breakfast the following morning. 'The boss just phoned to invite the two of us to his box. He apologised for the late notice. Apparently we're needed to "make up the numbers".'

'I suppose it's a command rather than an invitation, then?' Will chuckled. He couldn't help a frisson of delight at the thought he might catch a glimpse of Connie there with her family.

Reggie laughed wryly. 'Boss's daughter has just arrived from England. I expect Mrs Hartley Smith is keen for her to meet "suitable young men".'

'Rather you than me, old chap,' Will said.

'Is there a girl back home?' Reggie lifted a brow.

'Something like that.' Will forked scrambled egg into his mouth. 'So, tell me more about racing in Hong Kong...'

'It's strictly amateur, "gentleman jockeys" from Hong Kong, as well those who come down from Shanghai, Tientsin and Foochow. They have day jobs and don't ride thoroughbreds but horses imported from Australia. The Chinese weren't admitted as members until 1926 and all the wealthy elite instantly joined. It has become a Saturday activity for the entire colony. The locals love to gamble, and they throng to the public area in their droves. That's it in a nutshell.'

'What's the dress code?'

'We can't wear our shorts, I'm afraid. Linen suits are the order of the day. Oh, and topees, of course.'

'Of course.'

Will went to change, then met Reggie downstairs where a taxi was already waiting for them.

Soon, they were on Hong Kong side boarding a tram to Happy Valley. Will eyed the rows of sedan chairs lining the pavements opposite and gave a shudder. There seemed to be no lack of passengers getting into them. Coolies shouldered pairs of long bamboo poles, one standing at the front and one behind, to carry like beasts of burden both men and women—Chinese as well as European.

The tram made its way through Wanchai district, its bell clanging non-stop. Colonnaded shophouses covered in Chinese writing lined the dirty streets, where rickshaws vied with handcarts and hordes of people on foot or on bicycles. Will's ears rang with the clashing of cymbals and high-pitched songs emanating from what must have been hundreds of wirelesses.

He got off the tram with Reggie at the racecourse in front of the tall clock tower dividing the members' stand in two. 'This way,' Reggie said before striding through the entrance and up a short flight of stairs.

The Colonial Secretary introduced them to his wife, Muriel, and his pretty blonde daughter, Deborah, before he and Muriel went to circulate among their other guests. From the look on his face, Will could tell that Reggie had already taken a shine to Deborah. They immediately struck up a rapport based on a mutual interest in tennis. 'Do both of you come and play at our place,' she said, including Will in the invitation. 'Mummy and Daddy would love to have you, I'm sure.'

Leaving Reggie and Deborah to chat, Will went to lean over the balcony and take in the sights. A range of hills surrounded the racecourse on three sides, dotted with white mansions, villas, and low-rise blocks of flats. Will had known that Hong Kong Island was mountainous, but he'd been surprised by how steep and craggy the ridges were. A barren rock when the British had taken possession of the island nearly a hundred years ago, afforestation had turned the slopes verdant, and they'd been given thoroughly English names. Will smirked to himself as he thought about them—Mount Kellett, Strawberry Hill and Mount Gough in the Peak district; Mount Cameron and Mount Nicholson enclosing Happy Valley, Mount Davis towering over the western approach to the harbour. He resolved to find out what they were called in Cantonese and to refer to them in that language, *Kwan Tung Hua*, whenever possible.

A roar came from the crowd below as a harass of horses raced towards the finish line. 'We should place a bet on the next race,' Reggie said from where he'd come to stand next to Will.

But Will's attention had been distracted. The box to the right of the Colonial Secretary's was occupied by a group of attractive, interesting-looking people. And they were Connie's people, for there she was, jumping up and down amid them, a betting slip in her hand. Her gaze locked with his, her mouth forming an *Oh* of surprise. He lifted his hand and waved.

Without apparent hesitation, she waved back.

'Who's that?' Reggie asked.

'Constance Han Fung. We met on the *Carthage*.'

'Ah. Is she the "something like that" you mentioned?'

'We're friends. You know why we can't be more than that...'

'Sorry, my friend. I wish for both your sakes things were different, but Hong Kong being Hong Kong...'

'You and Deborah appear to be getting on well.' Will changed the subject.

'We are.' Reggie grinned. 'Come on, let's go and place that bet.'

Downstairs, the betting hall was heaving, but Will's eyes found Connie straight away. Somehow, he'd known she would be there. She was standing at the counter chatting to Margaret Wyn-Jones. Will went up to them. 'Hello!'

'Oh, hello, Will.' Connie's tone was nonchalant. 'Margaret has been telling me about the thousands of refugees pouring into Hong Kong from China. She desperately needs help in her clinic. I'm a qualified first-aider from when I volunteered with St John's Ambulance in London and, as I've got some free time before I begin a secretarial course, I've offered to give her a hand.'

'Marvellous,' Will said.

'Connie will be a huge asset,' Margaret chipped in. 'I speak Mandarin but my Cantonese is rudimentary. We're trying to convince the refugee women to use birth control and limit their families. There are just so many of them, and resources are stretched.'

'Sounds as if you have quite a task ahead of you,' Will said. Reggie was clearing his throat behind him, so Will introduced him to Connie and Margaret.

'You must come to dinner.' Margaret swept her arm to include all three of them.

'I'd love to.' Connie's response took Will by surprise. But then he realised that he wouldn't be alone with her and therefore she wouldn't be contravening any conventions. She picked up her winnings from the counter. 'I'd better get back to my box.' She smiled tentatively. 'Nice seeing you again, Will.'

'Likewise.'

And again he found himself once more staring after her longingly as she walked away.

# THE FLAME TREE

Later that evening, back at home in La Salle Road, Will told a white lie when his housemates suggested a night out on the town. 'Got a bad stomach,' he said. 'Sorry.'

He just wasn't in the mood and, besides, he wanted to jot down a poem. One day he might try and write a poem in Chinese, he decided, but for now he'd have to content himself with English, albeit inspired by the beautiful poem he'd learnt with Connie.

Ah King brought him a cooling glass of Tiger beer. Will thanked him and, after several drafts, wrote a version he felt he could give Connie.

*Why does Lion Rock challenge me so?*
*See how amid the dragon hills it stands*
*Cloaked in emerald majesty*
*Clouds rise in tiers, refreshing the mountain*
*Would that I could fly like a bird*
*Up to its heights*
*One day I shall climb*
*Clear to the summit*
*See how small the ships in the harbour appear*
*How small I must appear*
*To those below me.*

Will put down his pen with a sigh. Perhaps Connie would agree to translate the poem into Chinese for him? Would that work? He gave a rueful laugh. She would probably think it was awful.

# CHAPTER EIGHT

Connie climbed aboard the Peak Tram. She sat at the front of the car and the narrow track before her dropped steeply down to the city below. The bell rang and the funicular started its almost vertical descent. How many times she'd made this journey as a child! Mother had insisted she and her siblings attended a girls' school in Kowloon, because Mother had been told it would give them the best English education—which Mother valued almost above all else. Connie sighed to herself. The Peak School only admitted English children, so she and her sisters had been constrained to make an arduous daily journey. They rode donkeys led by trusted servants to get from home to the tram station. In the city below, sedan chairs carried them to the ferry pier. After crossing the harbour, they took rickshaws to the school. So many hours of her childhood spent toing and froing.

She remembered the Peak children being envious of the Han Fung donkeys. But that was the only thing they'd envied. Connie gritted her teeth as she thought about the blonde girl she'd seen chatting to Will and Reggie at the races. Was she one of those girls who used to tease her? When Connie was little, Gloria often took her to the Peak playground and would sit gossiping with other governesses while Connie played on the swings, roundabouts, and slides. What Gloria didn't know was that Connie was bullied mercilessly by the European children, who'd called her a "chink" and had berated her for even daring to even think she could play with them. Connie often wondered if it was because she wore different clothes to them. After all, she didn't look fully Chinese. Mother had no idea about western fashion, but she'd wanted her offspring to fit in and so she dressed them in what she thought were the right outfits. Even though Mother would get their garments made by a tailor in town, her sartorial standards didn't meet with the sensitivities of the Peak community. One time Connie had to wear a voile dress trimmed with a pink ribbon in the middle of winter. The brightly coloured frock was made warmer by a woollen singlet underneath, which had an annoying habit of peeping out from under the voile neckline—a source of great amusement to the other children. Nowadays Connie would brush it off, but as a child she'd found the teasing laughter extremely hurtful.

As the cable railway progressed down the mountain, Connie's thoughts turned to Will. He'd looked so incredibly handsome last Saturday, dressed in his cream-coloured suit, his face already tanned by the Hong Kong sun. She'd felt a big thrill when she'd seen him the day before in the Botanical Gardens and had been even more delighted to bump into him at the races. Oh, if only they came from the same background. Except, would she be quite so fascinated by him if he were Eurasian? She'd never experienced such overwhelming attraction towards someone of her own race let alone towards an Englishman. Why couldn't she stop thinking about him? It was ridiculous, so unlike her, and would surely end in tears. She needed to get a grip on herself and dismiss all thoughts of there ever being anything other than friendship between them.

She resolved to focus on where she was headed instead. Of course, she'd obtained Father's approval before confirming with Margaret about helping at the clinic. Apparently, "family planning" had become a fashionable phrase in Hong Kong. Debates about the ethics of artificial birth control had caught the headlines of virtually every local newspaper after an American woman, Mrs Sanger, leader of the international birth control movement, had visited the colony three years ago upon the invitation of the Chinese Medical Association. She gave a public lecture on the subject to over five hundred people in the roof garden of the Hong Kong Hotel. Many of the local elite viewed Sanger as a symbol of salvation for a city haunted by poverty, abortion, and infanticide. Consequently, Father said he was in favour of Connie working with Margaret and offered to make a donation.

The funicular shuddered to a stop at the terminus. Connie made her way out of the building to where rickshaws queued up at the side of the road. She negotiated a fare to Wanchai and, before too long, she'd arrived at the clinic, on the ground floor of a grimy porticoed shophouse in Hennessy Road. Reeling at the stink of human ordure, Connie covered her nose with a handkerchief. The filthy pavement was lined with the grass mats of street sleepers—refugees from the war in China who hadn't been able to find anywhere to live. The raucous sound of voices filled the air, punctuated with the noise of tramcars, buses, and taxis passing by. Connie felt a rush of compassion for the mothers sitting on the kerb, clutching babies to their breasts. Flies swarmed around them and Connie wished she could invite them all to stay with her. She couldn't help a wry smile at the thought of how the "Peakites" would react if she did that.

Inside, Connie found a square room crowded with women, children clinging to their legs. Margaret welcomed her with open arms. Literally. She enfolded Connie in a warm embrace. 'I'm so glad you've agreed to help. As you can see, we're inundated. Jean here is also giving me a hand.' Margaret indicated towards a younger woman, Chinese, who was dressed in a western style blouse and skirt.

'Hi. Pleased to meet you, Connie,' Jean said in an American-sounding accent. She tucked the permed curl of her short black hair behind an ear.

'Jean's husband, George Robinson, is in charge of the refugee camp in Kowloon,' Margaret said. 'But it's overflowing...hence the number of street sleepers.'

Connie was curious about Jean and her husband, but now was not the time to ask. She'd barely taken a breath before Margaret thrust a small, square box into her hand. 'It's a Dutch cap or diaphragm. We're giving them out for free, but first the women must make an appointment with our gynaecologist to get one fitted. You'll need to record the appointments then teach the women how to use the diaphragm.'

Connie felt the heat of a blush. 'I'm sorry...but I don't know how to use one myself.'

Margaret smiled kindly, then turned to Jean. 'Can you explain everything to Connie, please. I need to make a phone call.'

She should have realised what she'd let herself in for, Connie thought as Jean went into details about the contraceptive device and how a recipient should insert it to cover her cervix. Connie squared her shoulders; she wouldn't let embarrassment put her off. She'd agreed to help and help she would.

Eventually, after talking to what seemed like hundreds of women and making appointments for them, Jean suggested they go for some dim sum. Connie accepted with pleasure. She was hungry and wanted to find out more about her new acquaintance.

'I know a great tea house around the corner,' Jean said to Connie as they headed out of the door.

Connie walked with her and soon they were sipping tea and nibbling steamed beef balls, char siu buns and yeung chow fried rice under slowly revolving ceiling fans in a teak-panelled room—where they were served by waiters in long white gowns.

'George is Canadian,' Jean clarified after Connie had asked her about him. 'As you can probably tell from my accent, I'm from there too. We met in Vancouver when we were both at the University of British Columbia.'

'Ah, I thought your accent was different. How did you end up in Hong Kong?' Connie took a sip of dark pu-erh tea, enjoying the earthy, slightly bitter rich taste.

'George is a mining engineer. He had his own company across the border in Southern China, but all that came to an end with the arrival of the Japanese. We moved to Hong Kong and he got a job with the government here.'

'That's interesting,' Connie said. And it was. Highly unusual for a man married to a Chinese—even one as westernised and well-educated as Jean—to have a career in the Colonial Secretariat. And what was a mining engineer doing running a refugee camp? There had to be more to George than met the eye, Connie thought.

Jean asked her about her own family, but Connie got the impression the question was only posed for politeness' sake as, when she mentioned that her father was Sir Albert Han Fung, Jean said she knew all about him. They finished their meal with walnut cake, then headed back to the clinic. There, Margaret repeated her invitation to dinner. 'Do come on Friday night,' she said. 'Jean and George will be there, also William Burton.'

'I'd love to,' Connie said. How could she possibly refuse?


'You're having dinner with "Septic" and his wife?' Father sounded surprised when Connie told him the next day.

'Why do you call him that?'

# THE FLAME TREE

'The British are always giving people nicknames, you know. He's known as "Septic" because he got involved in a controversy about night soil.'

Connie remembered the Chinese custom of using human excrement for fertilizer. It was composted with ashes and mainly used to fertilise mulberry trees in the silk-producing districts. Only wealthy people in Hong Kong had toilets in their homes. Everyone else used chamber pots. The contents were collected by female coolies in buckets at night and emptied into junks that came alongside the waterfront at specified points in the early hours of the morning. Locals paid the cost for collection themselves. Contractors made a big profit from selling the night soil to farmers.

Connie tilted her head towards her father. 'I know Europeans think the practise causes dysentery and cholera.'

'Harry Wyn-Jones maintains those diseases are caused by flies and the careless preparation of food. And I tend to agree with him.' Father smirked. '"Septic" provoked the coolies, who rioted when he proposed setting up tanks to contain the excrement. Hence his nickname.'

'Oh, how funny,' Connie giggled. 'He was kind to me on the *Carthage*. And I do like his wife.'

'I like her too. Did you know she is Honorary Secretary of the China Defence League, which raises funds to help the mother country in its fight against the Japanese?'

'Oh, my goodness. I didn't realise. How remarkable!'

'Indeed. Enjoy dinner with the Wyn-Joneses, daughter. Go with my blessing.'

'Thank you, Father,' Connie bowed her head and swallowed the guilty pang at the back of her throat. She had no reason to feel guilty, she told herself. She was a grown-up woman who had every right to a social life. The fact that Will would be there was incidental.

For the rest of the week, she focused on her voluntary work at the clinic. Friday came and she hurried home to get changed, excitement bubbling in her chest. Mother was busy entertaining a group of friends who'd come to play mah-jong, but that didn't stop her from asking Connie to see her before she set off up the road to the Wyn-Jones residence. 'That dress suits you,' Mother said, her gaze roving over Connie's demure silver-grey silk cheongsam. 'Look in on me when you get home.'

'I'll do that,' she promised.

Number One Elder Sister had gone to fetch a chair for her, and soon Connie found herself being deposited outside a Victorian-style red brick villa, perched on porticoes in Mount Kellett Road. A manservant opened the door and led her through to a lounge furnished with ornate black wood furniture. The other guests had already arrived and were sitting sipping cocktails and chatting. The men got to their feet as Connie approached. She shook hands with Will and her heart thrilled at the touch of his hand. Flustered, she kissed Jean and Margaret, and then was introduced to George Robinson, a burly man with a bulbous nose and thick, curly dark brown hair.

'What'll you have to drink, Connie?' Harry Wyn-Jones asked.

'A brandy soda, please.'

Instead of getting his house boy to pour the drinks, Harry served Connie himself. 'Here you are,' he said. 'Cheers!'

'Cheers!'

She settled herself on the sofa next to Jean and listened to talk about the Chinese Admiral, John Chang Wei, who had lately arrived in Hong Kong.

'He's a tough little guy with a body that's been battered in every war and dust-up since the 1911 revolution,' George said. 'I met him in Canton in '35.'

'Why is he in Hong Kong?' Jean asked.

'He was fighting the Japanese at the old Tiger Gate fort at the mouth of the Pearl River last year when he was wounded in the left foot,' Harry responded.

'The wound festered and he came down with blood poisoning,' Margaret added. 'He's been receiving treatment at Saint Theresa's Hospital in Kowloon, but they've just had to amputate his leg.'

Connie stiffened. 'How terrible. The poor man...'

'He'll be fine.' George swigged his gin and tonic. 'Chang Wei won't be daunted. He's one of the most resilient people I've ever met.'

'Sounds fascinating.' Will leant forward in his seat. 'I hope to meet him one day.'

George chuckled. 'He's quite a character. You'd like him, I'm sure.'

The Wyn-Jones's manservant reappeared. 'Supper ready, Missy,' he said to Margaret.

'Let's go through to the dining room,' she said, getting to her feet.

They sat at a rosewood table, laid with fine porcelain and silver cutlery.

Servants arrived with dishes of mushroom soup while Harry filled his guests' glasses with sherry from a crystal decanter.

While they ate, conversation turned to the war in China. 'Isn't your brother a lieutenant-colonel in Chiang Kai Shek's army, Connie?' Harry asked.

She felt everyone's eyes on her. 'He is indeed,' she said. 'I expect he knows the Admiral.'

'Your father must know him as well,' Margaret said. 'He supports the Kuomintang, doesn't he?'

Connie nodded. 'So do I, of course.'

'I just wish they would stop using all their resources fighting the communists and concentrate on beating the Japanese instead,' Margaret muttered.

'The communists are better at fighting the Japanese than the nationalists,' Jean chipped in.

George shot his wife a stern look. 'Let's not talk politics right now, sweetie.'

'Ok.' Jean smiled at Will. 'I hear you've only recently arrived in the colony. How are you getting on?'

'Very well. I started Cantonese classes this week. A tutor comes to my place every morning and I've been spending four hours in intensive language study. So far so good.'

'Didn't Connie give you some lessons on the *Carthage*?' Harry asked, filling everyone's glass with more sherry.

'She did and my tutor said he was impressed with how good my pronunciation is.'

'Marvellous,' George raised his glass. 'Here's to Will and his future in Hong Kong!'

They all clinked glasses and chorused, 'To Will!'

Connie's eyes locked with his, and their shared gaze felt so personal. How desperately she wanted to see him on his own. Sunday couldn't come fast enough.

The manservant cleared their plates and served them with sweet and sour fish, boiled rice, and crunchy vegetables. Connie was relieved not to have to face heavy English food. She couldn't stomach it at night. The meal passed in polite conversation, Margaret advising Will about getting his clothes tailor-made, Harry telling Jean about his service in West Africa before being posted to Hong Kong, and George speaking to Connie about his work with the refugees. She was horrified to learn that the population had doubled to one and a half million since the fall of Canton a year ago.

# THE FLAME TREE

After mango pudding with sago and pomelo, Connie and Jean went upstairs with Margaret, leaving the men to smoke cigars and drink brandy.

'Is there something going on between you and Will?' Jean said to Connie, sitting next to her on a soft sofa while Margaret was in the bathroom.

Connie sat bolt upright, her heart missing a beat. 'Why do you ask?' Her cheeks burned.

'I saw the way you were looking at each other, honey. I hope you don't think I'm prying but from my perspective it's obvious.'

'There can't be anything between us, Jean. I'm expected to conform to tradition and marry someone from my own background. If I'm seen alone with Will, it would spoil my chances and Father would never forgive me.'

'Oh, sweetie. I'm so sorry.'

Margaret appeared in the doorway. 'Is everything alright?'

'Yes,' Connie breathed. 'I'm just a little tired.'

'You've worked hard at the clinic. I'm proud of you.' Margaret went to her dressing table, powdered her nose, and put on lipstick. 'Let's go and join the men.'

'If you don't mind, I think I'll ask for a chair to take me home. Sorry to be a party-pooper.'

'No need to do that, Connie.' Jean gave her a sympathetic glance. 'George and I drove up in our Ford roadster. There's room in the flip-down back seat for you. Oh, and we'll give Will a lift down the Peak as well.'

And thus Connie found herself squashed next to him. She inhaled the sandalwood scent of his after-shave, his firm thigh against hers making her long for his touch.

'It's rather warm tonight,' Will said.

'Yes, it is,' Connie agreed, though she guessed he'd said it on purpose—the heat between them had made her breathless. She caught his gaze, the twinkle in his eye, and couldn't help but smile back at him.

'Thank you,' she said to George as the car pulled up in front of the Han Fung gates.

Will leapt out and held out his hand to help her. 'Good night, Connie. See you on Sunday,' he whispered.

She squeezed his hand and fought the urge to brush a kiss to his cheek. 'Good night, Will.'

# Chapter Nine

On the first Saturday in September, Will was hiking up to Lion Rock with Reggie. Will wiped sweat from his brow and wondered when the unforgiving Hong Kong summer would ever come to an end. It had been nearly four months since he'd arrived in the colony. Four months of sweating so much he'd had to resort to taking salt tablets to treat cramps and smother himself with prickly heat powder to prevent skin rashes. Thank God for Ah Jun, who washed and ironed the sweaty clothes he needed to change twice a day. Will had also resorted to scraping mildew off his leather shoes—mouldy on account of the constant high humidity. Apparently, drier weather would arrive in October, and he'd been told that the short Hong Kong winter would start before Christmas. It was something to look forward to. Despondency had settled on him like a shroud, spoiling his enchantment with being in China. All to do with Connie. He wanted so much more from her than friendship. He wanted her to be his girl and to take her out and show her off to the world like Reggie was doing with Deborah. Reggie knew where Will's heart lay and he'd encouraged him to tag along when he and Deborah set off to explore the New Territories and swim off remote beaches. Will had felt like a third wheel, however. At least, today, it was just him and Reggie. Deborah suffered from vertigo and had forgone the climb.

They'd left La Salle Road in the late afternoon, thinking it would be cooler, and had walked to the end of Prince Edward Road, past what remained of the old walled Kowloon City, then alongside the airfield until they'd come to a wide, unmetalled street. From there, they'd headed north, strolling through countryside where farmers, their wide-brimmed straw hats shaped like giant mushrooms, held wooden ploughs pulled by water buffalo, tilling the muddy paddy-fields to ready them for rice planting.

At the foot of the mountain, immersed in tropical forest, Will and Reggie set off up a steep trail, the incline testing their calf muscles. The narrow, beaten path was slippery and Will was glad they'd brought walking sticks. They paused occasionally, where gaps in the dense foliage and openings in the glades of tea-trees afforded enticing views of the curved roofs of the village houses and paddy-fields below.

Granite boulders edged the track, and uneven stone steps had been cut into the rock. The ascent grew steeper as they were nearing the summit. Their breath rasped and Will's legs ached. The impenetrable vegetation had given way to smaller shrubs and his spirits lightened at the panorama spreading below. It was as if he were up in the gods at the theatre. Kowloon represented the dress circle. The harbour the orchestra pit. And Hong Kong Island a magnificent stage etched against the evening sky.

The climb levelled out at the ridge cresting the summit. They walked along it, taking in the three-hundred-and-sixty-degree views. Indeed, they were on top of the world. Below, to the right, on the other side of Kowloon, lay Shatin Valley—an entirely rural area blanketed with paddy-fields and dotted with small villages, where the Shing Mun river flowed into a tidal cove.

# THE FLAME TREE

On the far horizon, the mountains of China formed a stunning backdrop to the scene.

They came to a stone ledge with an almost vertical deadly drop overlooking Kowloon. 'Let's take a break,' Reggie suggested, lowering himself.

Will followed suit. From here the eroded granite profile of the lion was unmistakable. Proud, majestic, gazing down at his territory. The beauty of Hong Kong tugged at Will's heartstrings. He'd come to love it just as he'd come to love Connie.

'Penny for them?' Reggie asked.

'Penny for my thoughts, ha,' Will chuckled. 'You're intuitive.'

'Does Connie know that you've fallen in love with her?'

'No,' Will sighed. 'There's no point me saying anything...'

Reggie offered him a Player's, which he accepted. He leant into the proffered match, sat back, and took a deep draw.

'You've been seeing each other in secret every week for months now.' Reggie exhaled smoke from his own cigarette. 'You can't go on like this.'

'I know,' Will groaned. 'It's tearing me apart.'

'Then you should say something. Find out if she feels the same. And, if she doesn't, then perhaps you should make a clean break of it?'

'That would be even worse.' Will shook his head. 'I'm truly caught between a rock and a hard place.'

'Hmmm.' Reggie refrained from further comment.

They sat smoking, watching the sun go down. 'So,' Will said, changing the subject to the other matter on his mind. 'Do you think we'll declare war on Germany?' They'd heard the news of the German invasion of Poland on the radio that morning.

'I'm afraid so, Will. Hitler is bound to ignore the ultimatum. He won't cease military operations.'

'Would you go back to England and enlist? I was thinking I should...'

'If war is declared, and I'm almost certain it will be, then there is a very real danger it will escalate into a global conflict. Japan will take advantage of the situation. It would be better if you and I joined the Hong Kong Volunteers. Don't forget that the Nips are at our border.'

'But everyone tells me the Japs wouldn't dare take on the might of the British Empire.'

Reggie laughed ruefully. 'To my way of thinking, people have underestimated them massively.'

'What makes you say that?'

'The way they have fought in China.'

'Ah. Yes. You have a point there.'

Next day, at seven in the morning, Will strolled across the central plaza of the Botanical Gardens for his weekly meeting with Connie. He meandered past the shadow boxers, men and women practising the ancient Chinese art of tai chi, their gentle, flowing movements a form of meditation in slow motion. He saw them every Sunday and they always lifted his sprits as he headed towards his and Connie's secret place.

She was sitting on their bench under the flame tree. No longer flowering, its dark green canopy spread over the gazebo turned the pavilion into a haven of privacy. So early in the day, that part of the garden was empty. On the rare occasions anyone passed by, they practised their ruse of Will getting up and walking away. He hoped it would not be the case today—he needed to talk to Connie and lay his cards on the table.

'Nei Hou Maa?' He asked her how she was.

'Ngo Hou Hou.' She said she was fine, her beautiful smile going straight to his heart. 'Nei na?'

'Ngo do gei hou.' He said he was fine too and sat next to her, glancing around before kissing her sweet lips. They'd only started kissing recently and Connie's apparent willingness had given Will so much hope. But, when he'd suggested taking her out to dinner, she'd clammed up and said it was impossible. Then he'd suggested going out on a double date with Jean and George, but she'd told him she would instantly become the subject of gossip and her father would find out.

'I finally hiked up to Lion Rock yesterday,' he said, reaching for her hand. Holding hands was another novelty. 'I went with Reggie.'

She repeated the first line of his poem, which she'd translated into Cantonese for him. *Why does Lion Rock challenge me so?* 'Was it how you'd expected?'

'Even better.' He grinned. 'But the climb was definitely a challenge.' He met her gaze. 'Did you have a good week?'

'I did. But I was sad to finish at the clinic.' She was starting her secretarial course tomorrow and would be too busy to do both, he remembered. 'How were your Cantonese lessons?' she asked.

'Vocabulary building is coming along. I know about eight hundred words now.'

'Excellent! You'll soon be able to get by in most situations.'

'Still a way to go. My teacher said I'll need about two and a half thousand under my belt for basic fluency. And about five thousand to be really fluent.'

Mr Tsui, a wonderful old gentleman, slim with a thin face, who always wore a long silk gown with black slippers, taught through the medium of Cantonese, using a picture book with Chinese characters written next to the images. Will spent half of each morning on his speaking skills, and the other half practising reading and writing. He enjoyed every minute of it.

He cleared his throat. 'Did you hear the news about Poland?'

A frown wrinkled Connie's brow. 'It's terrible. Those poor Polish people…'

'I'm afraid this means Britain is bound to declare war on Germany.'

She clamped a hand to her mouth. 'Oh, no!'

'I had thought of returning to England to join up. No doubt there will be conscription into the Armed Forces before too long.'

'But you won't be conscripted from here?' Her voice trembled.

'No. So, instead, I've decided to offer my services to the Hong Kong Volunteer Defence Corps.'

'Why?' She gripped his fingers.

'I know most people believe the Japs will never invade the colony. I hope they won't. Except it's better to be safe than sorry. There aren't enough battalions in the regiments making up the garrison to defend us if there's a full-scale attack. I talked with Reggie, Mike, and Nigel about it last night and we've all decided to do our bit.'

'You could get killed if you fought the Japanese, Will.' Her eyes shone with fear. 'I couldn't bear that.'

'You couldn't?'

'Of course, silly. You're… my friend.'

'I was hoping we could be more than friends, Connie.' He took a deep breath. 'I've fallen in love with you, my darling.'

She visibly stiffened and withdrew her hand. 'No, Will. You mustn't. We can never be a couple.'

'Don't you love me?'

Her pearly teeth caught at her lip and her frown deepened. 'I care for you very much. But I can't allow myself to fall in love with you.'

'What if we were to marry? Surely there would be no shame in that?' He looked her in the eye.

'It would mean leaving Hong Kong. There would be no future here for us. My family means everything to me. I couldn't live apart from them.' Her voice choked. 'And what about you? Your career in the colonial service? You'd be ostracised…' She was crying now, silent tears furrowing her cheeks.

He put his arms around her and held her close, kissing the top of her head and whispering, 'I'm sorry. I shouldn't have pressed you.' He pulled a clean handkerchief from his pocket and dried her tears. 'Let's carry on as we are, then. I'd rather be just your friend than not have you in my life.'

'Are you sure? I mean, maybe you should try and meet a girl from your own background. Someone like Deborah Hartley Smith…'

'I doubt there'll be time for that, even if I wanted to. Which I don't. Between training with the Volunteers and my Cantonese lessons, I expect I'll be kept far too busy.' He leant back and made eye contact with her again. 'I might not be able to meet with you every week, Connie. It will depend on my schedule.'

'Oh.' She sounded surprised and, dared he hope, disappointed.

'How do I get a message to you if I can't make it?'

'Call Jean and she'll phone me.'

Connie and Jean had become close. Connie had even invited her to meet her mother, Will remembered. 'Alright,' he said.

'Now we must start your lesson. Turn your back to me and we'll begin.'

He did as Connie had requested, reciting the poem he'd learnt last week and then going through the pronunciation of another of Do Fu's poems.

*Wild beasts howl as they seek their prey*
*Sleep does not come to me*
*For still I worry about war*

*Knowing I have no way to set the world aright.*

The words of the poem, written over a thousand years ago, resonated with Will. Humankind and war were two words that always went together, it seemed. With what felt like a stolen kiss and a hug that tore at his heart, he took his leave of Connie and made his way to the USRC for a curry tiffin and a swim. After a game of tennis with a couple of chums, he went home. There, he found his housemates gathered around the wireless in their sitting room.

'The balloon has gone up,' Reggie said in a solemn tone. 'We're at war with Germany.'

## Chapter Ten

Another sultry summer had arrived, and Will was out on an exercise with the Field Company Engineers. He'd enlisted right after Hitler had ignored Chamberlain's ultimatum, his initial training taking place during Hong Kong's agreeable winter months, which had coincided with the period known as the "phoney war" in Europe.

And what a winter it had been! Letters from home complained about the cold in Bristol—the frost which began in late December 1939, and continued with few intermissions until mid-February 1940, had been the most severe in Great Britain since 1895, his parents had written. Will's first winter in Hong Kong, on the other hand, had been divine—daytime temperatures in the high sixties only fell about ten degrees at night. He'd spent a dry, sunny Christmas Day at the Wyn-Jones's, and it had been the best Christmas of his life because Connie had spent it with him. He closed his eyes now and remembered. In the corner of the sitting room a China fir tree had held pride of place, decorated with spun cotton icicles, glass stars, beads and multi-coloured ornaments. They'd had traditional fare—roast turkey with all the trimmings, followed by plum pudding, brandy butter, mince pies and Christmas cake. After lunch, they'd played charades with Margaret, Harry, Jean, and George, and had sat around the gramophone singing carols. At one point, he and Connie had found themselves alone, but only for a moment. He'd pulled her under the hanging sprig of artificial mistletoe and stolen a heady kiss. At the end of the evening Connie said how much she'd enjoyed herself, gladdening Will's heart.

He smiled to himself, remembering how he and Connie had exchanged gifts—he'd given her a book of Robert Frost poems—Frost was one of his favourite poets—and she'd presented him with a beautiful, padded silk Chinese jacket, which he put on straight away and had worn proudly throughout the cooler months. It was a personal gift, and it had meant the world to him.

Wiping sweat from his forehead as he stood on a secluded beach near Tai Po overlooking Tolo Harbour in the New Territories, Will longed for the heat of summer to be over and for it to be Christmas once more. He only hoped he would spend it with Connie again. Thank God her father approved of the Wyn-Joneses and seemed happy for her to visit them. Margaret and Harry were the soul of discretion as far as Will and Connie were concerned. Sometimes Will caught Margaret looking at the two of them, a wistful expression on her face. But she said not a word and Will was grateful for that.

Hot sunshine beat through clouds of humidity and the air was heavy with the stench of the rotting seaweed on rocks by the shore. He glanced down at the limpet mine attached to a keeper plate hooked to a belt around his waist, marvelling at finding himself doing something so out of character. He'd never in his life imagined becoming a sapper. But there was a war on in Europe and there might well be one on shortly in Hong Kong.

Reggie had an identical explosive. He ran a hand through his ginger hair. 'All set, Will?' He gave a nervous smile.

'Ready as I'll ever be...'

# THE FLAME TREE

They'd primed the fuses earlier. All they needed to do now was row out to the rusty abandoned tanker lying semi-submerged in the middle of the bay, attach the limpet mines to the hull six and a half feet below the waterline, set the timers, and get away before the explosives went off. Easier said than done, Will thought, wiping his hands nervously down the sides of his shorts.

Field Company's Captain Sutherland, Major Winspear's second in command, both of whom were managers at Jardine Matheson and had seen action during the Great War, came up to Will and Reggie. 'Good luck, sappers,' he said.

'Thank you, Sir.' His heart thumping, he climbed into the rowing boat and sat in the stern while Reggie rowed them out to the tanker. They tied up alongside, put on goggles, then lowered themselves into the tepid sea.

Will offered to go first. He took a deep breath and swam down to the required depth, a little more than his body's length. In the murk, he discerned a barnacle-free spot, took the limpet from its plate, and let the magnetic force do the rest. In a fountain of bubbles, he resurfaced before clambering back into the dinghy to wait for Reggie to attach *his* mine.

It was Will's turn to row, and he did so fast and furiously, sweat pouring down his face. He beached the boat and hurried up the shore with Reggie. 'Ready for the countdown?' Will said, placing a tin hat on his head.

As soon as the words had left his mouth a muffled explosion reverberated, and then a massive plume of smoke and water shot up into the air.

Debris from the tanker rained down on them.

Will crouched low, his hat slipping. More sweat beaded his brow.

'Good God,' Reggie exclaimed. 'I didn't expect such a show.'

'Spectacular.' Will grinned.

'Well done, lads,' Sutherland said. 'You did a fine job.'

'Thank you, Sir.' Will saluted.

'Take the rest of the day off.' Sutherland waved his hand. 'You've earned a break.'

Will and Reggie went for a beer at the nearby Fanling Golf Club, where they met a couple of chums from the Royal Scots, who'd been carrying out manoeuvres on a half-constructed airfield in Sek Kong.

Still reeling from the almost total annihilation of their comrades in the 1$^{st}$ Battalion during the defence of Dunkirk, the 2$^{nd}$ Battalion, who'd been stationed in the colony since January 1938, were a gloomy bunch of men.

Will propped up the clubhouse bar next to a pal of his, Captain Jones, whom he'd played rugger against. 'I miss Elspeth and my wee Jimmy,' the captain lamented like a lost soul. His family, along with over forty other armed forces families, had been evacuated last month, among the 3,000 or so British women and children sent to Australia "as a precaution".

Will commiserated with him then checked his watch. Time was marching on and he needed to go home for a wash and a shave. Tonight, he was having dinner at George and Jean's. And, joy of joys, Connie would be there.

George and Jean's flat in Gunter Mansions, May Road, had a fine view of the harbour. Will was on the balcony, enjoying the evening air, anticipation making his heart pound at the thought he would soon be seeing Connie. Junks and sampans clogged the waterfront below and myriad ships lay at anchor in the depths. He thought back to when he danced with her on the *Carthage*. How he missed holding her in his arms! He'd arrived in Hong Kong over a year ago already. He'd passed two

# THE FLAME TREE

Cantonese exams—one every six months. The flame tree had flowered again and he'd met with Connie under its canopy whenever he could. But training with the Volunteers had taken up most of his free time and it had been a month since their last meeting. He couldn't wait to see her again.

'Nice 'ere, innit?' a cockney sounding voice interrupted Will's thoughts. He smiled at General Morris Cohen, an old China hand also known as "Two-gun Cohen". A colourful character who had once been Dr Sun Yat Sen, the founding father of the Republic of China's bodyguard. Cohen was the son of a Polish Jew who had emigrated in his teens from the East End of London to Canada, where he'd learnt to ride, shoot, and gamble. Having moved on to China, he'd offered his services to the President, becoming a favoured retainer, and acquiring the rank of General in the Chinese army. He later made his living from arms-dealing and all-night poker sessions at Short-Time Susan's in Shanghai before winding up in Hong Kong, where he hung around the lounge of the Hong Kong Hotel, slightly drunk, but ever ready to let the jacket of his white suit fall open and reveal his trademark two guns, holstered at each side of his body. Cohen was ambidextrous, evidently.

'Yes, it is nice here,' Will said distractedly, keeping his ear tuned for Connie's arrival.

Reggie and Deborah came out onto the balcony and sat on big rattan chairs under a ceiling fan. Will and Cohen went to join them. The sound of the doorbell ringing echoed through the veranda doors, and Connie's tinkling laughter made Will's heart sing. He restrained himself from going to her and sweeping her off her feet. Dear God, it was hard having to hide his feelings from the world. George and Jean brought her through and she sat opposite Will, smiling so sweetly and looking so beautiful in her pale blue cheongsam, her dark brown hair pinned up above her swan-like neck.

Conversation buzzed around Will. Apparently, the Japanese Foreign Minister had just announced the concept of something called the Greater East Asia Co-Prosperity Sphere.

'What's on earth could that be?' Deborah enquired. She was one of the few European girls left in Hong Kong. When her mother had been evacuated, Deborah had been allowed to stay behind because she'd joined the VAD, the Voluntary Aid Detachment, where she was doing ciphering work. Only those women involved in so-called essential services had been permitted to remain, and Will guessed she'd foregone evacuation so that she could carry on seeing Reggie.

'Japan wants to create a self-sufficient bloc of Asian countries that'll be led by the Japanese and free from the rule of the West,' George explained.

'Sounds ominous,' Connie said with a shudder. She caught Will's eye and he gave her what he hoped was a reassuring smile.

'Roosevelt has just signed an Export Control Act, limiting the sale of military equipment to Japan.' George sipped his gin gimlet. 'Japs have responded by saying a showdown with the United States might be necessary.'

'A showdown?' Reggie chipped in.

'Surely Japan won't take on America?' Will frowned.

George smirked ruefully. 'Britain is focused on fighting Germany. I think the Japs will wait until the Nazis invade the Soviet Union.'

Will shook his head. 'But hasn't Hitler signed a non-aggression treaty with Stalin?'

'My bet is it won't last,' George responded. 'Hitler is greedy for conquest. And I expect he's already drawing up plans to march his troops into Russia.'

'He's a horrible man. I hate him.' Jean passed around a bowl of peanuts. 'Why can't the world live in peace?'

# THE FLAME TREE

No one had an answer to her question. They sat sipping their drinks, nibbling salty nuts, and chatting about the typhoon which had narrowly missed the colony last week.

The Robinsons' houseboy arrived to say that dinner was ready, so everyone rose to their feet.

In the dining room, which boasted another stunning view of the harbour through a picture window, Will was pleased that Connie had been placed next to him. He found her hand under the tablecloth and held it. Her eyes met his and sent him the message that she'd missed him. He returned the message with his own eyes before mouthing the words when no one was looking, 'I've missed you, darling girl.'

After dinner, the ladies went to powder their noses and Will sat with the men, smoking a cigar, and sipping brandy.

'So,' George said, without preamble. 'There's something I'd like to discuss with you, Will and Reggie.' He indicated towards Cohen. 'Morris is here to back me up.'

Will straightened his spine and listened.

'You might have wondered what a mining engineer is doing looking after a bunch of refugees?'

Will *had* wondered. He'd discussed the anomaly with Reggie on several occasions.

'Well,' George carried on. 'I'm in charge of setting up a secret services commando unit.'

'A commando unit?!' Will almost fell off his chair.

'It's called Z Force,' Cohen clarified.

'Hasn't Churchill just set up the British Commandos in the UK?' Reggie's eyes had widened with surprise.

'Yep. Our unit will allow itself to be overrun if the Japs invade, then use guerrilla tactics to harass them,' George went on to say. 'We'll blow up bridges, create diversions, gather intelligence, and send reports back to any remaining defenders. If the enemy wins, the plan is to escape into the part of China which hasn't been occupied, bringing out as much information as possible from Hong Kong.'

'And you want us to join?' Will leant forward in his seat.

'You've both done explosives training in the Volunteers and are competent in speaking Cantonese. You're exactly the men we need.'

Five million Chinese soldiers were confronting the Japanese invaders in a virtual stalemate along a 2,000-mile front. There was no disputing the fact that the tiny nation of Japan now controlled the north and much of the east and south of the world's most populous country—including almost all its key cities, ports, and communication lines. Hong Kong was a likely target and Will knew where his duty lay. But he needed time to consider George's proposal, and maybe even run it by Connie. 'Can I think about it?' he asked.

Reggie relit his cigar. 'I need time to think too.'

'George has many contacts in southern China.' Cohen took a snifter of brandy. 'He's formed links with the guerrilla groups that are springing up in the no-man's-land between areas held by the Japanese and by the Kuomintang Government. Many of these irregular forces are pro-Nationalist, acting as a buffer for the Chinese government troops. But there is also an increasingly strong communist guerrilla movement. It's the communist units that are most active against the Japanese, and therefore, the most useful to us.'

'Interesting,' Will said. 'I'm tempted to say yes. Can I let you know in a day or two? Would it involve me stepping down from the Volunteers?'

# THE FLAME TREE

'You'd both be seconded to me, so no need. I work for the government, remember.' George exhaled cigar smoke. 'This is all top secret, by the way. You mustn't mention it to anyone.'

'Ah, of course.'

The door to the dining room swung open and the ladies came in, bringing the scent of their perfumes with them. Will reached for Connie's hand under the table again while coffee was served. 'Can Reggie and I give you a lift home?' he asked.

'My parents have gone to Macau for a brief holiday in our house there and to visit my brother, so yes, please.' She smiled.

In the back seat of Reggie's Morris, Will put his arm around Connie. 'Nei Hou Maa?' *How are you?*

'Ngo Hou Hou. Nei na?' *I'm very well. And you?*

'Ngo do gei hou.' *I'm very well too.*

And then, he kissed her. How warm and sweet were her lips. He felt the pounding of her heart, trembling in her mouth. Oh how he wished he could share his love for her with the world. But kisses snatched in secret were better than no kisses at all. So he carried on kissing her until Reggie pulled up outside the gate to the Han Fung estate. 'Goodnight, darling Connie,' he said. 'I hope to see you soon.'

'I hope so too, Will. Goodnight.'

He leapt out of the car to open the door for her, longing to crush her to him and feel her lithe body pressed to his. She made her way down the path and, with a heavy sensation in his chest, he kept his eyes on her until she disappeared.

# Chapter Eleven

The weather was still too hot to be dressed in a traditional Chinese ceremonial jacket, Connie thought as she stood in line with Mamma, Father, Mother, and her siblings on the front steps of the Peninsula Hotel—also known as the finest hotel east of Suez—in the early evening of the first Monday in October. But Mamma had insisted that hers and Father's 50$^{th}$ wedding anniversary should be celebrated in style, and it was customary for women of the Han Fung family's background to dress formally on such occasions. Made of heavy red silk embroidered with gold metallic thread flowers, her high-collared coat, worn over a long brocade skirt, felt inhibiting and Connie couldn't wait to take it off.

She fidgeted with the cuffs of her long sleeves. That morning, at "The Manor", Mamma and Father had received deputations from the local community, represented by officials of the Chinese Chamber of Commerce, the Tung Wah Hospital, and twenty-four merchants' guilds. The entire family was on parade, listening to interminable congratulatory speeches, drinking champagne, and eating canapés. And now a dinner-dance, in the Rose Room on the sixth floor of the Peninsula, was about to begin.

# THE FLAME TREE

Connie's breath suddenly hitched. Will had come into the periphery of her vision. He was getting out of a rickshaw over by the fountain gracing the forecourt of the hotel. She'd told him on Sunday two weeks ago about the celebration. It had been one of their rare meetings under the flame tree. All through the summer, she'd barely seen him. He appeared to be busier than ever and, when she'd asked him about his activities, he'd said he couldn't talk about them. Connie frowned. It was all very hush-hush and she feared for his safety.

She was standing at the back of the reception line. Hierarchy meant her brothers came before her and her sisters, and she, being the youngest, came last. She wondered if Will had seen her. He'd turned away and was heading towards Salisbury Road.

She mustn't think about him. She did that far too much and it was becoming more and more difficult to deny her feelings. Common sense told her that she should break off their liaison. It was a miracle none of her family had found out. But, whenever she'd geared herself up to suggest not seeing him anymore, her heart had overruled the sensible voice in her head. She briefly brushed a finger to her lips. How she loved being kissed by him, the slide of his hands around her back, the warmth and press of his mouth. He made her come alive at his touch, and delicious sensations spread through her. It was wrong, she knew it was, but it felt like the most perfect thing in the world.

With a quick shake of her head, she made herself focus on greeting the invitees. Special launches decorated with gold-coloured bunting had ferried them over to Kowloon from Hong Kong side, a fleet of motor cars conveying them from the landing stage to the hotel. Young bellboys in white uniforms opened the doors of the vehicles, and the guests, dressed to the nines, lined up to enter the building. The press was also there, camera flash bulbs going off left, right and centre. It was all so overwhelming.

The Governor arrived, followed by the Colonial Secretary, the Commander of British Forces, and the Secretary for Chinese Affairs. All the European men were without their wives, who'd been evacuated from the colony. But the Colonial Secretary had brought his daughter, Deborah. Connie smiled as she shook her hand. They'd become friends—not close like her and Jean, but more than acquaintances—and Connie was grateful the English girl had kept hers and Will's closeness a secret.

Connie walked with her family across the marble floor of the lobby, then rode the lifts to the Rose Room. Floor-to-ceiling windows, lined with pillars topped with Corinthian capitals, opened onto a splendid view of the harbour. Ceiling fans hung from ornately decorated joists. At the sides of the rectangular room stood many tables covered with crisp white linen, silver cutlery and crystal—enough to seat eight hundred guests—with space to spare for the parquet-covered dance floor in the centre. A jazz band was playing *Puttin' On the Ritz* and Connie swallowed the lump of nostalgia in her throat as she remembered dancing to that song with Will on the *Carthage*.

After checking the table plan, she found herself seated next to the one-legged Admiral John Chang Wei. Her brother, Matthew, looking tall, dark, and handsome in his tuxedo and black morning coat, had been placed on the other side of the Admiral's wife, Shiuchi.

Short, sturdily built, with a round face, a defiantly jutting jaw and sparkling eyes, the Admiral immediately endeared himself to Connie when he insisted that she called him "Uncle Wei".

Waiters arrived, carrying silver trays laden with plates of consommé soup. Connie fell into polite conversation with the Admiral, who told her he was forty-six years old.

'You look much younger,' she said.

'I have a young heart.' He winked and glanced at his wife. 'I still take Shiuchi out dancing to nightclubs every weekend…

Even with this.' He rolled up his trouser leg and showed Connie the artificial wooden limb.

'Oh,' she said, not knowing what else to say.

'Uncle Wei is a legend,' Matthew said. 'Did you know he once saved the lives of Dr Sun Yat Sen and Chiang Kai Shek when he rescued them both by boat from rivals who'd penned them in?'

'That's wonderful.' Connie gave the Admiral an admiring smile, thankful he'd rolled down his trouser leg again.

'So, Connie,' he said. 'I hear you studied in London. What are your future plans?'

'I've just finished a secretarial course and now I'd like to get a job.'

'Interesting.' The Admiral spooned soup into his mouth, then turned his attention to his wife, who was sitting on the other side of him.

The meal progressed with duck à l'orange, rice and sautéed vegetables, followed by tropical fruit salad and mango ice cream. After Mamma and Father had cut a multi-tiered fruit cake iced with golden flowers, the Governor made a congratulatory speech and everyone raised their glasses of champagne to toast the happy couple.

'Care to dance, little sister?' Matthew asked when the band launched into *The Very Thought of You*.

'Yes, please.' She got to her feet. 'Shame Esther couldn't be here...'

Matthew led Connie onto the floor. 'It's safer for her in America with James.' Connie remembered that her nephew's school in Chungking had been bombed by the Japanese.

Connie thought for a moment. 'Uncle Wei seems like a fascinating character.'

'He's remarkable.' Mathew smirked at the Admiral, who was managing to foxtrot like a professional. 'After Sun Yat Sen died and Generalissimo Chiang Kai Shek became our leader, he gave

Uncle Wei what amounted to his own fiefdom along the South China coast.'

'You mean he was a warlord?' The Kuomintang was made up of such men, who exercised effective governmental control over well-defined regions by means of military organisation that obeyed no higher authority than themselves.

'Indeed. But Uncle Wei never abused that power.'

'I see.' Connie nodded. 'What's he doing in Hong Kong?'

'Can you keep a secret?' Matthew looked Connie in the eye.

'Of course.'

'He's the Chinese government's political and military representative here.'

'But, why is that a secret?'

'Because the Kuomintang is not allowed to have an official ambassador in the colony.' Matthew huffed. 'It's because the British don't wish to provoke the Japanese, I believe.'

'Ah.' Uncle Wei was gliding past again, twisting and turning to the music with his wife. What an extraordinary person, Connie thought.

'So, little sister, have you decided to let Father find you a husband yet?' Matthew said teasingly.

Connie gritted her teeth. She'd passed her secretarial course three months ago but her father had said there weren't any positions available for her in any of his businesses. She'd gone back to helping Margaret at her clinic, worried he was planning to try and arrange a marriage for her. 'I want to get a job,' she said. 'Do something useful before I become a tai-tai.'

'So you should, little sis. So you should...'

The song came to an end and Connie excused herself to go to the ladies. After she'd used the facilities, she went to wash her hands and refresh her lipstick. The door swung open and Deborah came in.

'I was hoping I'd bump into you.' A smile lit the English girl's blue eyes. 'Reggie and Will are down on the terrace. How about we sneak out there and join them?'

'I'm not sure,' Connie said. 'I'm supposed to be with my family.'

'It won't be for long. We can have one drink then come back upstairs. Everyone is busy dancing with everyone else. No one will notice our absence.'

Connie's chest tightened with indecision. Surely there could be no harm in going with Deborah. It wouldn't be as if she'd be on her own with Will. 'I'd love that,' she said.

The balustraded veranda bar overlooked the forecourt of the hotel. Will was sitting on an upholstered armchair pulled up to a small, round, marble-topped table, opposite Reggie. Both men leapt to their feet as Connie and Deborah approached.

'You're looking absolutely gorgeous,' Will whispered as he came to stand next to Connie.

She'd managed to shrug off her jacket earlier, and the cool night air caressed her bare arms. She cast her gaze over Will. Dressed in his smart linen suit, he was looking so terribly handsome she could cry. The sound of a ship's horn reverberated in the distance, and across the harbour the majestic night spectacle of the Peak, festooned with myriad lights, made Connie smile.

'What'll you have to drink?' Will inclined his head towards her.

'A brandy soda, please.' She glanced around. The bar was quiet at this time of night. She wouldn't be seen. Oh, how she wished she didn't have to go behind everyone's back.

Reggie went to place their drinks orders. Connie sat next to Will. Without warning, the hair on the back of her neck prickled. Someone was staring at her, she was sure of it. But when she turned around to look, there was no one.

The brief interlude was over almost as soon as it had begun. Connie glanced at her watch. 'Sorry, but I've got to get back to the party.'

'Must you?' Will's brow creased.

'I'll come with you, Connie.' Deborah brushed a kiss to Reggie's cheek. 'See you tomorrow, darling.'

Connie's eyes met Will's. When would she see him again? They hadn't even arranged their next meeting in the Botanical Gardens...

'I'll leave a message with Jean,' he said.

'Father wants to see you,' Matthew announced while Connie was having breakfast the next morning.

Connie's heart skittered. Had someone seen her out on the Peninsula's terrace? 'What does he want?'

'Search me. But he asked if I would bring you to him forthwith.'

Connie put down her table napkin and rose to her feet. Better get it over with. If she had been seen, there'd been nothing untoward. She'd slipped out for a drink with Deborah, who was meeting her boyfriend. Will just happened to have been with him, Connie quickly made up the excuse in her head.

Matthew walked along the path to Father's with her. They found him in his study, seated behind his antique blackwood desk.

'Sit, both of you,' Father said. He turned to Connie. 'Daughter, you have been noticed.'

Connie's blood froze. 'I haven't done anything wrong.' Heat bloomed up the sides of her face.

'Hmmm.' Father made a steeple with his fingers. 'It appears not.'

# THE FLAME TREE

'Oh?' She caught the twinkle in his eye.

'Admiral John Chang Wei would like to offer you a job.'

'Me?!' Her mouth had dropped open. She shut it rapidly.

'He needs a private secretary. Someone with your background who will be discreet,' Father said.

'Uncle Wei has set up a small stockbroking company as a cover for his secret activity running the Kuomintang's vast underground network in Hong Kong,' Matthew chipped in. 'It's on the second floor of Shell House in Queen's Road Central.'

'But he has another office on the fourth floor of Pedder Building, just across the street,' Father added. 'For the past year, he's been carrying out undercover work against Japan and trying to ensure that China remains supplied with fuel and other essential materials, despite the Japanese trade embargo.'

'I would be honoured to work for him,' Connie said. And she would. She didn't need to even think about it.

'Good.' Father smiled. 'It will only be until I find a suitable husband for you, though. Remember where your duty lies, daughter.'

Connie bowed her head. How could she ever forget? 'Yes, Father,' she said resignedly. 'Of course.'

# CHAPTER TWELVE

It was two days before Christmas and, from her desk in the anteroom of the Admiral's private office in Pedder Building, Connie was watching three burly men who were sitting just a few feet away from her, slurping tea and cracking sunflower-seed shells between their teeth. They were Big Eared Tu, the Shanghai mobster's White Russian bodyguards, and were nothing more than uncouth thugs, she thought with a shiver. No wonder she felt chilled to the bone. Big Eared Tu was already with the Admiral, in his office. She sat erect, her hand near the buzzer. Cheng Jin, Uncle Wei's own bodyguard, was a skilled kung fu fighter. She didn't like the way the three Russians were looking at her, undressing her with their eyes.

It had been eight weeks since Connie had started working for the Admiral, eight weeks of answering the phone, typing letters and reports, taking minutes at meetings, filing documents, and making sure the Admiral was kept supplied with endless cups of tea made by the office boy. But this was the first time she had come face-to-face with anyone like Big Eared Tu and his henchmen. Connie shivered again.

Matthew had once told her that Tu was the leader of the Green Gang Triads and had dominated Shanghai's opium and heroin trade during the past ten years. What was Tu's connection with the Admiral? The emperor of the underworld was all-powerful in Shanghai. It was the world's most blatantly wicked city—where vice, crime, and even virtue, were far less inhibited than they were in sleepy, provincial Hong Kong. Why was he in the colony? Could he be one of Colonel Yiu, the Admiral's chief of staff's agents? The majority were northern Triad members, but Tu was too big a fish to swim in the Colonel's pool of small-time spies.

A bell summoned her and she picked up her shorthand notebook. Cheng Jin let her into the Admiral's sparsely furnished office. Maps studded with coloured pins had replaced the scrolls that had once marked dark stripes on the faded blue walls. Only one painting remained—a crimson splendour of peonies in the foreground framed a shaded hillside where a tiger, half-hidden in the long grass, was stalking a pair of grazing deer.

Connie stepped across the teak wood floor. Uncle Wei was sitting behind his big blackwood desk. 'There you are, Constance,' he said. Creepy, thin-faced Colonel Yiu Kai Pao stood on the Admiral's left. Connie was slightly afraid of the thirty-seven-year-old powerfully built, immaculately dressed man. He spoke excellent, accentless English and posed as an insurance salesman, but she'd heard that his civilised exterior hid a killer instinct. It was a relief that he kept himself to himself, only coming into the office from time to time to report on his activities.

The Admiral's Aide-de Camp, Robert Lau Yeung was on Uncle Wei's right. He'd made Connie feel at ease right from the start. Fresh-faced, clean-living and a lover of sport, he'd requested that she called him, "Bob". Later, she'd found out that he had won gold medals at the Far East Games in Tokyo and Manila for volleyball and football and was the current Hong Kong freestyle swimming champion. Like the Admiral, Bob was a product of the prestigious Whampoa Naval Academy in Canton. He was a lieutenant-commander, an impressive rank for someone still in his twenties. But just as Uncle Wei was now an Admiral without a fleet, his ADC was a commander without a ship—there simply weren't enough in the Chinese Navy to go round. Bob, a staunch Christian, had invited Connie to go to church with him, but she'd declined, telling him she was a devout Buddhist—an exaggeration as she hadn't wanted to encourage him. There was no denying that Bob was good-looking, however. At six-foot-three he was more than a foot taller than the Admiral, and charming to boot.

'I have discourteously left Mr Tu's associates alone in the anteroom,' Connie said.

'Don't worry, Constance.' A smile teased Uncle Wei's lips. 'Mr Tu and I are old friends. His ... ah... associates will not be offended.'

The gangster's sleek reptilian head nodded to acknowledge the compliment. Relaxed in an ebony chair, Big Eared Tu appeared as self-assured as the Admiral himself.

Uncle Wei fixed Connie with a business-like look. 'We are having an important meeting. I would like you to take the minutes.'

She perched on her customary stool at the side of his desk and lifted her pen.

'You are much maligned, my old friend.' The Admiral addressed the brigand. 'You and I have striven together against the bullying Japanese. You are a great patriot. Has not your Green League resisted both the Manchus and the foreigners for decades?'

'We have.' The gangster smirked. 'And now we must crush the bullies. They've split our country in two. Some Triads are even supporting them. The glory of China is the unity of the Chinese people and their leaders. As it has always been, so must it be today.'

# THE FLAME TREE

Big Eared Tu had grown wealthy and powerful by exploiting the same Chinese people he professed to glorify, Connie reflected as she took notes. At its core the Green Gang was an organised crime syndicate that thrived from the profits of drug trafficking and prostitution. Nothing more. Nothing less.

'Can I count on your support if the Japanese should invade Hong Kong?' the Admiral asked Tu without preamble. 'Some secret society members here have decided to take sides with Japan and others are waiting to see what will happen.'

'It will depend on the compensation.' Tu grinned. 'For a big enough reward, I will be delighted to help.'

'I'm sure that can be arranged.'

'Good.' The gangster glanced at his watch. 'It is time for me to go.'

Colonel Yiu and Bob saw him out. After the office door had shut, Uncle Wei muttered, 'Ham gaa chan.'

Connie gasped at the curse, one of the worst in the Cantonese language. *May his whole family be bulldozed.*

The Admiral grinned. 'I trust I haven't shocked you, Constance. Big Earned Tu is a ruffian. But I will have need of him in the difficult times to come.'

She shook her head. 'I'm not shocked, Uncle. I agree with you wholeheartedly.' She paused. 'I just hope those difficult times you speak of will never come.'

'I vehemently hope so too, Constance.'

Two days later, Connie's sedan chair bearers dropped her at the Wyn-Jones's house. Her second Christmas Day to be spent with them. How time had flown since her return to Hong Kong. Soon it would be 1941. Two years ago she was in London, living with the Huang family, friends of Father's. Mr Huang had been her guardian and his wife, Helen, had taken Connie under her wing when she was at the university. Her heart had wept for them when she'd learnt that the Luftwaffe had dropped an incendiary bomb on their house in Mayfair. Thankfully, no one had been home at the time. But it was still a complete and utter tragedy.

Connie sighed. Whenever she went to the pictures with one of her sisters and the Pathé newsreel came on before the feature film, she watched images of the Blitz and horror twisted her stomach into knots. She hoped fervently nothing like that would ever occur in Hong Kong. The horror was going on right now in Chungking, however, where Japanese air raids were becoming increasingly intense and destructive.

It was terribly worrying, but today was Christmas, and she was determined not to dwell on the war. She hadn't seen Will for a month and couldn't wait for his vibrant blue eyes to smile at her and for them to kiss below the mistletoe like they did last year.

At home, she'd exchanged gifts under the tree with her family straight after breakfast. Although they weren't Christians, they'd always celebrated the holiday. Mother said she hadn't wanted her children to feel left out. So, Santa had filled their stockings with toys until they'd been too old for such childish delights. Mother had tried her best to give her children everything they'd needed and Connie loved her for it.

Her mouth watered at the thought of the meal she was about to enjoy. The Han Fungs had never gone in for a traditional Christmas lunch. Father couldn't abide English food, he always maintained. Connie had got used to following a more western diet while she was in the UK, and roast dinners were her favourite. It was her excuse for accepting the invitation to the Wyn-Jones's and Father had acquiesced. 'Go, daughter,' he'd said. 'Enjoy yourself and wish them a Merry Christmas from us all.'

Connie rang the doorbell and a houseboy came bustling out to help with her bag of gifts.

'Merry Christmas, Connie,' Harry exclaimed from where he was standing in the hallway. 'Welcome, my dear. Come and have a glass of sherry!'

Jean, George, and Will were there already. Reggie had been invited to Deborah's, apparently. Connie placed her gifts under the tree, then greeted everyone with a kiss. At first she'd found the familiarity of friendly kisses among the expatriates to be a little unsettling. It had taken some time for her to become used to the habit. Now she was glad for a reason to press her lips to Will's cheek and savour his fresh sandalwood aroma. 'How are you, darling girl?' he whispered into her ear.

'I'm well,' she responded in Cantonese. 'And you?'

'I got the results of my second last exam yesterday. Passed with flying colours.'

'Oh, Will, that's marvellous.' She knew he was champing at the bit to start work in the Secretariat for Chinese Affairs. Reggie, who'd arrived in the colony before him, had just taken up a position in the Education Department.

Connie sat on the sofa next to Will and accepted a glass of sherry from Harry. 'Got some champers for later.' He winked and raised his glass. 'A very Merry Christmas, everyone!'

Lunch was just as delicious as she'd remembered. Rich mushroom soup, roast turkey with potatoes, Brussel sprouts, chipolata sausages, gravy, and cranberry sauce. She loved the plum pudding best of all, especially the brandy butter served with it.

'I can't eat another mouthful,' she said when Margaret offered her a mince pie. After two helpings of dessert, she was fit to burst.

They went through to the sitting room to exchange gifts. Connie exclaimed in delight at the Elizabeth Arden eau-de-cologne and Yardley's bath salts she received from Margaret and Jean. They, in turn, appeared pleased with the hand-embroidered linen tablecloths she gave them.

Connie held her breath while Will unwrapped his present. Would he like it? A small jade flame tree emerged from its packaging. His smile went straight to her heart. 'Thank you, it's beautiful. Open yours now,' he said.

It was a novel. She examined the cover. *Of Human Bondage* by W. Somerset Maugham. One of Will's favourites, he'd told her about it some time ago. 'Thank you,' she said. 'I shall treasure this.'

'Let's go for a walk around the Peak,' Margaret suggested out of the blue. 'It's a fine day for it.'

They shrugged on their light coats and set off along Mount Kellett Road. Thick, sub-tropical vegetation—wild banana trees, acacias, and eucalyptus—initially obscured the view of the south side of Hong Kong Island. But, once they'd passed the War Memorial Hospital, the vegetation thinned out and they caught glimpses of the sea twinkling in the afternoon sunshine far below.

Connie breathed in the fresh air, remembering winters in the UK when her breath came out as steam. That rarely happened in the colony—frosts would only occasionally occur on the top of Tai Mo Shan mountain.

Before too long, she and Will found themselves falling behind the others. It was as if they'd deliberately slowed their footsteps so they could be alone. There was no one else about, and Will gently pulled her through a gap in the trees to a thicket, where he spread out his coat so they could sit.

'I've been wanting to do this all day,' he said, wrapping his arms around her.

# THE FLAME TREE

They kissed for the longest time. Hot kisses, open mouthed, tongues dancing. Connie threaded her fingers in his hair and gazed deep into his eyes. 'I love you, Will,' she said, her pulse beating in her throat. 'I love you so very much.'

'I love you too, my darling. I wish with all my heart that we could be together.' He kissed her again, deeply. 'Whatever is to become of us, Connie?'

'I don't know, my love. It's hopeless.'

'Don't say that, sweetheart.' Tears ran down her cheeks and he kissed them away. 'There is always hope. Don't despair. Whatever happens I'll always love you, Connie.'

'As I shall always love you.'

With his strong arms wrapped around her, her head tucked into his chest, it felt like she was in another world. A world where only love mattered. *If only it could really be so.*

# Chapter Thirteen

On the last Sunday in November, Will was perched on a smooth rock at the entrance to Z Force's main refuge—two natural caves 1,800 feet up the southeast face of Hong Kong's highest mountain, Tai Mo Shan, right below the source of a stream which fed the Shing Mun Reservoir in the New Territories. He reflected on how, over the past year, he and the other commandos had set up four such hideouts—to house food dumps, weapons caches and sleeping quarters for stay-behind groups if ever the Japanese were victorious. The Royal Scots Engineers had camouflaged and enlarged the Tai Mo Shan caves last week, and Will had just given them the onceover. They were now as ready as they would ever be.

He lit a Player's and contemplated the view. Below, through the dense sub-tropical forest, the pineapple-shaped reservoir glistened in the morning sunshine. How Will loved this time of the year. The intense heat and humidity of Hong Kong's difficult summer had given way to pleasantly dry, temperate weather. It was still warm enough to swim, but he no longer dripped with sweat.

Will exhaled a puff of smoke, remembering how much he'd enjoyed going to the pictures and sitting in an air-conditioned cinema soon after he'd started his job as Assistant Secretary

# THE FLAME TREE

for Chinese Affairs in June. He'd been given a Chinese name, Kiu Ming Jeun and he smiled now as he thought about the meaning—smart, handsome tall man. What an accolade! It was a good thing he could just go by this surname and introduce himself as Mr Kiu when working with the locals. He spent a lot of his time giving advice and dealing with people having family problems. It often struck him as ironic that he, an English bachelor of twenty-five, had been called upon to act as a mediator between feuding couples. When all else failed, if they had married according to Chinese custom, it was simple for them to divorce. Will took a deep draw of his cigarette. He'd learnt so much about ordinary life in Hong Kong and liked helping people. The opportunity to unburden themselves in front of him brought relief to some and reconciliation to many, he believed. When he wasn't dealing directly with individuals, he was required to sort out matters that were deemed too unimportant to be handled by anyone with experience, such as backlogs in filing and ordering new equipment, but it was only temporary. With all the refugees arriving from China, a great deal of work would need to be done vis-à-vis social welfare and he was eager to get stuck into it.

He glanced at his watch. Time to get a move on. He stubbed out his Player's and put the butt in his pocket to dispose of later. There was a natural pool at the bottom of the stream not far from where George and Jean rented a bungalow for weekends, which Z Force had been using as their base. Today, though, George had sent Reggie and the others north to a disused lead mine on the border with China near Sha Tau Kok, where they were to establish another refuge. Will smiled to himself. Jean had invited Connie for tiffin. Yesterday, her father had left for Macau where he would be treated for a gastrointestinal disorder. He'd taken his wives, concubine, and most of his trusted servants with him, leaving Connie at home with a skeleton staff.

Will couldn't help hoping this turn of events would give her greater freedom. Their snatched moments together had been few and far between of late. Connie would be driving over in the car Sir Albert had bought for her birthday in September and Will's heart sang at the thought of seeing her. For once, they could be alone with no questions asked. Connie had revealed that Jean knew she and Will were in love. He deduced George was also aware of their relationship, although he hadn't said anything.

His thoughts drifted to the likelihood of war in the colony—it was ever on his mind. He shaded his eyes, trying to identify the location of the Shing Mun Redoubt defensive position on Smugglers' Ridge just to the south. While training with Z Force last month, he'd visited the underground military facility—referred to as the Strand Palace Hotel by the Royal Scots. Four nearby pillboxes with a capacity of 120 men, linked by a network of tunnels and fitted with Vickers machine guns and Bren LMGs, were known as Regent Street, Shaftsbury Avenue, Charing Cross, and Piccadilly Circus for ease of identification. The redoubt acted as command HQ of the Gin Drinkers Line, which Will had learnt stretched from the eponymous bay at Tsuen Wan in the west to Port Shelter in the east. Over the past three years eleven miles of fortifications had been constructed on the hills and mountains separating Kowloon from the New Territories. Earth trodden paths linked the bunkers, machine gun posts, trenches, and artillery batteries, which everyone believed would stop a Japanese advance. Will prayed to God they were right.

He got to his feet, then set off down the forest trail running parallel to Dragon Valley and the stream which fed the reservoir. The narrow path was steep and rocky—he was grateful for the occasional exposed tree roots forming natural steps. He stopped by a tiny cascade to catch his breath, marvelling at a grey-green

## THE FLAME TREE

dark spotted frog poking its head out from behind a moss-covered rock. Birdsong and the chatter of rhesus macaque monkeys echoed in the lush sub-tropical vegetation as he battled his way through myriad spider webs, clutching at his face and arms whenever he copped the full force of the arachnids' handiwork.

Eventually he emerged from the treeline at the base of Tai Mo Shan. He quickened his pace and followed the road to a creek where George and Jean's long, narrow bungalow came into view. Connie's Studebaker was parked out front and Will couldn't stop smiling as he hurried to greet her.

Later, after pre-lunch drinks on the veranda, Will reached for Connie's hand under the tablecloth after she'd helped Jean serve tiffin in the sparsely furnished dining room. She squeezed his fingers in response, a smile lighting her beautiful eyes. They were sitting at a rectangular wicker table opposite George and Jean. A deliciously spicy chicken curry, served with steamed rice and crowned with chopped hard-boiled eggs, sliced cucumber, tomatoes, peanuts, desiccated coconut flakes and mango chutney, was making Will's tastebuds tingle.

'So, the caves are all in good order?' George asked as he passed Will a bottle of Tiger Beer.

'Spick and span. Just hope we'll never have to use them.'

Connie took a sip of water. 'Maybe the recently arrived Canadians will make Japan think twice before attacking.'

Around two thousand young Royal Rifles of Canada and Winnipeg Grenadier soldiers had disembarked two weeks ago to reinforce the garrison and act as a deterrent, not to mention reassure Generalissimo Chiang Kai Shek of Britain's intension to defend the colony.

'They've had practically no training whatsoever,' George huffed. 'Hopefully they'll get up to scratch and familiarise themselves with the terrain in time.'

'You think an invasion is imminent?' Will inclined his head towards him.

George shrugged. 'My sources inform me of an increase in Jap troop movements on the other side of the border.'

Connie gave a gasp. 'Oh, no!'

'There've been false alarms before.' George reached across the table and patted her hand. 'Try not to worry.'

'Are you going to the Tin Hat Ball next Saturday in aid of the Bomber Fund, Connie?' Jean asked, in an obvious attempt to change the subject. 'George and I have a table booked at the Peninsula for the occasion.'

'I'll be there with my sisters and their husbands. We're all looking forward to it.'

The ball was to raise money towards the purchase of a plane for the RAF in Britain and Will had been invited to join the Colonial Secretary's party. Life in the colony was carrying on as usual despite those worrying reports from over the border. Perhaps the reports had been exaggerated or deliberately fostered by the enemy, like many people believed? Certainly, a spirit of optimism prevailed. 'What does your boss think of the situation, Connie?' Will asked.

'The Admiral is convinced the Japanese will try their hand sooner or later.'

'All this talk of war,' Jean chipped in. 'Let's enjoy our lunch. Eat up, drink up, and then we can relax in the garden. It's such a beautiful day.'

# THE FLAME TREE

Connie leant into Will, her arm threaded through his as they set off for a walk after a brief post-lunch rest on rattan chairs placed in the shade of the bungalow's flame tree. Will's breaths sped up as he relished the feel of her lovely body pressed to his. He wrapped his arms around her and, when she lifted her face, he kissed her so thoroughly they both needed to come up for air.

'God, how I love you, my darling,' he said.

'As I love you, dearest Will.' Her eyes locked with his. 'All I want is to be with you. I only wish it could be more often.'

'I'd like to see your father and ask his permission to court you. I've been thinking about it and I believe if I'm honest and lay my cards on the table, there's every chance he'll agree.'

She froze. 'But what if he says no?'

'Then I'll just have to kidnap you.' He chuckled. 'Joking aside. I would never expect you to leave your family. But we can't go on like this. It's driving me crazy.'

A lone tear tricked down Connie's face. 'I would give up everything for you, Will. I love you so much.'

He kissed away the tear. 'No, my darling. It won't come to that. I'll talk to your father. I'm sure I'll be able to convince him.' He'd sounded more confident that he felt, but what else could he say? That Connie had even mentioned splitting away from the Han Fungs had touched him to the core.

'I hope so.' Her voice trembled, and Will held her close. He hadn't referred to the possibility of losing his job. It no longer mattered. Connie was all that mattered and there were plenty of opportunities in the colony for someone like him.

They resumed their walk and soon they'd come to the concrete bridge spanning the pool formed where the stream levelled out before flowing into the reservoir. 'It's a bit hot. Shall we go down there for a paddle?' Will suggested.

'I'd really like that.'

He took her hand and led her down the stone steps to a small pebbly beach. They removed their socks and shoes—Connie was wearing shorts like he was—and waded into the fresh, cool water.

With a giggle, she bent and began to splash him.

How could he resist? He splashed her in return, and soon the two of them were thoroughly drenched. 'Come on into the deep end,' he said. 'We might as well have a swim.'

A small waterfall gurgled into a basin a couple of yards in diameter. Connie came into his arms again and they kissed. Desire spread through him and he pressed himself against her.

She looped her legs around his waist and trailed kisses down his face, his lips, his jaw.

'God, Connie. I want you so desperately.'

'I want you too, Will.'

With her still clinging to him, he walked them both to the other side of the pool. He'd discerned a dell hidden between the trees. Only visible from where he was standing, it would be totally private. He laid her down on the grass. 'We're soaked. Better take off our clothes and let them dry a bit before we return to the bungalow.'

Her gaze glued to his, she sat up, unbuttoned her blouse, and slipped out of her shorts to reveal a white lace bra and knickers. He contemplated her in awe. 'You're so beautiful...'

She smiled, a sparkle in her eye. 'Get undressed, Will. You need to dry off.'

Like her, he kept his underwear on. He took her clothes from her and spread them over a shrub together with his own shorts and shirt. Then he stretched out beside her and gently pulled her on top of him. Feeling her tremble, he reassured her. 'I'll only go as far as you want me to, my love.'

He kissed her. Oh, how he kissed her. Heat sparked between them, and he wrapped his arms tighter, his groan echoing in his ears. Their heads tilted, their breath mingled, their souls danced. He rolled over and tucked her into his side. 'Can I kiss you all over?'

She nodded and he kissed his way down from her mouth until he'd arrived at her most intimate part. He pressed more kisses there, ran his tongue over her knickers, creating a hot wetness that made her moan. He pulled down her pants and breathed in her sweet musky scent. Her back arched and she whimpered delightfully as he cupped her with his mouth.

'Oh, God, Will.' She rocked against him, her hands in his hair as he drew circles with his tongue.

He carried on, harder, faster, stronger. Her shoulders lifted and she quivered. He soothed her with his lips until her tremors became spasms and the spasms stilled. 'I love you so much, darling Connie.' He sat and pulled her into his lap. 'You're the most gorgeous girl in the world.'

'I love you too, my dearest.' She nestled into his chest. 'You're everything to me.'

'As you are to me.' He kissed the pulse behind her ear. 'Will you marry me, my love?'

She smiled. 'I want that more than anything. Let's try and get my father's permission first. If he doesn't give it, I'll still marry you. But there's no harm in trying, is there?'

'Indeed.' He stroked her cheek. 'When is he expected back from Macau?'

'That will depend on how he responds to treatment. But I think he'll be home before Christmas.'

'Good. I'll ask him then.'

A sudden rustle in the canopy above, followed by the *oo oo ah ah* of a monkey, made Connie startle and then laugh. 'Seems we had an audience.' She blushed. 'Maybe we should get dressed...'

Will laughed with her. 'I'll see you at the ball next Saturday, I hope?'

'Of course. It will be so hard not to be able to dance with you, though.'

'I don't see why you can't. I mean, we met on the *Carthage* and danced in front of everyone there.'

'Maybe if I tell my sisters about meeting you then, it won't be a problem...'

He stood and helped her to her feet. Their clothes were still damp, but they put them on. His arm around her, they made their way back to the bungalow, stopping every now and then for a kiss.

# Chapter Fourteen

Connie was getting ready for the ball, her senses heightened as she smoothed the silk of her cheongsam. She'd debated whether to order a western style dance frock from Chiffon, the tailor Mother used in the central district, but had decided against it for it would have been frivolous. Father discouraged frivolity and Connie had been brought up to make do with what she had. Besides, Will had told her on many occasions how much he liked her oriental dresses. Adorned with sequins and beads, the red brocaded gown clung to her body and was one of her favourites. She couldn't wait to show it off.

Connie sighed. It had been six days since she'd seen Will. Six days of longing for him. Her love for him caused her to alternate between feelings of euphoria and anguish. Her insides trembled constantly; it was as if she were on a ship being tossed by the waves of a mighty storm. Everything around her had become so intense, so vibrant. A bar of soulful music, a line from a sonnet, melodic voices, the vivid colour of flowers—all made her want to weep and laugh at the same time. When she was with Will, happiness overflowed and her life was complete. Separated from him, everyday sounds—the chatter of sparrows in the garden, the swish of wind in the trees, the vroom of a car engine—filled her with the pain of missing him. She could almost smell the golden sunbeams, and the beauty of the full moon prickled her eyes with emotional tears. She literally ached for him. How had this happened? She hadn't wanted it to but love for him had grown slowly like a strong-rooted tree. The difficulties ahead were not to be ignored, of course. But they paled into insignificance when compared with the magnitude of her passion.

Oh, how she prayed Father would be understanding. Except he always maintained that east and west couldn't mix, that they'd always be separate, that one had to choose between the two like he'd done. Connie hoped she wouldn't have to make a choice but, if she did, she would choose Will. *It would break her heart, though...*

She checked her reflection in her bedroom mirror, imagining Will's smiling face when he saw her. And there was that ache again as she recalled the concrete bridge and the pool beneath where they'd paddled and splashed... and...She caught herself blushing, heat building at her core, thought instead of Christmastime, chastised herself, then made her way out of the house. Number Six Elder Sister materialised in the hallway, her thin black hair scraped into a bun, her gold teeth gleaming. 'You look very beautiful tonight, Miss.'

'Nei Zan Hai Ho Jan,' Connie said. *So kind of you.* 'I will be home a little late, I expect. There's no need to wait up for me.'

Her trusted servant nodded, then went to open the door.

Outside, Connie's car was in the driveway. She'd decided to drive down from the Peak and park the Studebaker in front of the ferry pier, take the boat across the harbour, then a rickshaw to the Peninsula. Her sisters would meet her there with their husbands. Her heart raced at the thought of seeing Will, dancing with him, and sharing what they'd been doing since last Sunday. Smiling, she slipped into the driver's seat and started the engine.

# THE FLAME TREE

An hour or so later, Connie got into a rickshaw which took her past the Kowloon railway station, past the YMCA to arrive at the Peninsula. She paid the puller and climbed the steps to the hotel entrance, glancing upwards at the horseshoe-shaped structure. Two bellboys in white uniforms opened the double doors into the cream and gold lobby—with its long line of chandeliers and pillars, potted palms, and ornamental gilt.

She stepped across the marble floor to where Mary, Veronica, Dorothy, and Edith were sipping cocktails with their husbands. All four men—Howard, Leo, Eddie, and Walter—had joined the Hong Kong Volunteer Defence Corps last year but had taken this afternoon off to go to the races. She'd met them there earlier and had listened to the Royal Scots band play the same jaunty tunes they played every week—despite the red clouds of war which appeared to be gathering.

Connie kissed her siblings on the cheek, then ordered a brandy soda from their waiter.

'Did you know that Madame Sun Yat Sen will be at the ball, Connie?' Edith's face reflected her delight. 'It's such an honour...'

'That's wonderful,' Connie said. And it was. The widow of the founder of the Chinese Republic lived in splendid isolation in a villa overlooking Telegraph Bay near Aberdeen and was rarely seen in public.

Connie's drink arrived and she sipped it in silence while her siblings chatted about who else would be at the ball. 'Everyone who is anyone has bought tickets,' Dorothy said. 'We've worked hard on the organisation, so it's extremely gratifying.'

Entirely arranged by the Chinese community, the ball was a sign of their solidarity with the British, Connie surmised.

Although, from what she'd learnt in the Admiral's office, not all the local population felt that way. In fact, there was a growing group of fifth columnists who supported the Axis powers. She couldn't stop a shiver of apprehension from chilling her spine.

They finished their drinks and made their way up the elegant, carpeted staircase to the mezzanine floor. The ballroom's wide doors opened onto the same terrace above the hotel's entrance where Connie had enjoyed that drink with Will during Mamma and Father's anniversary celebration. The parquet glistened after its daily polish and glittering crystal chandeliers hung from the slightly domed ceiling, painted rain-washed blue. On a podium at the far end of the long room a swing band had launched into playing *The Best Things in Life are Free*.

Connie caught sight of Madame Sun Yat Sen, tiny and fragile looking, who was with her sister, Madame H. H. Kung, wife of the Chinese Minister of Finance. Two Guns Cohen stood behind them, vigilantly. But it was Will who drew Connie's rapt attention. He was with Reggie, Deborah, George, and Jean, and looking so incredibly handsome in his black tuxedo. Connie went up to them, her heart thudding. 'Hello, everyone,' she said nonchalantly. 'How lovely to see you.'

Deborah kissed her on the cheek. 'Lovely to see you too, Connie.' Deborah's father was due to retire from his position as Colonial Secretary before Christmas, and she would return to England with him, much to Reggie's sorrow. The couple had recently become engaged and had decided to marry as soon as the war was over. Connie couldn't help feeling envious of their freedom to reveal their love to the world.

She squeezed Will's fingers in a formal handshake. 'I need to go and join my family at our table,' she said.

'I wish you didn't have to,' he whispered in her ear.

'I'm sorry.' She made a regretful face.

He met her gaze. 'Do you have a dance card?'

She retrieved the item from her evening bag and showed it to him.

'I'd like to book every dance with you.'

Connie shook her head regretfully. 'Not tonight, my darling. We mustn't be foolhardy until you've spoken with Father. I'll pencil you in for the first one.'

Her feet dragging, she went to join her siblings. The Governor then arrived and dinner was served. Conversation at the table revolved around Father's illness. He'd been diagnosed with tropical sprue, a malabsorption syndrome, but the disease was being treated successfully and the entire family expected he would be home soon. 'Jonathan will bring him back,' Mary said.

'That'll be wonderful.' Connie hadn't seen her brother since the anniversary celebration. 'With a bit of luck we can all have Christmas together.' She crossed her fingers under the table. If Father asked her to choose between the family and Will, her life could be extremely different. Now was not the time to think about such matters, however. Instead, she chatted with her sisters about their children. Dorothy told her that Gloria had been thinking about retirement, possibly next year if the conflict in Europe came to an end. 'We'll all miss her when she goes,' Connie said. And it was true. Gloria had played a big role in their upbringing.

The meal seemed interminable while the master of ceremonies made draws for the donated prizes, but finally the bomber fund was near to reaching its target. How strange it was to be gaily raising money for something that would bring death and destruction, Connie thought with an inward shudder. *War was a terrible thing...*

Eventually, coffee was served and the men began to pencil their names on the ladies' dance cards. Connie accepted requests from all four of her brothers-in-law as well as Harry, George and even Reggie. 'Who's that?' Veronica—her second sister—asked, leaning over Connie and pointing out Will's name.

'Oh, I met him on the *Carthage*. He's very nice.'

'Hmm.' Veronica gave her a quizzical look. 'Be careful of your reputation, little sister.'

Connie was spared a response as Will chose that moment to approach. She introduced him to her family before letting him lead her onto the ballroom floor. Hilda Yen, a local singer, took to the podium and launched into a Chinese folk ballad in her sweet, high voice—*Dream Girl of the Autumn Water*. Connie fell into Will's arms with a happy sigh.

He waltzed her past Margaret and Harry, Jean and George, Deborah and Reggie, Uncle Wei and his wife, and myriad other couples. Her body melded to his. This was where she belonged. When she was with him the world, albeit out-of-kilter, resumed its rightful rhythm. 'I love you,' she breathed the words into his ear.

'I love you too, my darling,' he said.

Without warning, the music came to an abrupt halt.

Connie froze. *What was going on?* A man she knew as Mr Johnson of the American President Lines, had appeared on the balcony above the dance floor, and was waving a megaphone.

'Would all naval personnel, including merchant service personnel, return to their ships and report for duty,' he announced before adding forcefully, 'immediately!'

Connie felt her blood freeze.

She caught Will's eye. He seemed just as shocked as she was.

Everyone around them was silent.

People began to stir and talk excitedly. Some of the men were hurriedly saying goodbye to their partners, collecting their hats and coats and leaving.

'What does this mean?' Connie asked.

# THE FLAME TREE

'I don't know, my dearest.' Will shook his head, clearly at a loss for words.

Dorothy and her husband, Eddie, came striding up. 'We're crossing over to the island.' Dorothy folded her arms. 'Say goodnight to Mr Burton and come with us, little sister.'

It was an order, not a request. 'I'll see you down in the lobby,' Connie acquiesced.

Once Dorothy was out of earshot, Connie told Will she would meet with him in the Botanical Gardens early next morning. 'We might know more about what's going on by then.'

'I'll find out as much as I can,' he promised, squeezing her fingers. 'Good night, my love. Try not to worry...'

'Good night, Will. I'll see you tomorrow.'

She walked with her family to the ferry, pulled along by the chattering crowds. A keen wind whipped around them, ship lights gleaming on the choppy water.

Once they'd arrived at Hong Kong side, she bade goodnight to her siblings and drove home with a fearful heart. There could only be one reason for shipping craft to be ordered to leave the harbour. The enemy must be about to make a move.

Trembling, she undressed and collapsed into bed. There, she tossed and turned, thoughts of Will mingling with the delightful folk tune they'd danced to, contending with Mr Johnson's dramatic order for the men to man their ships. She distracted herself by focusing on the flame tree instead, imagined dancing under its branches with Will. What would be their future? *If only she knew...*

Early the next morning, Connie tiptoed past the tai chi exercisers in the Botanical Gardens. She wrapped her arms around herself in the chilly December air. Winter had arrived and it was cold at that time of the day. She sat on hers and Will's stone bench and waited for him. It was hard to believe it had only been a week ago that they'd swum together by the reservoir. Just thinking about how Will had kissed her so passionately, how his mouth had given her such pleasure, made her insides melt. She vehemently hoped last night's announcement was just another false alarm. There had been so many of those in recent times…

But when she glanced up as Will approached, she could tell by the look on his face that matters had become grim. 'I can't stay long, my dearest,' he said. 'A state of emergency will soon be announced and all the Volunteers are about to be mobilised.'

'Oh, no!' Her hand flew to her chest.

He sat next to her, took her hand. 'Reggie has gone to help Deborah and her father board the *Ulysses*. Apparently as many as 20,000 Japanese troops have been spotted moving up to the border. And a Jap armada is reported to be steaming across the Gulf of Siam.'

'How true do you think the reports are? I mean, there've been so many false alarms…'

'This is the first time that ships have been ordered to leave the harbour. And it's the first time the Volunteers are being mobilised.' He squeezed her fingers. 'It's serious, darling. Very serious indeed.'

'Oh, Will. I'm so worried for you.'

'As I am for you, my love.'

'Promise me you won't get killed!'

He gave a wry laugh. 'I'll try not to.'

'Kiss me, my dearest. I don't care if anyone sees us.' She couldn't bear it that this might be their final kiss. She wanted to rant and rage against destiny. She wanted to scream her anguish to the gods.

## THE FLAME TREE

He kissed her. Heat sparked between them, the intensity so strong she thought she might faint.

'How beautiful you are, my Connie. I will write you a new poem and give it to you when we meet again.'

She rested her head on his shoulder, inhaled his wonderful scent. 'I will think about you every second of every minute of every day. Come back to me, Will. I am nothing without you.'

'As I am without you. Take care of yourself, my darling. Stick with Admiral Chang Wei. He'll look after you, I'm sure.'

She nodded. What else could she do?

He kissed her again. Kissed her with such passion it felt like it could be the last time.

'Goodbye, my love.' He brushed his thumb across her trembling lip.

'Goodbye, Will.'

With tears streaming down her face and her heart breaking, she watched him as he made his way from under the flame tree and out of the garden.

# Chapter Fifteen

On Monday morning Connie set off for work as usual. Although she'd sobbed until she had no tears left and had barely slept, she knew where her duty lay. She parked her car opposite the Peak station before getting into the burgundy red tram car to make her way down to the office. Her mind buzzed with the events of yesterday. Saying goodbye to Will had turned her into a nervous wreck, not helped by distraught phone calls from her sisters who'd also had to bid farewell to the men they loved. How Connie hoped against hope the mobilisation was a false alarm.

With a sudden screech of brakes, the funicular railway came to an abrupt halt. Connie wasn't unduly concerned. The tram often stopped on its decent as it worked on a pulley system and would halt when the car coming up did so.

The shrill wail of air raid sirens cut into the air. Connie stiffened with sudden fear.

'Big trouble now,' the conductor shouted.

An uninterrupted view of the harbour lay before Connie. Her heart pounded. Twelve silver-coloured planes were droning in a V-shaped formation, tilting their wings to reveal the red sun of the Japanese flag as they few through the clear skies.

She gasped. The aircraft were swooping down towards the Kai Tak Aerodrome.

# THE FLAME TREE

Black, egg-shaped pellets spilled from their bellies. Bombs!
*Boom! Boom! Boom!*
Massive explosions ricocheted around the Kowloon hills.

Connie squinted through the golden sunlight, and the bitter taste of fear coated her tongue.

White puffs burst alongside the enemy planes. Was it flack? Whatever it was, it wasn't very accurate, didn't go high enough and, although one enemy bomber turned away, the others weren't put off at all. Where were Hong Kong's fighter aircraft? They should have been scrambled and sent aloft to combat the Japs.

Connie's stomach churned and sweat beaded her lip. Will and her brothers-in-law, were they alright? A sick feeling spread through her and she prayed they hadn't been stationed anywhere nearby.

The planes at the back of the formation began to dive bomb Kai Tak. Crimson flashes winked from their wings. A deafening explosion, and Connie clutched at her stomach. The four-motored Pan American Clipper seaplane had been hit and was sending up coils of black smoke.

A gun started banging away from somewhere near the Botanical Gardens. Against the loud crash of the Japanese bombs it sounded weak and futile.

Finally, one by one, the attacking planes gained height, turned, and headed back in the direction of China.

With a shudder, the tramcar recommenced its descent. Connie gazed at the shocked, pale faces of her fellow-passengers—British taipans on their way to the office, muttering to each other, 'Bloody Japs! How dare they? We'll give them a damned good hiding. Just wait and see!'

She made fists of her hands to stop them from trembling. On shaky legs, she debarked from the tram and stepped into Garden Road. The sky was black with acrid smoke and her eyes stung. In the business district, however, people were scurrying about with their usual purpose. Across the water, the green Star ferries were still shuttling back and forth. A feeling of unreality took hold of Connie. It was as if she'd imagined what had just occurred. But no. The sting in her eyes and the taste of metal on her tongue brought home to her that Hong Kong had been attacked. All was quiet now, though. Could the Japanese have merely been flexing their muscles and carrying out some kind of drill? Holding onto that slim hope, Connie made her way quickly towards Admiral Chang Wei's office.

'I had a phone call at dawn from Ben Clarke, the British army's chief intelligence officer,' the Admiral said to Connie and the rest of his staff, gathered in Pedder Building half an hour later. 'Clarke was monitoring a Japanese language broadcast and heard them announce the start of hostilities against the British and Americans.'

'The enemy has bombed Pearl Harbor in Hawaii,' Bob, the Admiral's ADC, clarified. 'We've only just got the news. They've sunk most of the American battle-fleet.'

Connie's heart skipped. 'How terrible!' Her hand flew to her mouth.

'The USA has declared war on Japan.' Colonel Yiu smirked. 'Those piratical dwarves have just signed their own death warrants. They will never be able to resist the force of America and Britain united against them.'

Connie stared at the sinister man. He was bouncing on his toes and smiling gleefully. She gave herself a quick shake and asked the Admiral, 'Will you go back to China now, Uncle?'

# THE FLAME TREE

'No. I'll arrange for my wife and children to travel north to safety. But I must stay in Hong Kong and rally the Chinese community.'

Other individuals would surely have taken the chance to get out while they could, and left the colony to sink or swim, Connie thought. But the indomitable Admiral seemed positively enthusiastic about the idea of fighting alongside Hong Kong's defenders.

'Two Gun Cohen is arranging transport for Madame Sun Yat Sen and her sister,' Bob chipped in. 'They'll return to Chungking tomorrow.'

Connie's pulse set up a fearful beat. If the Soong sisters were leaving the colony, it would be like rats leaving a sinking ship. Not that the elegant ladies in question could ever be compared with rodents. 'Will China send a relief army?' She met the Admiral's eye.

Since she'd started working for Uncle Wei, the Nationalist Government had offered several times to dispatch troops to reinforce Hong Kong's garrison. The British had been hesitant, however. Perhaps they saw no need for it, so confident were they of western superiority. Or maybe they feared the Chinese might carry on and take the colony back for themselves.

The Admiral smiled. 'The British are sending a liaison officer to request help from the Generalissimo.'

'Good.' Relief swept through Connie. 'The Kuomintang forces will soon stop any Japanese advance.'

'I agree. But, in the meantime, we must play a leading role in Hong Kong's civil defence.' Uncle Wei puffed out his chest. 'I will step up our efforts to assist the police in rounding up pro-Japanese fifth columnists. At the same time I will offer to mobilise my contacts to help maintain order and keep vital services going in the rear. That way, British troops can fight at the front, free from any worry.'

'It's an excellent plan.' Colonel Yiu smirked again. 'I can't wait to get my hands on any son-of-a-bitch traitors.'

Connie stared at the thin-faced man, trying to ignore the revulsion flowing through her veins. Colonel Yiu was so ruthless he brought her out in a cold sweat. 'How about I go and organise some tea for us all?' she suggested. The habits of the past year persisted. It was time for morning tea. She wanted to cling to routine, hold on to the normality of everyday activities. Her world was spinning out of control. Kai Tak had been bombed into a mess of craters and rubble. Men had been blown apart. Buildings crumpled into debris. And where was Will? She was so worried about him she could almost be sick.

The morning wore on and the Japanese planes came back again and again, bringing with them the dull thump and rumble of heavy guns and bombs. For some reason, the central district of the island was being spared. *For now.* Bob went out to reconnoitre the situation. 'Kowloon is being hammered,' he said. 'People are crowding the ferries to Hong Kong side.'

A communique came over the radio advising the population that it was safer for them on the Kowloon peninsula and that congestion in the crowded streets of the island would inevitably lead to unnecessary casualties. There hadn't been any sightings of the Japanese Navy steaming towards Hong Kong, the broadcaster announced. He told everyone to keep calm.

Connie tried to focus on typing the letters the Admiral dictated to her, a lengthy process involving the use of a revolving cylinder containing thousands of Chinese characters. She couldn't stop worrying about Will. He'd been mobilised, but he wasn't a member of any Hong Kong Volunteer Defence Corps unit as far as she'd been able to ascertain. Will had kept his activities close to his chest these past several months, telling her they were top secret and that, for her own safety, he couldn't provide her with any details. But Jean had let slip that Will

# THE FLAME TREE

and Reggie had joined George in something called Z Force. It occurred to Connie that Jean might be able to set her mind at rest. Should she stop off at Jean's on her way home and ask her friend to spill the beans? It was worth a try...

But when the hour came to knock off work, Bob informed her that the trams and buses had all stopped running. 'Would you like me to drive you up to the Peak?' he offered. 'The all clear has sounded again. We'll be safe enough...'

'Thank you.' It would have been impolite to refuse. She could phone Jean when she got home. 'I left my car parked in front of the station at the top of the line.'

Admiral Chang Wei fixed her with a firm look. 'If the Japanese start bombing the island, it will be too dangerous for you to travel down from the Peak, Connie.'

Her chest tightened. 'Perhaps I can take a room at the Gloucester Hotel?' She chewed at her lip. 'I want to work. If I don't, I think I'd go mad.' *Mad with worry.*

Uncle Wei touched his hand to her arm. 'If that is what you want, I gratefully accept. Your help will be invaluable. There is much to be done before the Nationalist army arrives. And you have become my... my...'

'"Girl Friday",' the Admiral's ADC finished the sentence for him with a smile.

She glanced at Bob. 'Could you wait for me on the Peak while I drive my car home and pack a suitcase?'

'It will be an honour,' he said.

Connie went to fetch her coat. She would phone Jean once she was settled in the hotel, she resolved. She would also contact Father and her sisters. There might be arguments against her decision, but she would confront them firmly. She wanted to play an active part in defending Hong Kong; allying herself with the Admiral would be the best way of achieving that aim. And

Will? What would he think? She hoped he'd be proud of her. As proud of her as she was of him. *Oh, my love, where are you?*

## Chapter Sixteen

Calves aching and carrying a fifty-pound load in his rucksack, Will was climbing the southern face of Tai Mo Shan with six of the seven other members of Z Force who'd arrived at George's bungalow that afternoon. Will had got there before them and had made his way over to the Royal Scots position to collect ammunition. There, he'd had a beer with Captain Jones and they'd discussed the horrific bombing of Kai Tak, which they'd both witnessed from Smugglers' Ridge. Will had felt sick with fear for Connie's safety.

How he'd wanted to rush to her, gather her up and keep her by his side; he'd had to swallow the lump of worry in his throat and soldier on with a stiff upper lip. Hostilities had commenced, they weren't engaged in some large-scale exercise, and Will was in it for the duration. All he could do was pray for Connie and hope Admiral Chang Wei would keep an eye on her in her father's absence. Will wondered if Sir Albert would return to Hong Kong or if he would stay in Macau. The latter scenario was more likely. In that case, would he send for his daughters? The Portuguese enclave was neutral territory and they'd be safer there.

Will trudged on with his fellow commandos, stones scattering beneath their feet as they hiked up the steep trail. On returning to the bungalow earlier he'd found the complete unit had turned up—Payne, Green, Dunn, Cotton, Walker, Edwards, and Will's housemate Nigel Bridges. Reggie had been sent to liaise with a group of Chinese communist guerrillas near the border and George had yet to arrive. They'd had a quick tiffin of ham sandwiches, after which Bridges had gone into town to fetch their portable transmitter, and Will and the rest had started on the removal of stores to No. 2—as the hideout was known. They were about half way up the mountain and he couldn't wait to put down his pack and ease his sore muscles.

Without warning, the crump of shell fire sounded. Range-finding shots from the Royal Scots position, Will surmised. Unused to being fired upon, he swore and clammy sweat slicked his body. Terrified monkeys screeched their fear in the forest around them. Will crouched down to avoid being hit by flying shrapnel, and his friends did likewise. Up, down, up, down, the process repeated while shells whistled left, right and centre. 'Wish they'd stop ranging,' he grumbled, lifting his heavy load for the umpteenth time.

They continued up the trail, and before too long they'd arrived at the caves. 'That was interesting,' Bertie Walker chuckled wryly. 'Being shot at by one's own side, I mean.'

'Not much fun, I agree,' Will concurred. 'Let's park our loads and return to the bungalow.' He glanced skywards. 'It'll be dark soon. Time for some food and then bed.'

'Enemy forces have crossed the border,' George announced as Will and the others trudged into the small house.

Will's pulse raced. How complacent they'd all been. The Japanese had been loudly announcing their intentions from every international podium at every opportunity for years. Before the two-month-old embargo, their air force had been flying planes with American engines running on American fuel and loaded with bombs marked "made in England". George had once let slip that Churchill deemed Hong Kong to be indefensible, that he wished they had fewer troops in the colony, but to move any would have been "noticeable and dangerous". Were they all to be abandoned like lambs to the slaughter? Will hoped to hell not.

George had brought a beef stew with him and placed it on the stove. 'Go and get cleaned up, men,' he commanded. 'We'll eat while we wait for Bridges, then we'll head to the caves.'

They did as George had requested and Will soon found himself sitting in the middle of a group of sombre faces around the same rectangular wicker table where he'd enjoyed that wonderful lunch with Connie just over a week ago. His heart ached with longing for her and he missed the usual banter he associated with his friends. War had come and removed all the joy from their lives.

Eventually, Bridges arrived and they tuned in to the latest news. At 3 pm 2/14th Punjab had engaged the Imperial Japanese Army in the northeast New Territories, managing to eliminate several IJA platoons at 6.30 pm just south of Tai Po. The Volunteer Defence Corps armoured cars and Bren Gun Carriers had also successfully exchanged fire with Japanese forces. Despite these successes the Punjab battalion had withdrawn towards Grassy Hill, about an hour's hike from Shing Mun, to avoid being outflanked. The enemy was now advancing down the Tai Po Road in the direction of Sha Tin.

The skin at the back of Will's neck tingled. 'They've managed to come closer than I'd imagined.'

George grunted. 'We'd better go to our position.'

Without a word, Will and his fellow commandos got to their feet, picked up more supplies, and set off with heavy packs for the second time that day. It was pitch black outside and the only noise came from their footfalls. Will found it difficult to distinguish the figure trudging in front of him in the darkness. His nerves jangled and he imagined sounds and saw movements where there weren't any. Up the mountain they climbed and, for the last 300 yards or so, Will's legs were so tired he could barely feel them. His rucksack cut into his shoulders and his back hurt. To make matters worse, it had started to rain.

Finally, they reached the hideout. In the smaller of the two caves, Will hunkered down in between boxes of gelignite, his feet among Bren ammo. He was so exhausted he fell asleep immediately. He woke in the night to the pitter-patter of the rain. The box of explosives dug into his ribs. It was a far cry from his bedroom at home in La Salle Road. He thought about Connie, wondered if she'd woken and was listening to the rain as well. From his kit bag, he retrieved the jade flame tree she'd given him last Christmas and held it to his chest. *Darling Connie, how I love you and pray you are safe.*

Next day, Will blinked his eyes open at first light. He rolled over with a groan and pushed himself to his feet. Outside, mist cloaked the mountain and rain fell on him as he washed in the stream. He returned the jade flame tree to his bag, slung it over his aching shoulder, and clambered down to the main cave to join the others for breakfast.

George said they should wait for orders, so they spent the morning huddled at the entrance to their hideout. Just before tiffin, the fog began to clear and George lifted his binoculars. 'Bloody hell,' he said. 'Japs are coming over Lead Mine Pass to Grassy Hill.'

# THE FLAME TREE

Will took the binoculars from him. A sudden explosion rent the air and a shell landed in the middle of the advancing enemy troops. The Punjab battalion must still be in the vicinity, fighting on.

George cranked up the field telephone. He shook his head. 'I was just answered in goddamn Japanese...'

'What the...?' Will's mouth felt as if it had filled with sand.

'With no wireless set, we're totally cut off up here,' George muttered. 'We'll wait for nightfall then you come with me, Will, to the redoubt. We can let the Royal Scots know what we've seen of enemy activity and help them mine the paths around their position.' He turned to the others. 'You lot can go back to the bungalow to collect the rest of our gear and the radio then head to Sha Tau Kok.'

They set off at dusk and made good time before splitting ways. Will proceeded with George down to the reservoir catchment above the Royal Scots. They were on fixed lines of fire, so gave a pre-arranged Morse signal at intervals by flash, to which they received only one half-hearted reply. 'Not very happy about potentially being shot at by my fellow countrymen,' Will grumbled, remembering what had occurred earlier.

They came to a narrow bridge. 'Wait until I've crossed over, just in case there's a tripwire,' George said. 'Don't want to be blown up by one of our own mines.'

Will hid behind a rock and watched his burly commander's backside slither across the concrete. In the darkness, he looked like some mythical beast. If the situation hadn't been so serious, he would have doubled up with laughter at the incongruous sight.

Once George had arrived at the other side, Will crawled after him and they fought their way through the undergrowth to the road, halting every few yards for George to call out, 'Friend, can we come through?'

No reply came, so they walked up the road talking and smoking, hoping their demeanour would proclaim them as friends not foes.

'Who goes there?' came a shout at last.

They introduced themselves to Lieutenant Phillips of the Royal Scots and his platoon sergeants, Arnott and Whippy.

'Japs have come over Kaplung and Telegraph Pass. They're already on the roads to Taipo and Castle Peak,' Phillips told them dolefully before picking up his field telephone to inform the command centre about George's proposal to lay mines.

But, before he could get through, a scout approached. 'There're hundreds of Nips heading this way,' he said, ashen-faced.

'Everyone, take cover,' Phillips barked.

Will tumbled into a trench overlooking the valley, his heart hammering.

Lit by gunfire, Japanese officers were leading their men through the barbed wire entanglements, using torches and waving swords in a feudal manner. They were skilfully camouflaged, their helmets and tunics covered with nets into which they had stuck sprays of leaves. They also appeared to be wearing rubber-soled boots, which would render their movements completely silent. It seemed as if the whole hillside was moving. Their dark eyes peered out from amongst the screens of foliage in their helmets and some of the soldiers had even smeared their faces with mud.

Suddenly, distant machine guns banged, grenades hissed, men shouted, sharp orders echoed. Nausea built in Will's throat at the thought of his friend Captain Jones and his men in "The Strand Palace Hotel".

Orders then came through to withdraw to B Company HQ at the foot of the Shing Mun valley. Will and George set off with Phillips and his platoon. Once they'd arrived at the command station, George got on to a phone. 'I'm leaving for the island to make a full report to the Major General,' he said after disconnecting the call. 'I'll be back as soon as possible.'

Will guessed George would also get in touch with Jean. 'If you see your wife, could you find out if she has any news of Connie?'

George placed his hand on Will's shoulder. 'Of course.'

Will and the others moved back up to the knoll overlooking their former position and took cover among some bushes. Will couldn't help noticing a decided "lack of morale" among the men, and no wonder. Their brothers-in-arms stationed in the redoubt had been sitting ducks. Will remembered the steep steps leading underground, the only light coming in from gun slits in the concrete and from air shafts. He'd be surprised if any of them had made it out alive.

A Bren had been laid aside on the ground by Will's feet. He picked it up to use as his weapon, thinking ironically that he'd now become a Royal Scot. A steady drizzle rained down on him and, when they were withdrawn at about 3 a.m., Will went gladly. On learning there would be no "sport" till next morning, he found his way to a bunker and grabbed himself a makeshift bed.

Snores resounded from his "roommates" and Will struggled to drop off to sleep. His thoughts turned to Connie. Would George manage to get news of her from Jean? He alternated between hoping she'd got away and praying she hadn't. How would he carry on without her if she'd joined her father in Macau?

He retrieved his notebook and pen from his kit bag, touched his fingers to the jade of the flame tree ornament, and wrote.

*Was it only last week*
*We were together*
*My lips on yours*

## SIOBHAN DAIKO

*Your lips so keen*
*It seems like a dream*
*How cruel is this war*
*Keeping us apart*
*Our love suspended*
*Paused like a dragonfly in amber*
*Until we can be united again.*

# Chapter Seventeen

It was the following afternoon, and Connie picked up her notebook and pen. Admiral Chang Wei had called her into his office together with Bob and Colonel Yiu.

'The Royal Scots have been driven from the Shing Mun redoubt,' the Admiral said without preface. 'The Gin Drinkers Line or what the British like to call their "Oriental Maginot Line" is under threat.'

Connie gasped. 'What happened?'

'The Japanese discovered there weren't many men defending the position, only about thirty or so, and they mounted a sneak attack under cover of darkness. From all accounts, the Royal Scots were fast asleep. Apparently they assumed the enemy didn't wage night battles. My sources told me that Jap troops climbed to the top of the redoubt and threw hand grenades into the air vents of the connecting tunnels. Infiltrating teams then went into the pill boxes and engaged in fierce close-quarter fighting after they'd blocked the tunnel exits. The Royal Scots who'd survived the initial attack offered stubborn resistance, but eventually the position fell into Japanese hands.'

Connie grabbed hold of the edge of Uncle Wei's desk. The redoubt wasn't far from George and Jean's bungalow. And Connie had found out from Jean when she'd phoned her last night that Will and the other members of Z Force were stationed nearby. Connie began to shake uncontrollably.

'What's wrong?' The Admiral stared at her, a worried look on his face.

'I'm feeling a little faint, Uncle.'

'You do look very pale.' He turned to Bob. 'Go and fetch Connie a glass of water.'

She lowered herself to her chair. 'It's all so terrible. Those poor men…'

'Indeed.' Colonel Yiu gave his habitual smirk. 'But they shouldn't have relaxed their guard.'

Connie nodded. 'You're right. They shouldn't have. But it's too late to change things now.'

'Supply lines to the front are also breaking down.' The Admiral creased his brow. 'I expect a withdrawal from Kowloon is imminent.'

Bob came through the office door with a glass of water, which Connie accepted gladly.

'All the villages in Kowloon are being evacuated to the end of the peninsula, and from there on to Hong Kong side,' the Admiral went on to say. 'Together with the mass of refugees already on the island, the authorities will have difficulties controlling them.'

'Fifth columnists have begun overt operations. They've taken their Japanese arms out of hiding and have begun a campaign of arson, looting and robbery,' Colonel Yiu said.

'Spies and collaborators have been reporting on the British gun positions and troop concentrations to the enemy. Since the invasion started, they've been brazenly going about spreading alarmist propaganda and false rumours.' The Admiral slammed his hand down on the desk. 'It is time for us to put a stop to it.'

Connie drank down her water and told herself to get a grip. Her job supporting the Admiral and his men was just as important as the actual fighting, and by supporting Uncle Wei she was also supporting Will. 'I want to help, Uncle,' she said.

'Good girl.' Uncle Wei smiled. 'I will dictate my plan. Afterwards, kindly translate it into English so that I can put forward my proposals to the colonial government.'

Connie lifted her notebook and pen. 'I'm ready.'

'I propose to group together all the Nationalist organisations in Hong Kong into one single body, with its own general secretariat, military police, finance, foreign affairs, and other departments. We will enlist thousands of volunteers to lend a hand with food supplies, transport, medical and other services. All the Kuomintang groups in the colony must co-operate fully. We will use our underworld connections to tackle any saboteurs, snipers, and other collaborators. They must help restore order to the streets. We will use a combination of threats and payoffs to persuade the Triads to deal with the vandals—many of them from rival gangs in the pay of Japan.' The Admiral glanced at Connie. 'Have you got all that?'

'Yes, Uncle.' She rose from her seat. 'I'll go through to my office and start transcribing.'

'Thank you.' He waved her off.

She went to her desk, her legs still shaking. *Focus on the task at hand, Connie!* Now that she'd had time to think about it, her gut feeling told her that Will was still alive. She'd have felt something had he been killed she was so in tune with him. If the British were soon to abandon Kowloon, then Will would return to the island and she might see him. The thought lifted her spirits.

But what the Admiral was proposing was in effect a shadow government, led by himself. She doubted the British would agree to all his proposals, but she hoped they would swallow their pride and at least accept his assistance in tackling traitors.

With a worried sigh she turned to her typewriter and got to work.

After work, Connie went to her room in the Gloucester Hotel. She was about to call Jean when the ring of the phone stopped her in her tracks. She picked up the receiver.

'It's Mary,' Connie's eldest sister's voice came down the line. 'We're leaving for Macau. Taking Gloria, our trusted servants, and the children. All of us. Our husbands have insisted. Father is sending his biggest launch to Aberdeen first thing tomorrow. He's decided to stay in Macau and he sent me a message that he wants you to join him too.'

Connie groaned. She'd feared this would happen. 'Please tell him that I can't. My work here is too important.' And it was. She couldn't consider leaving the Admiral in the lurch. 'I'm needed, Mary. I'm sure Father will understand...'

'But, what about your safety? All these bombs...'

'Admiral Chang Wei is convinced a relief army will arrive from China within days. The Japanese haven't bombed the central district much. I'm safe enough.'

Mary huffed. 'You always were the stubbornest of us.' She paused. 'I hope you aren't staying because of that Englishman. You know Father would not approve...'

'I know.' *Oh, how she knew.* 'I just want to play my part in the defence of Hong Kong.'

'Father won't be happy.'

'Father's in Macau.'

'You know he's not well.' Mary was playing the sympathy card.

'His illness isn't serious. If the Japanese hadn't attacked he'd be returning to the colony any day now.'

## THE FLAME TREE

'Alright, little sister.' Mary sighed. 'On your head be it. If Hong Kong falls to the Japanese, it might be too late to get you out.'

'I'm prepared to take that risk.'

'I expect the Admiral will look after you.' Mary's tone had become resigned. 'Take care, dearest. I do wish you'd change your mind...'

For a second or two, Connie wavered. She loved her family and would miss them dreadfully. Unshed tears clogged her throat, but she swallowed them down. 'Please give everyone my love, Mary. I hope you'll all have a good Christmas.'

'You too, dear. You too...'

Connie replaced the receiver then immediately called Jean. 'It's Connie,' she said. 'How are you?'

'Not too bad, given the circumstances. George dropped by in the early hours of this morning. I was able to give him news of you to take to Will.'

Connie's heart leapt. 'Is Will alright?'

'Oh, yes. George is taking him some of his "toys" and they're going to use them to mine a strategic area.'

'Toys?'

'Explosives.' Jean laughed. 'Come up to May Road for some supper. Thus far, the Japs have held back from bombing us at night.'

'I'd love to,' Connie said.

'Wonderful! I'll pick you up in my car in about an hour, alright?'

Connie thanked her, then took a quick bath before changing into a pair of slacks and a jumper. The weather had turned chilly—not as cold as England in December but Hong Kong houses were built for the heat and could be draughty. Before she went down to the lobby, she phoned her family home on the Peak to check on how the staff were coping. Number Six Elder

Sister answered and said they were all terrified but would stay to hold the fort. She added that many of the expatriates' servants, especially those working in mansions near the anti-aircraft batteries, which had been bombed by the Japs, had fled for their lives. Connie was only thankful the Han Fung estate faced in the opposite direction.

Next, she phoned Margaret, who told her she had a houseful of people whom she'd invited to take shelter because her place wasn't in a direct line of fire from Japanese shells. All day in the office, Connie had heard them battering the north face of the island. Her nerves jangling, she'd kept her head down and had focussed on her work.

Jean picked her up, as arranged, and Connie's heart wept at the sight of the terrible craters caused by the shelling of May Road. 'I think you should come down to central during the day,' she suggested to Jean. 'It isn't safe for you up here.'

'Oh, I'm not here during the day, honey,' she said. 'I'm helping at a food kitchen downtown. I spent most of today ladling out rice to coolies.'

'How brave of you! I'm filled with admiration...'

At Gunter Mansions, Connie refrained from commenting on the Shing Mun debacle. Instead, she helped Jean by chopping the vegetables for their stir-fried supper and remembered the last time she was here with Will. They'd been laughing and joking, holding hands under the table, devouring each other with their eyes, stealing secret kisses when no one was looking. If she'd known what was in store for them, she wouldn't have been so reticent. She wouldn't make that mistake again, she resolved sorrowfully. The next time she saw Will, she would give herself to him heart, body, and soul. She loved him so very much.

## Chapter Eighteen

Will was in the lobby of the Peninsula Hotel, waiting for George who'd crossed over to the island to find Reggie. Panic infused the air. Terrified people were milling about, pushing and shoving each other. Rumours and counter-rumours were gaining in strength as they were passed along: the Japanese were close by in Jordan Road; the local Chinese were looting; traitors with Tommy guns were out in force; thieves were robbing houses. Will shook his head in disbelief that matters had taken such a drastic turn.

Earlier, he'd gone home—where he'd shaved and had taken a bath. The servants had fled, but his housemate, the policeman Mike Middleton had been there. Will told him what had happened at the Gin Drinkers Line and that he was heading to the Peninsula to meet George.

'Change into civilian clothes so as not to draw attention to yourself and risk being attacked by fifth columnists,' Mike had said. 'Take anything of value with you. Looters are about. I'm about to leave for the Star Ferry pier to organise the checking of permits for people crossing the harbour.'

Will had done as Mike had suggested and now, kit bag full, he was observing the placid hotel receptionist, who was standing behind her desk dealing with requests for information in a calm manner. She called Will to one side. 'I've just heard that orders have been received to evacuate to the island.'

Will's heart sank. This put a new face on things. If Kowloon were to fall it might be more difficult to regain contact with Z Force. 'Thanks for letting me know. Can I use your phone?' he asked.

'Of course.'

He dialled George's number at Gunter Mansions and waited. No answer. The line to Fortress HQ was busy, so Will decided to set off on his own and catch George and Reggie as they arrived at the Kowloon side of the harbour.

'If anyone asks for me,' Will said to the receptionist. 'Please tell them that I've gone to the police barrier at the Star Ferry.'

She assured him that she would comply with his request.

After thanking her, Will made his way down Salisbury Road, his steps slow and heavy as he reflected on recent events. The day after the redoubt had been taken, orders had come through to the Royal Scots to withdraw to the inner line. Will had headed off to report back to battalion headquarters and find a phone to contact George. But the adjutant had told him that George was on his way and in fact some "toys" had already arrived.

Later, in brilliant moonlight, with most of Kowloon lit by a huge blaze on the waterfront, Will had gone with George and three volunteer engineers to a ridge above Gin Drinkers Bay. There, they found that the officer in charge was drunk, having fortified himself too liberally with brandy against the cold, and the junior officers were obeying orders which they themselves believed were mistaken. The platoon sent to guard the area were all untrained men who'd walked to the top of the hill and were perched on the skyline, where the moonlight rendered them visible for miles. To crown it all, instead of the tracks which George had been assured would be up there, there was only bare hillside—impossible country for their particular "toys". After arriving back at the battalion headquarters, George had set off to find Reggie while Will had gone straight to bed.

The next day, he'd found out that orders had come through for a withdrawal. He'd hurried home through a terrified and paralysed city. Only a few shops were still open, seemingly defiant in the face of the chaos that raged around them. Others were sealed and shuttered as if they would never open again. Kowloon was a lost cause. Will—like most people, he deduced—had never imagined that the New Territories would fall in just four days. How had it come to this?

A chill wind whipped around him as he arrived at the ferry. Crowds thronged the gates, many trying to force their way through without the necessary pass—and, to add to the confusion, walking wounded, mainly Punjabis, were being helped to the front of the queue. Cars piled up five or six deep with Mike Middleton and his force doing what they could to immobilise them. It was evident now that looting had well and truly started. Massive fires were spreading a lurid glare over the waterfront to the accompaniment of loud shouting.

With caustic smoke hurting his eyes, and his wait for George of no avail, Will decided to take matters into his own hands and cross to Hong Kong side on his own. Mike Middleton waved him through and soon Will found himself crammed onto a boat like a sardine in a tin as it battled its way over the choppy water, shells exploding and sending up waterspouts all around.

His head reeled—he still couldn't come to terms with the realisation that they were evacuating Kowloon. Hong Kong Island would come under siege—troops and civilians packed into a small area. He thought about Connie and his skin prickled with fear for her. Had she managed to escape to Macau? The sensible part of him hoped that she had. But the other part, the part where his heart lay, ached with anticipation that he might soon be seeing her again.

Battle Box—as the Fortress HQ was known—consisted of a reinforced concrete bunker sixty feet below Victoria Barracks. It was Hong Kong's defence nerve centre with its own power supply, telephone exchange, and ventilation system. Will made his way up Cotton Tree Drive, then into the sunken entrance, which lay among the sleepy colonnades and sprawling banyans of the colony's original military encampment. Down thirteen flights of steps, steel doors opened onto a catacomb of pipelined passageways with a series of right-angled turns and small offices leading off the sides.

Will went into the last office, where he saluted and gave his report on Shing Mun to the intelligence officer Marcus Owen, a dapper-looking chap in his mid-thirties. Will enquired about George, but before Owen could respond, George came into the room with Reggie at his heels.

'We were about to set off and find you. You've saved us a trek across the harbour,' George said cheerfully, his eyes glowing with evident enthusiasm. 'The Major General has ordered us to join forces with Admiral Chang Wei to tackle fifth columnists.'

Will stepped back, speechless with surprise.

'We're to report to the Admiral now in Douglas McBride's office,' Reggie said in an excited tone.

'Excellent.' Will forced a smile. Rounding up spies would be an entirely different kettle of fish than commando activities. He hadn't signed up for this, but the war had taken a new turn and he'd have to do what he had to do.

They took their leave of Owen, and as they made their way down the corridor, George explained that McBride was head of the Hong Kong office of the British Ministry of Information and a good friend of the Admiral, having met him ten years ago when he was in China for the second part of his two-year Cantonese course. 'He's an "anti-colonial" civil servant,' Reggie said. 'Wants to modernise things.'

They shook hands with McBride, tall and fair, who smiled at them warmly. 'Glad to have the three of you on board,' he said before introducing the Admiral and his staff.

Will had seen Connie's boss at the Tin Hat Ball. He remembered being impressed by Chang Wei's agility despite his wooden leg. The Admiral's sparkling eyes bore into him as he responded to Will's salute. 'You speak Cantonese?'

Will answered in the Chan Wei's language. 'Gang hai la.' *Of course.*

'Tai hou la.' *That's great.*

Admiral Wei presented his Chief of staff, Colonel Yiu Kai Pao—a solidly built man with shifty eyes—and his fresh-faced ADC Lieutenant-commander Robert Lao Yeung.

'Call me Bob,' Lao Yeung said in excellent English.

'There's something the Admiral would like you to help him with,' McBride went on to say. 'A report has come in concerning a bright light seen shining across the harbour from a point about two hundred feet above the Battle Box.'

'It doesn't appear to have been signalling as it shines for a few seconds only,' Bob clarified. 'But the light is repeated at intervals.'

'We think fifth columnists are trying to indicate the exact position of Fortress HQ to the Japs,' McBride added. 'And now there are only 1,200 yards of water separating us, they'll use their heavy artillery in the daylight as soon as they can bring their guns up to the new front.'

'We go as soon as it gets dark,' the Admiral said. 'Meet me below on the waterfront at the naval dockyard at seven pm.'

'Yes, sir!' Will and the others saluted.

There was just enough time for Will to drop his gear off at George and Jean's flat in Gunter Mansions, where he'd been invited to form a "mess" with Reggie for the duration. They all changed into their jungle camouflage uniforms before taking their leave of Jean.

'Take care,' she said. 'Connie is dropping by for supper, by the way. Come back safe and sound.'

Will's heart leapt with joy. 'That's the best news I've had all day.'

Jean looked him in the eye. 'Connie's sisters tried to persuade her to go to Macau with them, but she refused on account of her job with the Admiral.'

Will nodded. How like Connie to put duty first. 'She's very brave,' he said. 'And so are you, Jean. George told me about you helping the refugees…'

'It's nothing compared to what you've been through.' Her expression darkened. 'We all have to put a brave face on things for to do otherwise would be far too depressing.'

George brushed a quick kiss to her cheek. 'We'll be home shortly, my love.'

Jean waved them off, and they piled into Reggie's Austin, which he drove down to the waterfront in darkness—due to the blackout—the only illumination provided by the moon. 'Any news of the rest of Z Force?' Will asked.

'None whatsoever.' George puffed out a loud breath. 'But they'll follow the plan to lie low then make their way to unoccupied China as soon as they can.'

At the waterfront, they found the Admiral waiting alone. 'I've sent my men to round up a group of collaborator gangsters in Wanchai,' he explained before indicating with his hand. 'There's the light.'

Sure enough, a bright light shone from about halfway up the Peak for a couple of seconds before going out again. 'Seems to be coming from a point just below the far end of May Road,' George said. 'Let's drive up there.'

Admiral Chang Wei got into the front of the car next to Reggie. Again, they set off in the gloom. 'We'll park then proceed on foot,' George suggested. 'Don't want to announce our arrival.'

Reggie found a space by some tennis courts and they made their way to the point about fifty to a hundred feet above what they deemed to be the light's location. The Admiral explained his tactics, then stealthily, he led them down the hillside to reach a thicket where they could take cover and listen.

Movement rustled in the bushes below and a bright light shone across the harbour.

Lit by the moon, the Admiral quickly took a hand grenade and a ball of string from his belt. He proceeded to tie one end of the twine around the grenade and the other end onto a tree trunk. With an exhale of breath, he pulled the pin from the grenade and threw it.

The purpose of the string was to stop the grenade from falling below its target. It was timed to go off in five seconds. Apparently and a dropping explosive could go a long way in that time and miss its objective.

They were the longest five seconds Will had ever experienced. He counted to five over and over again in his head. Suddenly, a massive explosion rent the air, followed by a flash, a yell, a crash and then…dead silence. He gave a sigh of relief.

'Job well done,' the Admiral muttered. 'Please, can you drop me off at Pedder Street? I've moved into my office there since the fall of Kowloon.'

'Yes, sir,' Reggie responded.

Mission complete, they made their way back to the Austin, and Will couldn't stop smiling to himself. Connie would be in Gunter Mansions. He couldn't wait to hold her in his arms. *To hold her tighter than ever before.*

# Chapter Nineteen

In Jean's steam-filled kitchen, bereft of the servants who'd all left for China, Connie was making wonton soup from scratch. She'd learnt the recipe from Mrs Huang when she was a student in London. At home on the Peak, Elder Brother, the cook, was hugely protective of his domain and would throw up his hands in horror if she ever tried to encroach on his territory, so she'd only started learning to prepare tasty dishes when she was in England. She stood back and surveyed her efforts. The result pleased her; she enjoyed cooking and was finding it a welcome distraction from thinking of Will every minute; she was so looking forward to seeing him again, she could barely contain herself.

She glanced at Jean. 'Everything's ready for when the men arrive.'

'They should be back any minute, honey.' Jean wiped her hands on a towel.

Connie untied her apron, sudden worry turning her mouth dry. 'I hope they're alright.'

'They're with the Admiral, aren't they? They'll be fine...'

Connie nodded. Uncle Wei would look after them; she had absolute faith in him.

The sound of the front door opening, followed by male voices, set Connie's heart racing. 'They're here. I'll go and say hello.'

She hovered in the hallway, drinking in the sight of Will. A warm, fuzzy feeling spread through her; he looked so heartbreakingly handsome in his camouflage uniform.

Reggie and George went through to the sitting room, but Will stood rooted to the spot.

'Connie!' He ran to her, swept her into his arms.

She gave herself up to his kiss, closing her eyes and savouring the feel of his lips on hers.

He hugged her tightly. 'I've been wanting to do this since the moment we parted.'

She snuggled against him. 'I have too. Oh, Will, I've been so worried about you.'

'As I have about you.' A frown creased his brow. 'You should have gone to Macau with your sisters.'

'I couldn't leave the Admiral, couldn't leave you either, my dearest.'

'My darling girl, I love you so much.' He stroked the side of her cheek, then touched another kiss to her lips.

'I love you too, Will. Being in the middle of that Japanese attack on the redoubt must have been terrifying. I was so...'

'You heard what happened?'

She nodded, unable to put the horror into words.

Will sighed, pulled her in tight. 'I'm here now, Connie. I'm here...'

At the dinner table, blackout curtains obscuring the windows, everyone praised Connie's soup, which they ate hungrily before tucking into the chow fan—egg fried rice—that Jean had thrown together to finish the meal. George raised his glass of

# THE FLAME TREE

Tiger Beer. 'Here's to Connie and Jean,' he said. 'Thanks for a superb supper.'

Talk soon turned to the Admiral and what would happen now that Kowloon had fallen.

'Your boss is remarkable, Connie,' Will said. He went on to tell her and Jean about the Admiral's tactics that evening.

'There can be no doubt that Uncle Wei is as cunning as a fox.' Connie chuckled. 'But he's also a thoroughly nice man and brimming with optimism. I love his positive attitude. It gives me confidence that all could be well in the end.'

Jean started to clear their plates. 'I hope the Chinese army gets here soon. I doubt we'll be able to hold out against the Japanese siege for long.'

'There's enough food on the island for a protracted blockade,' George said. 'We'll just have to fight the Japs off until help comes.'

Everyone pushed back their chairs and went to lend a hand with the washing up. Afterwards, they all trooped through to the sitting room, where George poured them each a glass of brandy.

Suddenly a short burst of gun fire echoed from the city below.

'What the...?' Reggie leapt to his feet and out through the veranda door.

Connie and the others followed him.

A deafening explosion ricocheted from the Western Bund, and an enormous pinkish-purple flame shot up, illuminating the waterfront for a couple of seconds.

Connie found herself shaking and Will put his arm around her. 'A Jap shell must have hit an ammo dump.'

'Hmm.' George shook his head. 'My guess is a ship of some kind has been blown up by British fire instead.'

The entire waterfront sprang into action. Searchlights swept the harbour and machine guns fired, reminding Connie of something akin to a fireworks display. Lines of tracer criss-crossed up and down. 'Maybe a large-scale attempted landing has started,' she murmured as explosions reverberated across the water.

Then, everything went quiet and she sighed with relief.

'Let's go back inside,' George said. 'Show's over.'

'I should return to my hotel.' Connie glanced at Will. 'It's getting late.'

Reggie tossed Will the keys to his Austin. 'Here you are, my friend. I'd offer to drive Connie myself but I'm dead beat.'

Will thanked him. 'Off you to go to bed. Sleep well!'

'We'll see you in the morning, Will.' Jean linked her arm with George's. 'Good night, Connie.'

And then she was alone with Will. She sat next to him on the sofa. 'You must be tired...'

'I'm as fresh as a daisy.' He spread his arms wide and she went into them.

He kissed her slowly, passionately, without stopping, running his hands down her sides, squeezing her hips, moulding her to him.

Desire spiralled through her. She clung to him and gazed deep into his indigo blue eyes. 'Make love to me, Will.'

'Are you sure? I mean, I love you and want you with every ounce of my being. But I thought you'd want to wait...'

She pressed her hand to his chest, felt the beating of his heart. 'The future is so uncertain, my dearest. We need to seize the moment. If anything were to happen to either of us, we might live the rest of our lives with the regret of not having truly known each other. I... I couldn't bear that.'

'Neither could I.' Reverently, he helped her to her feet. 'God, how I love you.'

Her pulse pounded. 'I love you too, Will.'

# THE FLAME TREE

He took her to his room. There, he laid her on the bed, stretched out beside her and kissed her over and over until she was begging him. 'Please, Will. Please...'

He chuckled. 'Your wish is my command.'

Slowly, he undressed her, kissing her all the while. She swooned in his arms, unaware that he'd taken his own clothes off until she felt his warm skin against hers. It was wonderful. He covered her like a blanket, and she parted her thighs. She was doing the right thing. Her heart was thudding for him and her body melting, at one with his as he thrust inside her. She lost all sense of time, of space, of right and wrong. She forgot about her father and the Japanese and the fact she might lose Will in the fighting or that she might die herself. All she knew, all she cared about, was that he was hers right now and she marvelled at their bodies' magical ability to replace all their woes with this bliss. *Oh, how she loved him.*

The following morning, Connie made her way to the office as usual. After Will had driven her back to the Gloucester the night before, she'd lain awake reliving their lovemaking, holding the poem Will had written for her when he'd been at the front line.

She'd always believed that the first time she made love it would be painful, and it had hurt a little at the start. But then pleasure had rocked through her and she'd lost herself in exquisite sensations. She loved him so much she hadn't wanted anything to spoil the moment, so she'd been glad Will had discreetly sheathed himself and she hadn't had to bring up the fact that she was in the safe period of her cycle. Thank God she'd learnt about contraception at the clinic.

Connie thought about how she hadn't felt at all self-conscious about going to Will's room. The fact that there was a war on, and they could be killed at any moment, had rendered such reticence redundant, she supposed.

From across the harbour came the boom of the enemy's big guns in Kowloon, their shells screaming overhead as she nervously dashed across the road, the shrapnel hot beneath her feet.

In the office, she translated into Chinese an official communiqué announcing the withdrawal from the mainland, "*We have retired within our fortress, and from the shelter of our main defences we will hold off the enemy until the strategical situation permits of relief*".

'Did you hear the racket last night, Connie?' the Admiral glanced up as she took him a cup of tea.

'I did. Do you know if the Japanese were attempting to cross?'

'It wasn't them, but our own side. Apparently, a British launch loaded with explosives from Green Island had arrived ahead of schedule. Thinking it was the enemy, a machine gun post fired on it, which caused the explosion. The boat was blown to bits and the entire crew killed.'

Connie winced. 'Oh, no!'

'The defenders were already in a jumpy state of nerves. They began shooting at imaginary boats containing imaginary Japs. Their action in turn spread to the artillery and the whole concentration of fire power was put up against nothing. Searchlights were playing, so why the truth wasn't found out sooner is anyone's guess.'

'What a terrible thing to happen.'

'Indeed.'

With a heavy heart, Connie returned to her office. She picked up the day's edition of the colony's leading newspaper, *The South China Morning Post,* to translate for the Admiral, whose command of English was rudimentary. Her breath caught. It was still providing its daily fare of official announcements, international news items, lists of coming events, and the usual host of advertisements. Jimmy's Tiffin cost one dollar and thirty cents, she read, while Lane Crawford, with twelve days left before Christmas, was urging buyers to let Aladdin lamps brighten up their homes. The Jockey Club even announced its forthcoming race meeting at Happy Valley. The only note of war was the Whiteaway's advertisement for emergency supplies: blackout materials, camp beds, volunteer requisites and nurse uniforms made to measure. Connie began her translation.

Later, in the afternoon, there was a lull in the shelling. She found out from Colonel Yiu that the Japanese had sent a peace mission over, to demand unconditional surrender... or else. 'A party of three Japanese officers crossed the harbour in a launch bearing at its bows a white sheet with the words "Peace Mission". One of the aides carried a small white flag on a stick. These signals were not immediately seen, and as the launch pulled out from the wharf at Kowloon it was fired upon but not hit.' Colonel Yiu smirked.

'How did the Governor respond?' Connie asked.

'He said he wasn't prepared to enter into any conference or parley on the subject of surrender.'

Connie couldn't help but feel proud of Hong Kong's defiance. It was as if the colony was infused with the same spirit shown during the London Blitz of 1940. From all accounts, the Chinese population were carrying on with their motto of "business as usual". During intense shelling, they went down to a network of air-raid shelters in Happy Valley or packed the corridors of the well-constructed buildings in the central district. Everyone was confident in the ability of Hong Kong's defences and there weren't any signs of apprehension.

It was better to be positive than negative, Connie told herself. In the lounge of the Gloucester, she'd observed the women who sat knitting unconcernedly, which had a calming effect on her. But, realistically, the situation couldn't remain as it was. The hotel was within 100 yards of the waterfront—the new front line—and she feared it might become a casualty station.

Unexpectedly, the Admiral's door crashed open. 'One of our paid inside informers just telephoned. There's a plot among pro-Japanese triads to massacre the entire European community.' Uncle Wei's voice had gone up a pitch. 'Colonel Yiu has got hold of Big Eared Tu. He'll be here momentarily with the five heads of the biggest Hong Kong criminal societies to meet with Douglas McBride of the Hong Kong Government. I want you to take notes, Constance.'

Her pulse raced. 'Of course, Uncle.' She grabbed her notebook and pen, then followed him into his office.

'You might think this is a fantastical and unlikely story, but Douglas McBride is taking it seriously.'

'Good.' What else could she say? She felt sick with worry.

She waited with the Admiral, his bodyguard and Bob. The office boy was sent to make tea and soon Douglas McBride arrived, followed by Colonel Yiu, Tu, and the top five Hong Kong triad leaders. Uncle stayed behind his desk, in command, and everyone else sat on chairs around him.

'I heard a silly rumour that certain organisations propose carrying out some sort of "celebration" tonight,' McBride opened the discussion. 'The only "celebration" the government will permit at present is the killing of Japanese.' He stared at each of the gangsters in turn. 'I've never had the pleasure of meeting you before, but I've heard you have considerable influence among a certain section of the community.'

'In other words,' Big Eared Tu clarified. 'A plan to murder all the British has come to our attention and we want it stopped.'

The eldest of the triads assumed a "holier than thou" expression. 'Nothing to do with us. But if some people are arranging to bump off the foreign devils, they could save the lives of hundreds if not thousands of Chinese.'

# THE FLAME TREE

'The Japanese have captured Kowloon and the British will be bombarding that densely populated area,' the plump man next to him added. 'Surely the siege should be ended now?'

'Our forces have been wary of shelling Kowloon for fear of frightening the inhabitants. We want to avoid killing civilians,' McBride said firmly.

'We're only mediators.' The third cut-throat held up his hands. 'We could try and get in touch with the gang leaders tomorrow and use what little influence we have to persuade them to cooperate with the government.'

'We're not prepared to let you go on the off chance as to what you might or might not do "tomorrow",' the Admiral growled, drawing his pistol. 'All the sub-heads of the organisations must attend a meeting tonight. If you can't arrange it, then we have no alternative than to throw you in jail.'

'I know someone who could organise a meeting,' the eldest of the gangsters blurted. Clearly he was still maintaining the role of "mediator". 'I'll phone him now.'

The Admiral indicated the telephone on his desk and the call was put through. 'We can hold a conference in two hours' time in the dining room of the Cecil Hotel. But it will cost a large, extremely large, sum of money to secure "co-operation",' the triad said after hanging up.

'You're holding the Hong Kong government to ransom?' Douglas McBride sounded incredulous.

'I can deal with providing the cash, Mr McBride,' Big Eared Tu leant forward. 'Provided you give me an undertaking to settle up after the war ends.'

McBride tapped his chin. He opened and closed his mouth, plainly struggling to find the right words. 'Of course,' he agreed eventually, obviously caught between a rock and a hard place.

Smiling like cats who'd got the cream, the triads left to carry out their promised task.

'Can we trust them?' Douglas McBride asked the Admiral.

'I think their demand is a good omen. It indicates the other side has something to sell and that if we buy it, they will keep to the bargain.'

'I hope so, John,' McBride said, calling the Admiral by his European name.

'We can only wait and see.'

The Admiral and his men were almost certainly triad members themselves—most people with pretentions to political power in China were triads, Connie reflected as she returned to her office. Father had once told her that Dr Sun Yat Sen himself had been one. And so was Chiang Kai Shek.

Connie sighed to herself as she began to type up her notes. The Admiral had been right when he'd said the gangsters would keep to their agreement. Of that she had no doubts. Money was involved and money meant everything to the Hong Kong Chinese. Nevertheless, she would ask Bob to ring her as soon as he knew the deal had been done. She wouldn't be seeing Will tonight; he'd told her earlier that he'd be on duty, on the lookout for anyone signalling across the harbour. But they'd planned to meet up tomorrow at Jean and George's. It would be Sunday, their usual day for meeting each other under the flame tree. Connie wondered if the Botanical Gardens had been bombed by the Japanese. Was it only a week ago that she'd danced with Will at the Tin Hat Ball? So much had happened in the interim. So much death and devastation. But she couldn't help the fluttery feeling in her stomach, the bubble of happiness when she thought about Will, for she loved him with all of her heart.

## CHAPTER TWENTY

Will woke and rubbed the sleep from his eyes; he was still dog tired from his exertions the night before, when reports had been received with respect to signals coming from Conduit Road in the mid-levels. Given that the enemy's artillery had been picking out British gun emplacements suspiciously quickly, George had said that a fifth columnist was obviously at work. They'd left immediately to patrol the area, making haste down May Road in the blackout, pistols at the ready. At first, all had been quiet. Then they'd spotted a suspicious character running into a block of flats. They'd pursued him stealthily and had kept watch on the building. They hadn't needed to wait long. A bright white beam flashed from a ground floor window. All three of them fired through the glass plane. A loud cry came, followed by silence, and exhilaration had coursed through Will's veins. But now, in the cold light of day, he realised he'd probably made his first kill. The target had been a spy, though, his actions causing many deaths, and Will felt no remorse for what he'd done. It was what he'd been trained for...

He crawled from his bed, used the bathroom, changed out of his pyjamas, and went through to the dining room. A crackly recording of "*The Old Folks at Home*", sung in a plaintive voice, was wafting through the veranda door. 'What's that music?' he asked.

George looked up from *The South China Morning Post*. 'Seems to be coming from that derelict old merchant ship lying in Lye Mun Channel.' He grunted. 'I've heard that the singer is Deanna Durbin, "The Sensational Canadian Songbird". Japs must be trying to make the young Winnipeg Grenadiers feel homesick and long for surrender. There's also been spoken announcements, exhorting the Chinese and Indians to join Japan's Greater East Asia Co-Prosperity Sphere and turn against the Europeans.'

'Good God,' Will exclaimed. 'Whatever next?'

'We don't know the half of it,' George said wryly. 'But no doubt we'll find out soon enough. We've been called to a meeting with Admiral Wei, Douglas McBride, and Major General Maltby in the Battle Box later.'

Reggie came into the dining room as the soundtrack changed to "*Swanee River*". He stopped in his tracks. 'What the...?'

'Get used to it,' George said, 'maybe we can have a singalong after breakfast.'


In the early afternoon, Will set off with George and Reggie for Fortress HQ. Inside the huge catacomb, the musty air and claustrophobic passages reminded Will of the Shing Mun command centre. He winced.

Douglas McBride was waiting in his office. 'The Admiral will be here shortly,' he said. He proceeded to tell them about how Chang Wei had helped to foil a pro-Japanese triad plot aimed at killing all the Europeans in Hong Kong.

'Sounds a bit far-fetched.' George raised a brow.

# THE FLAME TREE

'I can assure you it wasn't.' McBride had barely uttered the words when his young assistant, Fred Martin, escorted the Admiral into his office.

Chang Wei returned their salutes, then said, 'I was informed at 5.30 am this morning that the meeting with our "friends" was a success. They've agreed to cooperate with the Hong Kong government and do everything in their power to exterminate the Japanese enemy. They're fighting for their own country, after all, not just helping the British...'

'Wonderful!' McBride smiled. 'Major General Maltby would like to thank you in person, John. Follow me!'

They found the harassed-looking Commander in his operations room. A map on the far wall showed the Japanese positions in Kowloon. Telephones were ringing and the atmosphere was like that of an animated beehive. Terrible news had just come through that the British battleship *Prince of Wales* and the battlecruiser *Repulse* had been sunk by the Japanese in an attack off Singapore. Germany and Italy had declared war on the USA and the Japs had annihilated American air power in the Philippines. Will stared at his fellow commandos and they stared back at him, their faces pale with shock.

Admiral Wei shook hands with the Major General, who thanked him for his efforts with the triads. 'What do you make of the music coming across the harbour, Chang Wei?'

The admiral gave a lukewarm smile. 'Very nice...'

'I'm not so keen on it.' Maltby grimaced. 'Have you any ideas how it can be stopped?'

The admiral smirked. 'I have a fine idea.'

'Good. I'm grateful. I'll leave it to you, then,' the Commander said before getting back to his battle plans.

Once they'd made their way outside, the Admiral turned to George. 'Major General Maltby doesn't like the music. We must stop it.'

'How do you propose we do that?'
'With your "toys".' The Admiral chuckled.

The derelict merchant ship lay about a quarter of a mile out from Kowloon side. Not only were the Japanese using it for their broadcasts, George informed Will and Reggie after he'd received a phone call from the Admiral late that afternoon, but it had also been boarded by an observation team, who were almost certainly employing the vessel as a spotting post to study possible landing points on Hong Kong Island opposite. 'I've contacted the officer in command of the Taikoo Dockyard,' George went on to say. 'He's expecting us.'

They took their leave of Jean and set off in Reggie's Morris to make their way down the cratered roads towards Quarry Bay in the north-eastern part of the island. Shells exploded around them, some of which whistled so close overhead that Will broke out in a cold sweat. Eventually, they got through to the dockyard—the site of a sugar refinery and ship building enterprise. Will glanced around. Where were the hundreds of coolies who usually thronged the place? The area was eerily quiet. 'It's like a ghost town,' he observed as Reggie parked his car out front.

Inside the premises, they found Chris Edwards, the officer in charge. 'Sorry, old chaps,' Edwards said. 'I don't know the exact position of the ship, nor the pill boxes...which would be your reference points. The Middlesex battalion has only newly occupied them.'

George put down his bag of explosives. 'Anyone else here who can help?'

Edwards scratched his head. 'I'll find out.'

# THE FLAME TREE

He returned momentarily with a couple of dockyard workers and a map. 'It's anchored right here,' he pointed out the position.

'Perfect.' George picked up his bag and turned to Will and Reggie. 'I'll get the "toys" ready. You two go and find us a boat.'

Wont' be easy, Will thought. They could hardly go up to a fisherman and ask to borrow a sampan. 'Let's try the yacht club,' he suggested.

Which is what they did. An abandoned dinghy with two sawn off paddles lay beached on the deserted slipway. They found a lorry parked nearby and paid the driver to transport the boat to Taikoo, with them following in the car behind. 'Job well done.' Reggie clapped Will on the back.

On arrival back at the docks, they discovered that George has got the first "toy" primed. Once the second of the explosives had been readied, they had a quick supper with Edwards and then, at 21.00 hours—when the tide was turning—they established bearings and launched the dinghy. George had decided it would be Will and him carrying out the sabotage mission while Reggie would stay at the docks to fire from the Vickers machine gun mounted on the roof of the refinery building. 'It'll make the Japs keep their heads down and divert attention from Will and me as we approach,' George said.

Will sucked in a sharp breath. They'd overlooked something—the phosphorescent light caused by movement in the water. But it was too late to worry about that now and, nerves fluttering in the pit of his stomach, he stepped into the dinghy next to George. They took an oar each and began to row, the limpet mines attached to keeper plates hooked to belts around their waists.

Paddling out to the ship proved to be a hell of a job. The tide was running like the devil. 'Don't want to row too forcefully as we'll stir up more phosphorous. But we need to counteract the tide,' George muttered.

Suddenly a burst of machine gun fire rippled overhead. Will's blood froze. It took a moment before he realised it was Reggie shooting. *Phew!*

He rowed with George towards their first bearing—another ship, except this one was in flames. Bursts from Reggie came at irregular intervals. The blazing vessel spread a garish glow over the water . If only the wind were blowing the smoke in their direction, it would form a screen, Will thought.

They approached their target. Will's heart sank. Bloody hell, they'd made a mistake in judging the tide. They were about 200 yards astern of the vessel, with the tide against them; they'd need to paddle like mad and thus create more phosphorous not to mention make a noise from the oars splashing.

A light began to go on and off on the ship. One of the Japs could be sitting at the stern with an automatic aimed at them. What would it feel like to be hit by a burst? It would hurt like hell, that's what. Will drew a strange comfort from the realisation that any gunfire would most likely set off the "toys" and finish him and George off before they knew it.

When they were about 100 yards astern, another surge of shots from Reggie struck the superstructure of the ship. They rowed fast and furiously and slid safely to the stern, from where they took their bearings. A long lifeboat was attached to the gangway on the port side. They rowed up to it and used it to drag themselves around to a point about a quarter of the way up the vessel.

During supper earlier, they'd decided that Will, the strongest swimmer, would place the limpets. He pulled on his goggles and slipped over the side of the dinghy into the cold water, sinking down to get some depth before slapping his "toy" onto the ship. *Ouch!* He grimaced with pain; he'd taken most of the skin from the tips of his fingers off on some bastard barnacles in the process.

He surfaced. The bloody tide had swept him nearly as far as the sternpost. Inching his way along the lifeboat, he managed to pull himself back up the ship to where George was waiting.

Placing the second limpet proved to be more problematic. The barnacles might deaden the magnetic attraction. After attaching the "toy", Will tried to yank it off. He heaved a sigh of relief as the limpet behaved like its name and stuck fast.

He resurfaced, incongruously admiring the phosphorescent bubbles coming out of his battle pants.

'We'll drift down stream until we're clear,' George whispered after Will had heaved himself back onto the dinghy.

They did as George had suggested, then paddled back to the dock, trailing phosphorescence in their wake. Reggie was there with a big tot of rum and, after a change of clothes, they set off for home, Will more eager than ever to see Connie and hold her close.

After they'd gained some distance, the timers on the "toys" did what they were designed for. Two almighty explosions reverberated in the air. Will couldn't help but smile.

## Chapter Twenty-One

After a week of war, Hong Kong's once-teeming harbour had a desolate air, Will reflected as he stood on the Robinsons' veranda during a break in the shelling. The magnificent junks had been herded off into typhoon shelters. Those freighters and ships which hadn't left when the invasion started, had all been bombed or scuttled and lay keeled over at grotesque angles—like the derelict vessel he and George had blown up. The Royal Navy's huge old depot ship, *HMS Tamar*, had proved most reluctant to sink, even when a British motor torpedo boat had fired at it to keep it out of Jap hands. But finally, after forty-four years as home of the Far Eastern Fleet, it too had succumbed and had settled slowly down into the mud.

Will gazed across the water towards Kowloon. Thousands of Japanese soldiers were camped there, ready to try and cross over. Would the colony's forces hold out against them? Their only real hope lay in relief coming from China. But time was running out. Worry pinched at the back of Will's throat. What would happen to Connie if Hong Kong Island was taken? Japanese soldiers did terrible things to women; they'd beaten, tortured and raped thousands after they'd occupied Nanking in 1937. Will groaned to himself—he would do his utmost to protect her. He'd die for her if he had to. Though even that wouldn't guarantee her safety. How he wished she'd left for Macau with her sisters...

Warmth spread through him as he recalled making love to her after everyone else had gone to bed last night. She'd said she'd checked with Jean that she could carry on going to his room, and Jean had expressed surprise that she'd even asked. 'You must seize the moment,' Jean had said. 'We all must.'

Connie had lain in his arms afterwards and he'd described every detail of sabotaging the derelict ship, reliving the exhilaration with her. She'd told him how proud she was of him but also that she was concerned. 'Thank God you made it back safe and sound.' Her voice had trembled. 'I hope you never have to do anything so dangerous again.'

He couldn't make that promise, of course, but he'd hugged her tightly and had suggested she would be safer if she left Hong Kong. She'd kissed him, told him in no uncertain terms that she was staying, and then they'd made love again. Later, he'd taken her back to the hotel in Reggie's car, the road almost unpassable for the craters. It had been like driving in an obstacle race. 'Take care, my darling,' he'd said as he'd dropped her off.

'You too, Will. Jean has invited me for supper again...she's so kind. I promised I'd sit with her while you're all out on patrol.'

Will heaved a sigh, not relishing the chore he would carry out tonight. Earlier, he'd gone with Reggie and George to the Central Police Headquarters in Hollywood Road—a four-storey block opposite the barracks adjacent to Victoria Prison, which had been heavily hammered by the shelling. The ground floor and basement offices had been reduced to rubble, so preparations were being made for transfer of personnel to the Gloucester. The fifth columnist prisoners were to be "made an example of" and the job of making that "example" had fallen to Will, Reggie, and George.

Will didn't have much appetite and said little during supper. He caught Connie glancing at him, a worried expression on her face. She saw him off at the appointed time. 'Stay safe, my darling,' she said, kissing him on the lips.

'I'll be back soon.' He injected a fake cheerful note into his voice.

Police HQ was in complete darkness when Will, Reggie and George arrived. They went through to the bar where Mike Middleton was waiting for them. Lit by flickering candles, the room's atmosphere matched the gloom of the task they were about to perform. They sat in silence, scarcely touching their beers. At last, 10 o'clock came and Mike led them across the road to the prison.

Seven men were dragged out onto the pavement by three Punjabi guards. Will had expected to feel some sympathy for the prisoners, but instead anger rose like a red tide washing over him. The fifth columnists' actions had contributed to the fall of Kowloon. They'd leaked information about the location of the Shing Mun pill boxes to the Japs. Captain Jones and his company had died as a result. The bloody traitors deserved what was coming to them.

Mike signed off the prisoners, and George took charge. The march from Hollywood Road to Pedder Building lasted about fifteen minutes. It was so dark it was like walking through the halls of Hell itself. The guards' boots made a rasping sound, interspersed by an occasional whimper from one of the prisoners.

An alley separated Pedder Building from the structure next to it. Colonel Yiu met them at the entrance, his pistol drawn.

Not a word was spoken. They lined up the traitors, turning them to face the wall.

# THE FLAME TREE

Without warning, the tallest prisoner whirled around and set off running down the alleyway. A guard gave chase, his boots pounding the pavement.

Will went to follow them, gun at the ready. But the guard had already caught the prisoner and was marching him back to the wall.

'Step up to your marks,' the Colonel barked.

Will and the others did as commanded.

'Take aim!'

They raised their guns.

'Fire!'

With a sharp intake of breath, Will squeezed his trigger. *Bang!* The sound echoed like the crack of a whip. He felt the rush of adrenaline and the recoil of his weapon—it was over so fast he'd barely registered what he'd done.

He gazed down at the bodies of the collaborators, crumpled on the ground. The metallic smell of blood hit his nostrils and nausea swelled his gullet.

'We need to placard them, men,' Colonel Yiu commanded. 'As a warning to all spies that they will be dealt with in a similar way.'

He handed out boards with the characters □□ "Traitor" in thick black ink.

They looped the placards around the necks of the dead men, tying the cords before leaving them in full public view.

After Colonel Yiu had dismissed them, the guards returned to their barracks and Will, George and Reggie set off back up to May Road. It was a steep climb and they hardly spoke, each of them lost in thought.

Will tried to focus on seeing Connie but he couldn't get the image of those blood-soaked bodies out of his head. What a change there'd been in his life. Not long ago, he'd embarked on a future as a civil servant. The idea of killing anyone had been as remote from his mind as travelling to the moon. But war had come and turned everyone's life upside down. His old school and university chums were in the thick of it in Europe. Had any of them been ordered to take part in a firing squad? It had been a dirty kind of killing and had left a sour taste in Will's mouth.

'You're very quiet, my darling,' Connie said later, lying next to him in his single bed.

He stroked his finger down her cheek. 'Just tired, sweetheart.'

A sigh escaped her. She wrapped her arms around his waist and buried her face in his neck. 'You don't need to say anything. I can tell when something's upset you…'

'It was horrible. I'd prefer not to talk about it.'

She brushed a kiss to his lips. 'Would you like a massage? It might soothe you…' Without waiting for an answer, she began to knead his shoulders. 'Turn over and try to relax.'

He gave himself up to her ministrations. She stroked him deeper and deeper, massaging the tension from his muscles, trailing her hands down his body, squeezing and letting go again, and again, and again. He gave a moan of pleasure. 'That feels wonderful…'

'Good.'

He rocked into her hands, need spiralling through him. She kissed his face, his jaw, his lips.

'You're so beautiful, Connie. I love you so much.'

'I love you too, Will. Lie back…'

She sheathed him, then straddled him, rolling her lovely hips to take him deeper. Her long dark brown hair cascaded between them, and their eyes locked as their passion peaked.

# THE FLAME TREE

After, they laid in each other's arms. 'I wish you didn't have to go back to the Gloucester,' he said. 'I'd love you to spend the night with me.'

'Maybe this once?' She caught her lip between her teeth. 'As long as I get down to Central before the shelling starts, I think it will be fine.'

They snuggled together in the single bed, sharing their warmth until sleep claimed them.

Dread shook him awake in the early hours. Tramping boots. Colonel Yiu brandishing a sword. Blood everywhere. Will cried out.

'Hush, dearest.' Connie smoothed the hair from his sweat-beaded brow. 'You had a bad dream. Be calm, my darling. I'm here…'

He closed his eyes and drifted off again.

*Boom!*

Connie nudged him fully awake.

*Boom!*

The flat shook.

*Boom!*

Will sat bolt upright. 'We've overslept. The shelling has started. Quick, darling. We must go down to the basement.'

*Boom!*

They leapt out of bed and threw on their clothes.

*Boom!*

'Connie! Will!' Reggie's voice came from the corridor. 'Get a move on!'

Through the open veranda doors, they spotted four Japanese planes flying low.

Bombs whammed and thumped and the entire building quaked.

They rushed down four flights of stairs to shelter below ground. Every time a shell landed, the concrete floor beneath them shuddered. Their ears ached from the rumble of explosions, the crash of falling masonry and the shattering of glass.

'This is the worst attack yet,' George muttered. 'It's bloody relentless.'

The shelling went on all day. Will kept his arm around Connie. She burrowed into his chest, cringing each time an explosive hit Gunter Mansions. Jean had brought a thermos of coffee which she passed around. The other residents of the flats shared bottles of water. Terror made everyone tremble.

At last, it was over. The enemy had halted its attacks for the night as usual. Will and the others crept up the stairs.

Connie grabbed hold of Will's arm. The side of the block had been opened to the world.

'My home is destroyed,' Jean sobbed. 'Where do we go now?'

'You can come to my room at the Gloucester, maybe?' Connie suggested. 'It's small but there are two beds.'

George smiled with evident relief. 'Jean can share with you, Connie. Thanks for offering. It will be a bit cramped for us all. We men can join Mike Middleton in the police mess.' He glanced around. 'Where's Reggie got to?'

'There he is,' Connie said, pointing.

'I just went to check on my car.' Reggie swiped a hand through his ginger hair. 'It scored a direct hit, I'm afraid.'

'Bugger,' Will swore. 'I'm sorry about that.'

'Me too.' Reggie exhaled a loud breath. 'But at least we're all ok...'

'We've had a miraculous escape,' George grunted. 'I suggest we salvage what we can from the flat then head down to Central.'

There wasn't much to be salvaged, but they managed to fill their kit bags with some clothes. Will breathed a sigh of relief that the jade flame tree Connie had given him last Christmas was still intact. He wrapped it in a jumper and stashed it in his sack.

His arm around Connie, he headed with everyone down Old Peak Road. Skirting the burning shrapnel, they crept past many wrecked apartment blocks. Ahead, buildings were spewing flames and smoke billowed high while fire engines pumped water into them, their hoses snaking across the pavement.

They came across two dead bodies, sprawled on the street. 'This is all so terrible,' Connie wailed.

'Don't look, my darling,' Will said. 'We can't do anything for them now. Better keep going. There are live people needing us.'

Eventually, they arrived at Pedder Street. It was jammed with milling locals, carrying tables and chairs and small stoves and bundles of clothing. 'Looks like we're not the only ones bombed out of our home,' George observed.

Inside the Gloucester, mayhem reigned. But Connie managed to lead them up to her room, where they dumped their belongings. 'I'll just call the Admiral.' She picked up the phone, then shook her head. 'The line is dead.'

A rap sounded. 'Connie,' a voice came through the door. 'Are you there? Uncle Wei is worried about you. We all are...'

Will opened said door to reveal the Admiral's ADC, Bob. Will saluted. 'Connie is safe.' He didn't add the words, *for now*.

'Why don't you all come and have some supper with us.' Bob issued the invitation as if nothing out-of-the ordinary had happened. But that's what people did when everything around them had gone to pot, Will thought. Life carried on. People tried to make the best of things.

'Thank you,' he said. 'We haven't had anything to eat all day. Much appreciated.'

George and Reggie echoed Will's thanks, but Jean and Connie stayed silent.

Will glanced at his darling girl. Her face was so pale and she seemed so sad. How he wanted to take her in his arms and comfort her. But he couldn't. Now that Bob had appeared they needed to keep up the pretence of not being together.

*Damn the war.*

## CHAPTER TWENTY-TWO

Shelling from across the harbour reverberated constantly, but Connie felt secure in Pedder Building. Constructed of granite and hidden from view by the Hong Kong and Gloucester hotels, it was almost as safe as an air raid shelter. Earlier there'd been a pause in the bombing while the Japanese had sent over their second peace mission. Connie had translated the subsequent British announcement. *"The Governor received today a letter from the Japanese military and naval authorities repeating the suggestion that he should enter into negotiations for surrender. The Governor informed the Japanese authorities in reply that he was not prepared to receive any further communications on the subject."* Afterwards, it didn't take long for the enemy to restart the attack, and the air around Connie throbbed relentlessly while their shells rained down.

She looked up as the Admiral brushed past her desk. 'The cloak and dagger boys are about to arrive for a meeting, Connie. I'd like you to take the minutes,' he said.

She smiled to herself; it was how he always referred to Will, George and Reggie. Except, she found it hard to reconcile the tag "cloak and dagger" with Will. On her way to work the day after Gunter Mansions had been bombed, she'd come across a grisly sight. A crowd of people had gathered in the adjacent alleyway. She'd pushed her way between them, recoiling in shock when she saw blood-covered bodies lying on the ground. On reading the word "Traitor" inked on placards around their necks, it occurred to her that Will might have been involved in their deaths—given that he was working with the Admiral. If he had, he'd clearly been affected, judging by his subsequent silence. Dear Will, how she loved him. It cut her to the core that he could have been ordered to do something so alien to his caring nature.

But perhaps Will hadn't been there. It could have been the Admiral and Colonel Yiu who'd killed those fifth columnists. Bob had once told her about the time they'd surprised around a hundred traitors holding a secret gathering in a cinema. Twenty men under Uncle Wei's command had burst in with hand grenades and Tommy guns. She remembered the Admiral returning to the office looking exhausted and saying, 'We got them all.'

She couldn't help but be impressed by her boss's energy and bravery. He'd organised a force of two thousand vigilantes, whom he paid two dollars a day each to patrol the streets and seize troublemakers. Some wore identifying armbands. Others struck gongs. Led by triads from Shanghai and northern China, they'd adopted the innocuous sounding name, "Loyal and Righteous Charitable Association". Connie pulled in a deep breath; she was proud of the Admiral for keeping order among the local population. He'd saved the day and the island could await the next Japanese onslaught with something approaching a spirit of calm solidarity.

Her thoughts turned to Will again and how difficult it was to be alone with him these days. Their lovemaking seemed a beautiful dream to her now, a poignant respite from the harsh realities of the war. No one knew what would happen next. All

# THE FLAME TREE

Connie knew was that things would probably get a lot worse, and she trembled at the prospect.

A knock at the door interrupted her reverie. Cheng Jin, Uncle Wei's bodyguard, went to open it. He ushered Will, Reggie and George into the room. Connie greeted them and she shared a brief smile with Will before Cheng Jin took him and the others through to the Admiral. She organised the office boy to make tea, then retrieved her notebook and pen.

Will met her gaze firmly, his eyes burning with love as she took her usual seat opposite Bob's next to Uncle Wei's desk. She felt the heat of a blush and looked down at her notepad.

'So, what can we do for you Mr Robinson?' the Admiral asked George after pleasantries had been exchanged.

'Have you managed to establish contact with those guerrillas fighting the Japs near Sha Tau Kok? We've weapons for them to use against the enemy,' George said.

The Admiral smiled. 'I sent a man with a message, but no reply has come back yet.'

'Well, I've been given the go-ahead to arrange for the transport of the guns and ammo to the naval dockyard where our motor torpedo vessels are based in Aberdeen—and from there we'll run the ordnance to the insurgents across Mirs Bay.'

'Excellent.' The Admiral beamed another broad smile. 'Colonel Yiu is occupied at the moment, which is why he isn't here, but I'll get him to send a more reliable man with this latest news.'

Talk then turned to the British motor torpedo boats, or MTBs as George called them. 'I've heard they make a noise like thunder and look like sleek salmon,' Uncle Wei observed.

'But beware the sting in the tail.' George smirked. 'It's the warning on the flotilla's flying fish crest.'

'Why the tail?' Bob asked.

'When firing, the MTB must be accelerating, and the torpedoes come out backwards from the stern of the boat.'

'Ah, I see.' Bob nodded. 'Are the MTBs going to be any use when the Japs try to cross over the harbour?'

'Absolutely. I'm sure they'll be onto them straight away. They might not be the most modern or formidable of craft. But they're as fast as speedboats. With their 1500 horsepower engines and multiple Lewis guns mounted fore and aft they'll put up a bloody good fight.' George chuckled. 'We call them the spitfires of the sea.'

Connie's stomach twisted with dread. Events were moving at such a fast pace and she was so worried about Will she wanted to be sick.

After work, Connie made her way across Pedder Street to the Gloucester. She stepped into the lobby and her eyes widened. Her brother-in-law, Howard, was standing by the desk. 'Ah, there you are, my dear,' he said. 'I need to talk to you.'

She gave him a hug. 'Better come up to my room.' She glanced at the people milling around them. 'It'll be quieter.' Looping her arm though his, she led him up the carpeted staircase to her fourth-floor accommodation. 'My roommate works with the refugees, but she'll be back soon.'

'I can't stay long.' Howard accepted the glass of water she poured for him. 'Japs have stepped up their firing on our positions. They tried to come over the other night, but we foiled them with our guns and searchlights.' His shoulders drooped. 'They retaliated by shelling us mercilessly, added to some heavy air raids. I'm sorry to have to say that my battery has been evacuated.' He met her eye. 'The enemy will make another attempt to cross any day now, Connie. I've come to try and persuade you to leave.'

'Leave?' Her voice rose. 'When? How?'

'Jonathan sent a message. He has contacts among the fishermen in Aberdeen. One of them is prepared to sail to Macau with you on his junk.'

Connie shook her head. 'I can't leave the Admiral. It would be like abandoning my post. You wouldn't abandon your post, would you, Howard?'

'Put like that, I see your point.' He sighed. 'It was worth a try but, somehow, I didn't think you'd agree...'

'Do you have any news of Leo, Eddy and Walter?' She changed the subject.

'They're commanding Volunteer batteries at strategic points where the Japs might try and land.'

Fear for her brothers-in-law made Connie quake. 'I hate this war.'

'We all do.' Howard straightened his shoulders. 'But we'll fight the Japs off, you'll see. In any case, Matthew will be here any day now with the Chinese army. Those piratical midgets won't stand a chance against the Kuomintang forces.'

'Oh, Howard. I hope and pray they get here soon. And it would be wonderful to see my brother, Matthew, if he's with them.' She would welcome them all with open arms. 'Do you know how Father and my sisters are?'

'They're well. Things aren't as bad in Macau, from what I hear.' Howard glanced at her. 'I wish you'd reconsider and go join them.'

'Please, dear. Don't ask me again. It pains me to have to refuse.'

'Fair enough.' He checked his watch. 'I'd best be off. I still need to go and see my quartermaster about supplies.'

'I'll take you down to the lobby,' she said.

After she'd waved him off, she was just about to go back upstairs when Jean and George appeared.

'We're heading over to the Gripps for supper,' Jean said. 'Will and Reggie are already there. Would you like to join us?'

Connie's heart leapt. 'I'd love to.'

The rooftop restaurant at The Gripps, formerly a place where people treated themselves to a night out, had now been converted into a set price canteen. Gone were the days of sitting sipping gin gimlets and enjoying unparalleled views of the harbour, Connie reflected as Will led her away from their table after they'd eaten. The last vestiges of the old Hong Kong Hotel had disappeared with the arrival of notices informing clientele that chits could no longer be authorised and they would only accept cash. Whereas previously one ordered one's meal, sat over it at leisure, signed a bill and sauntered off; now cash was paid before covers were even laid. Lingering more than fifteen minutes after dessert was looked upon with stern disapproval.

Connie strolled over to the edge of the terrace with Will and the others, where they found some rattan chairs. The pitch-black night sky had filled with clouds of thick dark smoke, sent up by the oil tanks at North Point—ablaze after constant shelling.

Will offered everyone a Player's, then pulled out his lighter.

'Tell us about your visit to Aberdeen,' Jean said, leaning forward for him to light her cigarette.

'We met the man in charge, Lieutenant Commander Grainger.'

'Oh, what's he like?' Connie cupped her hand around Will's while he lit *her* cigarette.

'A bit of a crusty Great War veteran.' Will chuckled. 'But he came across as fair-minded.'

'How many MTBs are there?' Jean exhaled a puff of smoke.

'Eight,' Will said. 'Each with a lieutenant and a sub-lieutenant, and a crew of ten Royal Navy ratings.'

Reggie grinned. 'We were shown over the *French*. A snappy little cruiser on the lines of an MTB. Fast and quiet. Perfect for gun running. All that remains now is for the Admiral to contact the guerrillas and we'll be off.'

George pulled a flask of brandy from his pocket, took a sip and passed it around.

'I've a hunch we might be needed closer to home.' He shook his head dolefully. 'There's a high tide. It's as black as the Devil's waistcoat. The perfect night for a landing by the Japs...'

Connie met Will's eye, saw the resignation there, and her heart thumped loudly in her chest.

'Don't worry, my darling.' He reached for her hand in the darkness. 'I'll do all I can to protect you.'

'I know, dearest Will,' she whispered. 'And the Chinese army is on its way.' She tried to sound cheerful. 'All is not lost.'

# Chapter Twenty-Three

Will woke the next morning to the sound of Mike Middleton yelling, 'They landed last night. Three hundred of them, at North Point!'

*"They"—who are "they"?* Will rubbed his sleep-encrusted eyes. He'd partaken of rather too much brandy and had slept deeply, the alcohol numbing the ache of his fear for Connie's wellbeing. *Japs, that's who. Bloody, hell, it's started.* Will answered his own question as he shook himself fully awake.

All around him, men were stirring. The police mess overflowed with a dozen or more chaps hunkered down on camp beds filling every available space. Will got to the front of the queue for the bathroom, used the facilities, then changed into his uniform. He was just about to head to the dining room for some breakfast when Reggie gave a shout from where he was standing by the window. 'Look!'

Will strode up to him and peered through the grimy glass. 'Crikey!'

In the distance, Japanese barges, crawling with troops and armed with heavy machine guns, were coming across the oil-slicked harbour.

Will stood, transfixed, as the scene unfolded. A pair of British motor torpedo boats, their bows lifting proudly, suddenly ap-

## THE FLAME TREE

peared from behind Green Island. *Bang-bang-bang-bang-bang* went their Lewis guns.

Will's roommates jostled for a view, but he kept his feet planted firmly next to Reggie's. 'Blimey,' someone called out.

Japs had retaliated. Heavy rifle and machine gun fire exploded from their vessels and from positions on both sides of the harbour. A plane dived down, spraying bullets and artillery. *Ra-ta-ta-ta-ta!*

The brave little MTBs kept on going. In Kowloon Bay one of them sank two Japanese boats. *Oh, bugger!* It appeared to have been hit by cannon as its speed reduced. The MTB turned and attacked landing craft returning from Hong Kong island. Another shell struck and the MTB slowed to a limp. It stalled and the second MTB started towing it back in the direction of Green Island.

Will's heart swelled with pride when two more MTBs took their places. But the Japanese gunners met the new arrivals with a furious barrage from howitzers and mortars. One of the British boats began to weave a zig zag course as it headed out towards the western approach to the harbour. *Crikey!* The fourth MTB had taken a direct hit. With an almighty boom, it exploded in a cloud of black smoke.

Will stepped back from the window, met Reggie's eye, discerned the alarm in his friend's expression. 'Not a good start to the day, then,' he quipped.

'Indeed.' Reggie ran a hand through his hair. 'I suppose we'd better get a move on. Nothing else to be done, is there?'

Will nodded gloomily. 'Where's George?'

'Gone to the Battle Box.'

'Ah.' Will shouldered his Tommy gun. 'Fancy some breakfast before we go?'

'I've lost my appetite but could murder a cup of tea.'

'Likewise.'

They left the mess and stepped into the corridor. It had become home to masses of people who'd taken refuge from the shelling. The staircase was piled with sandbags, and all the glass in the dining room's windows had been blown out days ago.

After requesting a pot of lapsang souchong and some toast, they found an empty table and pulled out chairs.

'There's George,' Reggie said, indicating their burly commander striding towards them.

'Japs have established bridge heads in the neighbourhood of Taikoo. It's a bloody shambles.' He took a seat. 'We should have mined the area when we could…'

Will remembered the proposal had been put to them far too late. They'd have risked being shelled to smithereens. 'Did you hear about what just happened in the harbour?' he asked.

'Got the news as I was leaving HQ. Those chaps deserve medals when all this is over.' After Will and Reggie had agreed with him, George went on. 'You'll never believe what our next task is.' He poured himself a cup of tea, fixed them with a steely stare. 'Major General Maltby has ordered me to smuggle Admiral Chang Wei and his team out of Hong Kong and into China. But only if the worse comes to the worst and the island falls to the Japs.'

Will smiled broadly. 'Sounds like an excellent plan.'

'I agree.' Reggie gave a thumbs up. 'But why?'

'They'd be tortured if captured, to put it harshly.' George sipped his tea. 'Better they give information about secret agents, hidden arms dumps and mines to our allies than to the enemy. Under prolonged pain, most people have their breaking point.' He tapped his spoon against his cup. 'The Admiral would be a big catch. He's galvanised the resistance and emasculated the fifth column. Chiang Kai Shek would lose trust in us if we let the Nips capture his top man in Hong Kong.'

# THE FLAME TREE

Will tasted bitter bile. Connie had taken the minutes at all the Admiral's meetings. She would be a prime target for torture too. 'Have you any ideas about how we can carry out the task?' he asked.

'It won't be easy to get someone as conspicuous as one-legged Wei through Jap lines. I'm sure he and his team are being closely watched by fifth columnists.'

Will looked George in the eye. 'How about we use what's left of the motor torpedo boats? They'd probably leap at the chance to escape.'

'When we were in Aberdeen yesterday, I got wind of the flotilla's own plans to make a break for it if and when all was lost,' Reggie added.

'I did too.' George smiled. 'Commander Grainger has been summoned to meet Maltby in the Battle Box tomorrow, where the order will be given to him.' George smirked. 'We might even be able to combine the mission with contacting the guerrillas beyond Sha Tau Kok. If we can arm the reds, they'll be highly effective against the Japanese.'

Next morning, Will went with Reggie to help Mike Middleton on an anti-looting expedition at the French Store in Queen's Road. Mike shot an escaping looter, wounding him in the leg, and arrested a second man, who gave himself up. Apart from that, the Western District seemed quiet; Des Voeux Road and Queen's Road were practically deserted and, after patrolling for a couple of hours, Will and his comrades returned to the Gloucester.

George was waiting for them in the police mess. 'Everything's been arranged,' he said. 'We move to Aberdeen tomorrow morning.'

'Already?' Will's heart hammered.

'McBride and his assistant, Fred Martin, have been tasked with getting the Admiral and his party over to Aberdeen if and when the colony capitulates. In the meantime, we'll base ourselves on the boats. Grainger will prepare his men to leave as soon as he receives the word *"Go"*.'

'Sounds a bit vague to me,' Will said, worried for Connie.

'Your girl will be protected by the Admiral.' George sighed. 'It's Jean I'm concerned about.'

'Can't she come too?' Reggie asked.

'Not allowed, I'm afraid. I'll need to arrange for her to be taken to a safe house.'

'Sorry about that.' Will met George's eye.

'Can't be helped.' George shrugged, clearly putting a brave face on things. 'Let's enjoy our last evening with Jean and Connie. We must make the most of it...'

Reggie declined to join them, saying he'd already arranged to eat with Mike and his men. Will and George managed a quick wash before they went to Jean and Connie's room. There was no privacy to be had there, however. Two European women who'd been working as administrators for Major General Maltby, had been billeted with them.

'How about we try the Parisian Grill for dinner?' Jean suggested as they made their way downstairs. 'It's still open, I believe.'

'Would you like that, Connie?' Will whispered.

'I'd prefer to be alone with you, but that's not possible, is it?'

He shook his head. 'There's nowhere for us to go.'

During the meal, George told Jean and Connie not to worry if they heard nothing from him and Will over the next couple of days. They were being sent on a secret mission, of which they could reveal nothing—for Jean and Connie's safety.

# THE FLAME TREE

After they'd eaten, Will hit upon the idea of taking Connie for a stroll up to the Botanical Gardens to the pavilion under the flame tree but then dismissed the notion as being too dangerous. There was nothing for it but to return to the Gloucester.

George and Jean went ahead of them up the staircase, but Will dawdled with Connie. On finding the second floor landing deserted, he seized his chance.

He enveloped her in his arms, his nose pressed into her hair as he breathed in her sweet jasmine scent. With a groan, he tilted her chin up and brought his mouth down on hers.

Her breath caught, and she arched up to kiss him deeper.

'God, Connie. Ngo Oi Nei.' *I love you.*

'I love you too, Will. I've missed being with you so much.' She looped her arms around his neck and pulled herself against him.

Their heads switched sides, tongues dancing, lips sliding. The heat between them crackled like static electricity.

They clung to each other, breathless.

Connie's hands clutched at his hair, tugging.

He held her closer, then walked her backwards, kissing her until her back pressed against the wall.

Her teeth nipped at his mouth and their kisses became frantic.

He ran his hands down her sides. 'Oh, God, Connie. Please, stay safe. I can't tell you about my mission. Just stick close to the Admiral. Promise me, my darling?'

'I promise, dearest Will. Please stay safe too.' Her voice choked with tears.

He kissed her again, his heart breaking. 'Don't cry, sweetheart. Be brave and I'll see you again soon.'

She was sobbing openly now. 'I can't bear it.'

'You're strong, Connie. Your strength will get you through this. You are the most beautiful, courageous girl in the world.'

He wrapped his arms around her, rocking her until her sobs ceased.

She touched her hand to the side of his face, gazed into his eyes. 'You're everything to me, Will. I wouldn't be able to live without you.'

'You won't have to,' he said. 'We'll be together again before you know it.'

She nodded, catching her lip with her teeth. 'I hope so.'

'I know so,' he said. 'Can't say more than that.' He took her hand. 'I'd better get you back to your room before they send out a search party...'

Keeping positive was all he could do. For to do otherwise would lead to despair, he thought as he led Connie up the stairs.

# Chapter Twenty-Four

The Admiral glanced up as Connie placed his morning tea on the teak desk. 'Take a seat, Constance,' he said. 'There's something I'd like to tell you.'

'Should I fetch my notepad and pen, Uncle?'

'No need. Just sit and listen.'

She did as he'd requested.

'Remember I was at the Battle Box earlier?'

She nodded, wondering where this was going.

'Keep this under your hat. The "cloak and dagger boys" have been ordered to smuggle us out of Hong Kong if the colony is defeated.'

Connie gasped. *So that's what Will's mission was*. 'How do they propose to do that?'

'Using one of the British motor torpedo boats. Mr Robinson and his men have gone to Aberdeen to wait for us.'

'But where will they take you?' Connie sat back in her chair.

'When I said "us" I meant you too, dear. They will land us somewhere on the mainland, but not too far away given the limited fuel range of the MTBs.'

A tentative smile brushed Connie's lips. She would escape to China with Will. How wonderful! 'When do we leave?'

'Ah, I hope we won't have to leave.' Uncle Wei shook his head. 'I gave the British a report about the progress of the army being led by the commander of the Nationalist 7th War Zone. You know that area includes Guangdong Province adjacent to Hong Kong, right?'

'Yes, Uncle.'

'Well, I received information that our advance guard was on the frontier and poised to strike. But a telegram has arrived, clarifying that the main Chinese attack can't start for another ten days. Apparently, they need to move more troops up to the border. Fortress HQ has put out a signal to all units.' The Admiral handed her a piece of paper. 'Can you please translate this for me?'

'There are indications that Chinese troops are advancing towards the frontier to our aid,' she read the words in Cantonese. 'All forces must therefore hold their positions at all costs and look forward to only a few more days of strain.' A sigh escaped her lips. 'I hope Hong Kong will be able to resist until then.'

'I hope so too. I expressed my indignation to the government at accounts of how many of our people have been killed, raped or robbed by the Japanese troops, not to mention being kidnapped to be used as porters.' He slammed his hand on the desk. 'I said I could no longer tolerate my people's suffering. But when I proposed that my vigilantes should join the fighting on the front line and asked the British to provide us with guns and grenades, they seemed reluctant to do so. As soon as I brought up the subject, all of them expressed confidence in their ability to defend Hong Kong. They even quoted a message from Churchill... "Every day your resistance brings nearer our certain victory".'

Connie remembered that Uncle's vigilantes had now grown to a force of fifteen thousand. They would make a big difference if the British armed them, of that she was sure. 'I can't

# THE FLAME TREE

stop thinking about my brothers-in-law,' she said. 'I'm terribly anxious about them.'

'With reason. The British Prime Minister seems to be insisting that lives be sacrificed in Hong Kong to keep the enemy tied down and thus delay its advance elsewhere. But resistance in other parts of Asia is crumbling. Thailand succumbed to Japanese occupation within the first few days; in Malaya, Penang has been evacuated; in the Philippines, a large Japanese army has landed and is advancing on Manila.'

'It's all so tragic...'

The Admiral handed her a wad of papers. 'Can you file these, please, Constance?'

'Of course.'

She went to her office and, while she was working, she let her thoughts drift.

Would Hong Kong be able to hold out until the Chinese arrived? How were Howard, Leo, Eddie, and Walter coping? The battle ever since the Japanese had crossed over to the island had reminded her of the games of chess she used to play with Father. The British forces had their fixed positions, batteries and arms of varying fire power, the seventy-two pill boxes fortified with machine guns and rifles. Except some of these units had a limited range to counter the enemy's move. From what the Admiral had told her, the Japanese pawns of battle—the infantry men, armed with various weapons and grenades, were lightly kitted and wore silent rubber footwear, which gave them speed and surprise of attack.

Chess and war games were played according to rules and conventions, Connie mused. Pieces were taken and the opponent's field of action was relentlessly reduced to prevent counterattack, until no further lines of retreat were possible. But real-life battles and troops, both players and pieces in the game of death, could only follow the rules so far. Orders sometimes didn't get through or were disastrously garbled. The Admiral had divulged that a confused British officer, ordered to move his position and *bring* his guns out of action, mishearing the message, *put* his 4.5 out of action by spiking them with charges of high explosives. Consequently, the brigadier who'd withdrawn with his forces to Stanley had been deprived of vital support for the counterattack.

Connie's chest ached as she thought about those tired, dispirited men—without food, soaked to the skin, who'd retreated or surrendered when perhaps they should have stood firm. They'd been stranded in remote pockets of defence, the soldiers ignorant or oblivious of the sway of the change of the battle lines. They'd fought on to heroic, but futile deaths as they darted for shelter from the hail of enemy fire. The blood of hundreds of warriors—Canadians, Scots, English, local volunteers and even Japanese—had soaked into the earth of the hills and valleys leading to the southern shore of the island. She was only thankful Will had gone to Aberdeen, which was still some distance from the battle. *How she worried about him...* With a heavy heart, she picked up another of the Admiral's papers and placed it in the appropriate file.

On Christmas Eve, George came to visit Jean. He described the situation en route to the city centre as desperate. There were fires burning everywhere. Houses had collapsed and telegraph poles leant at crazy angles. Streets were pitted with shell holes, which were gradually filling with water from broken mains and sewers, drowning any of the wounded who might have been sheltering in them. Dead bodies lay on the roadsides. Small groups of British combatants had started occupying empty houses or hiding in doorways, and those buildings had turned into isolated strongpoints as they tried to hold back advancing enemy infantry. Artillery and small arms fire came from every direction. It was apparent the defenders wouldn't be able to hold out for much longer.

As Connie left for the office, Jean let slip that George was arranging for her to go to a safe house and she would be gone by the time Connie got back.

Connie hugged her friend tightly. 'Have as good a Christmas as you can, Jean. I'll see you in China...'

'God willing,' Jean said, kissing her on the cheek. 'Take care, honey.'

'You too.' Connie kissed her in return.

She made her way out of the Gloucester. By now, Central was the only no-man's land left. The island's reservoirs were all in possession of the invaders. The city's taps had run dry and the final reckoning was drawing ever closer. But Churchill had sent a message to the Governor which Connie had translated for the Admiral yesterday. "The eyes of the world are upon you. We expect you to resist to the end. The honour of the Empire is in your hands..." And so, Hong Kong was fighting on.

'The Royal Rifles have been withdrawn to the defensive lines at Stanley,' Bob informed Connie as she arrived in the office. 'Japs are advancing through Wanchai towards the dockyard but the British are holding firm. It's the most disheartening Christmas Eve of my life.'

Connie glanced at him, remembering that he was a Christian. 'It's terrible,' she lamented.

'Indeed.'

She startled as the intercom on her desk buzzed. 'We're summoned by Uncle.'

'We'd better go through,' Bob said.

The Admiral was sitting behind his desk, flanked by the Colonel and his bodyguard.

He told them all to sit and they did as he'd commanded. 'I'm sorry to have to say that Hong Kong is on the brink of capitulation.' His gaze was firm. 'Help will arrive too late. But I, myself, refuse to surrender. I will take the risk of trying to break through enemy lines. I'd rather die than be captured alive by the Japanese.'

'Me too,' Bob said, and they all agreed with him.

'It won't be easy.' Colonel Yiu smirked. 'We're well known to thousands of fifth columnists and Uncle Wei is easily identifiable by his physical disability.'

'For this reason, I intend to take up the British authorities' offer to use their motor torpedo boats, if there are any remaining when the colony falls. I want you, my immediate staff, to go with me.'

'Yes, sir,' they all concurred.

'We must wait in the city centre,' the Admiral continued. 'We'll be alerted one hour prior to the Governor's actual surrender and told where and when there will be the best chance of contacting the MTBs.'

'Why can't this be arranged now?' Bob asked.

'Impossible to fix a definite location.' The Admiral shook his head. 'The boats might be forced by bombing and shelling to dodge constantly from one hiding place to another. To make matters even more uncertain, orders for the MTB flotilla to leave must be given before the colony capitulates, since according to military procedure, once the command is received for an unconditional surrender, all armed forces' property immediately belongs to the victor.'

'We'll need to move quickly, then,' Colonel Yiu muttered.

'How will we get to the boats?' Connie risked asking.

'I told my intelligence officer friend, Douglas McBride, that he was welcome to join us,' Uncle Wei said. 'He mentioned he'd already been planning his own escape with his assistant, Fred

Martin, and asked if Martin could come too. I said yes but said he'd have to help us get to Aberdeen, to make the rendezvous. Martin has offered to drive us in his new Buick Special Station Wagon. He promised to make sure that the car was ready, filled with petrol and parked around the back of the Gloucester when the time comes. We'll meet them there. But McBride is concerned about the actual timing of the departure. He said they have no wish to make a break before the surrender and be called deserters.'

'I see,' Connie said, her heart quaking. She got to her feet. 'I'll go and organise some tea for us, shall I?'

'Thank you, Constance.' The Admiral gave a wan smile. 'That would be nice.'

She left his office, her stomach churning. She felt sick with worry for Will's safety. The Admiral's words that the MTBs might be forced by bombing and shelling to dodge continually from one hiding place to another had sent a shiver of fear through her. If Will died, her life would be without meaning. *She would want to die too.*

## CHAPTER TWENTY-FIVE

Will was waiting for George with Reggie by the bombed-out slipway in the Aberdeen naval dockyard during a lull in the shelling shortly before dusk. With a sorrowful heart, Will surveyed the scene around him. The mass of junks and sampans normally moored across the harbour, in front of the old fishermen's temple and the boatbuilding yards on the northern shore of Ap Lei Chau island had all but vanished. It was a miserable sight.

He accepted the cigarette Reggie offered him, bending to the proffered match. Taking a deep draw, he let his thoughts wander. It had been three days since he, George and Reggie had heaved their boxes of Bren light machine guns, grenades, explosives and various "toys" onto the MTBs. Three days during which the enemy had moved west with their light field guns. Three days of constant bombardment. There'd been little the MTBs could do other than try to avoid being hit while they waited for the order to go.

The men chafed at their lack of combat activity, but their only source of fuel was from a barge that had a defective pump—which meant the petrol needed to be transferred by bucket and therefore needed to be conserved. Since the dockyard had become untenable due to being constantly shelled, they couldn't load any new torpedoes, and they had no base in which to anchor. They hid from enemy planes behind small islands and in coves and bays, tucking themselves in close to the rocks under camouflage nets, and changing position several times a day. But when darkness fell and the Japs halted the war for the night, the MTBs moored alongside each other. The best time of the day, Will thought, taking another deep draw of his cigarette.

Despite missing Connie with every particle of his being, he'd enjoyed the camaraderie of the sailors and his spirits had been lifted by their high morale. Notwithstanding being under constant fire, and the loss of two boats and their comrades when they'd attacked the Japanese landing craft, they remained ever cheerful. Will found it a welcome change from the tension, gloom and confusion he'd come across on land. The flotilla's only protection against shells or bombs was the wit and courage of the men—and Lewis guns for any low-flying planes. Moored as they were, all they could do was duck and hope—yet the atmosphere was almost carefree, the relationship between officers and men relaxed and friendly. Will had been as delighted by the standard of cooking on board as by the level of camaraderie, and he'd been happy to make his acquaintance with those heavenly twins, Navy Rum and Navy Tobacco, whose praises, he told his shipmates, should be sung in verse and not in mere prose.

Everyone seemed to realise they were in a tough spot, yet there wasn't any sign of panic or disorder, and the crews simply ducked the shells or sat and smoked with an attitude of "oh well, what an effing life" that proved infectious. Will smiled to himself. Two days ago, the Coxswain, while climbing out of the conning tower with a rum jar, heard a shell coming, ducked, remembered the rum and reappeared, shielding the rum next his heart. Yesterday, when shrapnel exploded around him, instead of going flat, he bowed gracefully and wagged a shiny polished blue serge bottom at the enemy.

It was good to be with such optimistic people, with whom the war became a bit like a game played with good companions—and a shell burst something to occasion a joke. Naval hospitality was top-notch. In dealing with the Army, Will used to feel they had no objection to him being foisted upon them, but the Navy chaps somehow conveyed the impression that they would have objected to him *not* being with them.

When he, Reggie and George had arrived, they'd been split between three of the boats—Will on MTB10 with Commander Grainger, George on MTB 11 and Reggie on MTB 27—where they each shared the role of sub-lieutenant and bunked down in the wardrooms with the two officers on board. The presence of armed commandos in their jungle camouflage uniforms, who spoke Chinese like natives, had started a round of feverish speculation among the crews, so George had briefed the officers on who they were and why they were there. When news came through that the whole flotilla was coming on the expedition, Will's heart had soared. There was strength in numbers, which meant that Connie would be better protected.

George told the men what was afoot and gave advice on kit requirements. They were all sailors, many of whom would not have done much walking, but they seemed to be looking forward to the prospect of becoming guerrillas. Will had needed to be tactful when supervising the ratings in the packing of their kit—everyone had to be persuaded that a load of 50 lbs would weigh heavily even on a stalwart pair of shoulders after a few miles. But now the packing was done, Will found himself having to curb the enthusiasm of the men and make them see that, quite probably, they would not move off anytime soon. Playing the waiting game was just as difficult for him. He was on tenterhooks for Connie to arrive with the Admiral's party so they could make their bid for freedom. How he prayed she would make it out to Aberdeen safely.

The rumble of a car engine alerted Will to George's arrival. He stubbed out his cigarette and edged past the shell craters in the concrete as he walked up the slipway with Reggie.

George leapt out of the old, abandoned Ford he'd commandeered. 'Tomorrow, if Hong Kong surrenders, the Admiral and his party will be joining us,' he announced. 'All going according to plan, this will be our last night in Hong Kong.'

Will fell into step beside him as they made their way back down the jetty. 'How are Connie and Jean?'

'I've taken my wife somewhere safe. Mum's the word. Connie is fine. I expect she's looking forward to seeing you.'

Will looked George in the eye. 'Sorry Jean couldn't come with her.'

'As soon as we're settled in unoccupied China, one of my agents will smuggle her across the border and then convey her to me.'

Reggie matched his stride to theirs. 'You'll feel better for knowing that she's safe.'

Will patted his friend on the back. Reggie was still waiting to find out if Deborah and her father had made it to safety. The *Ulysses* had come under attack by Japanese bombers in the South China Sea as she'd headed for Manilla. From there, she'd gone on to Singapore but there'd been no further news. Reggie was keeping his chin up, though. He hardly ever let his stiff upper lip slip.

A fisherman sculled them in his sampan out to MTB10, where Grainger welcomed them on board. After George had reported on the situation in town, the commander said gruffly, 'We'll crack open some bottles of champagne as it's Christmas Eve. But only one glass each, men. There's a war on, unfortunately.'

The MTBs slipped their moorings at nightfall. Those hosting Will, George and Reggie were ordered to spread out to the west of Ap Lei Chau island. They left the harbour by the western route, threading through the masts of scuttled ships and attracting a burst of artillery fire from the ridges to the east. But it was preferable to taking the southern Aberdeen Channel, which was now open to machine gun fire from Japanese infantry infiltrating around Brick Hill. The remaining two MTBs went to take cover a little way farther up the west coast of Hong Kong Island in Telegraph Bay. Not a Christmas star was in sight, but bright flashes illuminated the scene and a steady roar came from the big guns at Stanley.

After a hearty chicken stew supper, Will went to take his turn on watch duty. A cool breeze lifted the hair from his forehead. After the noise of the day's shelling, utter peace and stillness reigned. The small island in the lee of which they'd dropped anchor boasted a small fishing village at its northern tip, just across the harbour from the Aberdeen waterfront. Otherwise uninhabited, it was made up almost entirely of three rugged hills which were etched against the inky blackness of the sky. Will took a cigarette from his pocket and lit it. Inhaling deeply, he thought about Connie. If Hong Kong surrendered tomorrow she would be on her way with the Admiral and his men. How would she feel about that? She'd be the only woman amidst them. It would be hard for her, but she was strong and, besides, she had him to protect her. Anticipation sparked through him. He couldn't wait.

On Christmas morning, Will woke to the sound of another bombardment. 'Japs are shelling the Hong Kong Volunteers' battery,' Commander Grainger grumbled, helping himself to a piece of toast at the breakfast table. 'Aberdeen is under heavy mortar attack. It'll be too dangerous for us to go in during daylight, even by the route we took yesterday, so we'll just have to sit tight. Oh, and Merry Christmas, by the way.'

'Merry Christmas,' Will said, thinking it was anything but. 'What about Admiral Chang Wei and his party? How will they find us?'

'Hopefully they'll rendezvous with the boats at Telegraph Bay. It's much quieter there, by all accounts.'

Will wiped nervous sweat from his brow. Telegraph Bay was sheltered by hills, both from the wind and the enemy's guns. But the MTBs were camouflaged and difficult to see from the road above. He hoped the Admiral would know where to look.

There was nothing to be done but wait. Will joined his shipmates for a cooked breakfast of bacon and eggs and, at midday, a traditional Christmas lunch—roast turkey with all the trimmings, plum pudding with custard and brandy butter, and a double whack of seasonal rum—which was relished by all. In the background, mortar fire continued intermittently, each blast sounding like a door slamming right next to Will's ear. He couldn't help thinking of the last two Christmases he'd spent with Connie, the snatched kisses under the mistletoe, their walk around the Peak when they'd embraced so passionately. Was she remembering the good times too? How he longed for her to arrive.

Soon after three in the afternoon, Grainger sent a message to MTBs 27 and 11. They came alongside and the men trooped into MTB10's wardroom, packing it to the gunwales. 'The word *Go* has come through,' Grainger announced. 'And our telegraphist has intercepted the signal ordering a ceasefire. Surrender is about to take place. We'll now carry out our escape instructions. If anyone feels unfit or unequal to the difficulties and hardships of guerrilla operations on land he should say so and he'll be put ashore.' Grainger swept his gaze around the men, but there were no takers. Will's heart thudded. Where had Connie got to?

'What about our expected passengers?' George asked, echoing Will's thoughts. 'We've a moral obligation to take the Admiral, after all that he's done during the battle. The British government has promised the Generalissimo we'll ensure his representative's safety. Besides, our chances of contacting the guerrillas in China will be greatly lessened without the local knowledge and contacts of John Chang Wei and his team.'

'Hmmm,' Grainger huffed. 'We'll give them until 6.30 then come together again for a parley.'

Will went up on deck to wait, his heart pounding painfully. He tried to distract himself with some writing. To no avail. All he could think about was Connie and all he could do was pray that everything would work out as planned.

The light began to fade and, at the appointed time, the three motor torpedo boats met up. Was it finally time to carry out their orders to "get away at all costs"? Or should they hang on in the hope that their passengers might yet arrive? Grainger put the questions to George and the other officers.

'We can't expect the Admiral and his party to show up here,' George said. 'They've either found the boats in Telegraph Bay or they're looking for us in Aberdeen.'

'Communications via wireless telegraph aren't working,' Grainger muttered. 'I'll send MTB11 over to the other boats to find out if they've turned up there.'

Will went up on deck to take his turn at aircraft watch. He stood scouring the area with a loaded, stripped Lewis gun in his hands.

# THE FLAME TREE

Without warning someone appeared on the beach opposite. A blond man, waving frantically. 'There are Japs behind me,' he yelled before striding into the sea and swimming towards the boat.

Two dark heads came over the crest of the hill.

'Bloody Japs', Will growled, letting them have a whole pan of tracer.

The heads quickly ducked down again.

Grainger materialised next to Will. He trained his binoculars on the blond man. 'Seems friendly enough,' he grunted before giving orders to a rating for the "visitor" to be hauled out of the sea with a boat hook. Blond man introduced himself as Hans Vestergaard. 'Your chaps are coming up behind me.'

Christ, the word "chaps" pronounced in a Danish accent sounded like "Japs", Will realised. He scanned the beach for Connie. But only Bob and the Admiral's bodyguard were on the shore.

The MTB didn't possess a dinghy, so they waited for Bob and Cheng Jin to swim the short distance to the boat.

His heartbeat racing, Will helped hoist them on board. *Where the hell was Connie?*

The Admiral's ADC introduced himself, saying, 'I'm Bob.'

'Come down to the wardroom,' Grainger suggested. 'You can fill me in on developments there.'

Bob and Cheng Jin's teeth were chattering from the cold. Will handed them blankets and stood by while they got out of their wet clothes. After they'd been given mugs of hot tea, he could contain himself no longer. 'Where's the Admiral?'

'He's injured so we came to get help.' Bob sipped his tea.

Shock wheeled through Will. His head spun and he sank into a chair. 'What happened?'

'It's a long story.' Bob shivered. 'I'll tell you everything as soon as I've warmed up.'

# CHAPTER TWENTY-SIX

*Four hours earlier*

Connie reached for the phone on her desk as it rang. She marvelled that it was still working when those in the Gloucester had been out of action for days. 'Admiral Wei's office,' she said.

'Douglas McBride speaking,' came the voice down the line.

'One moment, please.' She put the call through to Uncle, her nerves jangling. Had the time come to try and escape? Part of her couldn't wait—she'd be with Will again—but she was also terrified at the prospect of the journey. Escaping through Japanese lines would be perilous, to say the least.

Her intercom buzzed. 'Come through to my office, Constance.'

She went to her chair by the Admiral's teak desk. Colonel Yiu, Bob, and Cheng Jin were with him.

'The Governor and the General will go and surrender in person to the Japanese in about half an hour's time.' Uncle exhaled a long slow breath. 'We must dress inconspicuously, only take what we can carry, and meet McBride and his team in the Gloucester from where we'll make our escape. Go and fetch your things and I'll see you all in the lobby at a quarter past three. In the meantime, Cheng Jin will shred our documents in case they fall into enemy hands.'

Connie raced across the street to the hotel and up to her room. Hands trembling, she put on baggy black peasant trousers and a padded grey tunic. She placed a change of clothes in her wicker basket, a few toiletries, and the books Will had given her for Christmas. Holding them to her breast before packing them, she remembered their stolen kisses under the mistletoe and their walk on Mount Kellet road last year. How she yearned for him and prayed for his safety. It wouldn't be long before she saw him, she hoped, and holding onto that hope she made her way downstairs.

Douglas McBride, Fred Martin, and another man were waiting in reception with their knapsacks. McBride introduced Connie to the British intelligence officer, Marcus Owen. 'I was up on the Peak evacuating some women and children from one of the many houses on fire up there,' Owen said. 'When I got back to the Battle Box, it became clear all was over. The General told me I was free to escape if I could and wished me luck. So I gladly accepted Douglas's invitation to join the party.'

Connie shook hands with the debonair Briton. 'Pleased to meet you.'

The Admiral stepped into the lobby with Colonel Yiu, Bob and Cheng Jin. 'Has the colony surrendered yet?' he blurted.

'The Colonial Secretary came and confirmed the cessation of hostilities. When I asked if that meant "every man for himself", he said, "of course".' Douglas McBride heaved a heavy sigh.

'Plain-clothed Japanese agents have arrived ahead of the main body of troops and are converging on Fortress HQ,' the Admiral said, frowning. 'We must leave now or risk being captured.'

Colonel Yiu delved into his rucksack and handed Connie, Martin and McBride a revolver each. Owen already had one strapped to his chest.

Connie licked beads of sweat from her lip. 'I don't know how to use this.'

'It's not difficult. Just point and squeeze the trigger,' the Colonel said with his habitual smirk.

'We must go now!' The Admiral turned and set off.

Her heart hammering, Connie darted out of the hotel's side entrance on Pedder Street with the others. They dashed around the corner to Queen's Road, where Fred Martin had parked his Buick station wagon outside the King's Theatre.

Connie glanced at her watch. It was shortly after three thirty pm. Would they make it to Aberdeen in time? Her breath stuttered.

She clambered into the car with Uncle and the rest of the party, squashing into the front with him while everyone else squeezed into the back. Poor Cheng Jin was relegated to the boot, where he perched with his tommy gun trained on the road behind.

'Japs are approaching from the east,' Fred Martin said over the rattle of machine gun fire. He put the car into gear, revved the engine and roared off along Queen's Road.

Connie peered down Pedder Street towards Queen's Pier, past the neoclassical arches of Pedder Building and the stone columns of the Hong Kong Hotel. Flagpoles jutted from the offices of the big trading, shipping and insurance firms. Some displayed the white flag of surrender. Would they soon be replaced by the crimson red circle of the Empire of the Sun? Her vision blurred with tears. She wiped them away and told herself she must be strong.

In the heart of the city an eerie calm had now settled. Apart from a trickle of silent, fearful Chinese refugees, the streets were deserted. Fred Martin had only driven a few yards when a man sprang out from the kerb and lurched drunkenly.

'Stop! It's Two-Gun Cohen,' Connie cried.

## THE FLAME TREE

The car screeched to a halt.

McBride rolled down his window. 'If you want to escape, come with us. If you don't, get out of the way because there isn't much time, dear chap.'

Cohen pressed his boxer's nose up against the windscreen. 'Hell, no. I'm staying for the fighting.' His voice slurred.

'The fighting's over,' McBride assured the feisty bodyguard, who was living up to his name and brandishing two pistols.

'I'll take my chances.' Without another word, Cohen staggered off down the street.

'I hope he'll be alright,' Connie whispered.

'He's been in tougher scrapes than this,' Owen said. 'It wouldn't surprise me at all if we meet him in unoccupied China...'

Soon they'd arrived in the Western district, where the faded imperial grandeur of the city centre had given way to open-fronted shophouses festooned with signs and hoardings and grimy tenements, lined with balconies full of laundry and potted plants. Here, there were more people about—seemingly carrying on with their everyday lives. Martin kept one hand firmly pressed on the horn and one foot hard down on the accelerator. The car charged on through the winding streets, scattering stallholders and street-sleepers and skinny men in vests shouldering huge baskets hanging from bamboo poles. Connie wished the Englishman wasn't being quite so callous, but she supposed he felt the need for urgency.

The station wagon climbed the hill past the University of Hong Kong, the aerial roots of Chinese banyans—wild fig trees—reaching out high across the road. The Admiral's mentor, Sun Yat Sen, had qualified as a medical doctor in 1892 at the college, which was the university's forerunner, Connie remembered. He'd returned on a visit after becoming the founding father of the Chinese Republic in 1923 to tell students to carry Hong Kong's example of good government to every part of China. He'd once said, "I like the British and I understand them". But now the British had been humbled and the university reduced to a pitiful state of disrepair. More than two weeks of shellfire from across the harbour had demolished the roof of the students' union building, damaged the red brick and granite great hall, and replaced the clock face at the top of the handsome tower with an ugly, gaping hole. It was all too tragic for words.

Before too long the Buick was heading south along the narrow coastal Pokfulam Road, motoring past the forts at Belcher's and Mount Davis, past the Queen Mary Hospital, past Telegraph Bay and past an endless array of Chinese graveyards. The car hugged the edge of the rocky hillside and there was almost no other traffic, making them a conspicuous target for anyone who might be tempted to try to stop them or stage an ambush. But this was one part of the island the Japanese had yet to reach, and if any of the Admiral's fifth-columnist enemies had spotted him leaving Central, they had now lost track of him.

At last, the car swept on down towards Aberdeen and the advancing Japanese troops. Connie gripped her seat tightly. Craters studded the road's surface. Enemy guns pounded from almost every surrounding hillside, the explosions making her flinch. Hong Kong had surrendered, but the Japanese on the front line clearly hadn't got the message. Bursts of artillery, rifle and machine gun fire came from all directions and a plane soared above them, dropping bombs. The road they'd come to was obviously a prime target. Connie's heart thudded painfully.

Running the gauntlet of the mortar attack, the Buick crashed and bounced its way around the corner and down onto the Aberdeen waterfront. Connie gasped. The granite dry docks had been reduced to ruins and the nearby fish market buildings, the concrete praya and the two-foot harbour wall had all been decimated. Myriad dead bodies laid along the road, covered

# THE FLAME TREE

in thin straw sleeping mats. Out in the harbour, waterspouts trumpeted upwards from the exploding shells, and half-submerged wrecks littered the sea. A strong smell of raw sewage, salt and rotting fish infused the air.

Connie's stomach lurched. *There was not an MTB to be seen. Where were they?* She scoured the area. 'Look!' She pointed towards a group of European seamen working on a small launch tied up to a wooden pier. Fred Martin pulled up and she leapt out of the car with Bob. They ran down to ask if they had seen any MTBs.

'There was at least one here late last night,' a man with a Danish accent said, 'but they all took off again by this morning.'

Connie returned with Bob to the car. 'How will we find them?'

The Admiral indicated a large, battle-scarred building at the eastern end of the village, covered with camouflage netting and brushwood. 'We can go and ask there.'

Leaving Marcus Owen, Fred Martin and the Admiral's bodyguard to man the Buick, Connie and the others set off on foot. 'This was once an industrial school,' McBride informed them. 'It's now the garrison HQ.'

They made their way through the broken railings out front and presented themselves at the entrance. Inside, chaos reigned. News had just come through from the Battle Box that the British were to stop returning the enemy's fire. Runners were being sent to tell all fighting units in the area that they must return to the school, hand in their weapons, and wait for the Japanese to arrive and take them prisoner. Many were finding this hard to accept. 'The word, "surrender", they've always been taught,' Mc Bride said, 'is not in the Royal Navy's vocabulary.'

The middle-aged commander of the base stepped forward and the Admiral explained the purpose of their visit in his heavily-accented English.

'I'm most surprised to see you,' the commander said. 'I passed on orders for the MTBs to leave more than an hour ago.'

The Admiral stood firm. 'Do you know if they have left?'

The base commander shrugged. 'No idea. With all the confusion and speed with which events have been proceeding, no one has managed to stay in touch with them. I'm sorry, but enemy fire has been too heavy to allow the MTBs to come into Aberdeen by day, so they've been hiding out among the islands. The boats must be somewhere out there.' He waved his hand in the direction of Ap Lei Chau and beyond. 'Or they might have gone altogether.'

'Is there any chance we could use the little motor launch we just saw at the pier to help get the Admiral away?' McBride asked.

'That's not much of a boat. It doesn't have the range to get you across Mirs Bay to the Chinese coast. In fact, it might not be in a fit state to go anywhere at all. If you can wait four or five hours till high tide, we're going to re-float a bigger boat—a diesel tug that we've been using to run supplies into Stanley.'

Colonel Yiu folded his arms. 'We can't wait that long. We'll take a chance on the smaller one. At any moment the Japanese might appear along the road and cut us off.'

'There are still two hours of daylight left and the surrounding area is strongly held by the enemy. Perhaps if we take the boat, we might get as far as a small island nearby where we can wait till dark and see what happens,' McBride suggested.

The commander nodded. 'Fair enough. I'll accompany you back to the pier to find out whether the men working on the craft can get it going for you.'

'Thank you,' Connie said.

'You're most welcome, young lady.'

# THE FLAME TREE

The men labouring on the boat confirmed that all it needed was a battery and some fuel. But they wanted to be part of the escape group in return for the favour of getting it going. Connie learnt that the group included two Danes: a big, older man, Captain Anders Sorensen, who used to work on a Danish cable-laying ship, and Hans Vestergaard, a keen young merchant service cadet. There was also a middle-aged chief engineer, Taylor, who, like Vestergaard, had been serving on a Jardine's freighter before joining the corps of naval dockyard staff during the battle. And, finally, two men from the Naval Volunteer Reserve: a young warrant officer, Tom Harris, and a sub-lieutenant from Ulster, Miller.

Connie went with Fred Martin, Marcus Owen, and Tom Harris to the naval stores at the industrial school and returned with a battery and four one-gallon cans of petrol.

Then they all began loading up the little ship with other supplies from the Navy's depot: rifles, pistols, ammunition, food, and water. They took enough tinned food to last them for two days. Finally, they left the Buick standing beside the wharf. 'I'm heartbroken,' Martin lamented. 'She's my pride and joy.'

Connie touched her hand to his arm. 'I'm sorry.'

The base commander instructed the crew to take the escape party round to Telegraph Bay. 'I think the MTBs might still be hiding there,' he added.

'Bugger, we must have driven right past them,' Fred Martin lamented.

At 4.45 pm Captain Sorensen declared the launch to be in good enough running order and ready to go. Connie, the Admiral and the rest of the party climbed on board. The fierce bombardment that had been going on when they'd arrived had now subsided, leaving a silence broken only by the occasional distant boom of exploding ammunition and oil dumps. It was time to leave.

The boat's engine burst into life with a startling roar. Everyone looked at each other and scanned the hills anxiously as the echoes reverberated around the bay. It was still broad daylight with perfect visibility. Although the air was cool, the sky was brilliantly clear and sunny, and the South China Sea shimmered ahead of them.

They cruised past the mass of moored junks. The few fishermen and their families, sitting beneath their canvas awnings, stared at them with impassive interest as the launch threaded its way through their small floating village and headed down Aberdeen Channel to the east of Ap Lei Chau.

Suddenly a single rifle shot shattered the calm. A pause. Another rifle shot. Connie's heart thudded. Within moments they'd come under fire from yet more rifles. Then came the hateful rattle of machine guns followed by the screech of artillery shells. Water splashing just short of the boat had given the enemy their range, the Admiral muttered.

For a few minutes Captain Sorensen, at the helm, managed to keep the launch going. But bullets were piercing the flimsy wooden hull as if it was paper. Connie crouched down with a wince. She gave a gasp. McBride had taken a shot in the back of his shoulder. A burst of machine gun fire then silenced the engine and the boat chugged to a halt as Sorensen received hits in both legs, and Miller was wounded in the stomach.

The Admiral took charge. 'Everyone swim to Ap Lei Chau Island and meet on far side of hill,' he barked in English, his Cantonese accent even more marked than usual.

Connie froze. *Swim in the sea?* She hadn't swum in the sea since she was a child. It was full of sharks. And now, even worse, the Japanese were firing at anything that moved.

She gave herself a shake and went to McBride. 'Are you alright?'

# THE FLAME TREE

'I'm fine,' he said. 'But those two aren't.' He indicated Sorensen and Miller.

'I'm a trained first-aider,' she said, going up to them. Miller looked beyond help, but she found some rags and, with Marcus Owen's help, managed to make tourniquets which she tightened around the Danish captain's thighs.

In the meantime, with Bob's assistance, the Admiral had begun to remove his coat, trousers, shoes, and socks, and unstrap his wooden leg. Clad only in his underwear, he asked his aide-de-camp to strap his pistol and passport to his body. Everything else he said he'd leave on the boat, including his artificial leg which Connie noticed was stuffed full of bank notes.

'What do you make of our chances?' the Admiral asked his ADC.

Bob glanced across the oil-slicked water towards the island and put one hand on the bible he always carried with him. 'Only God can save you and you should pray for mercy.'

The Admiral raised his left hand and looked at his ADC. 'If I get out of this alive, I'll become a convert,' he promised.

Bob started to take off his clothes, readying himself to take his chances with the Admiral.

'Everyone into water,' Uncle Wei ordered in English.

Colonel Yiu stood firm. 'I can't swim. I'll stay on the boat.'

'Me too,' Connie added her voice to his. 'Captain Sorensen needs me to nurse him.' It was an excuse, but a valid one. Her heart was breaking, but she was too scared to jump overboard. She knew her love for Will should have made her risk everything, but she'd be no use to him dead. The Admiral and the others' chances of survival were practically zero. She would try her best to live through this and then find a way to reunite with him.

Without warning, a bullet smashed into the Admiral's wrist almost toppling him as he cried out. 'Look after Connie, Colonel Yiu,' he said through gritted teeth. Then, blood pouring from his wound, he threw himself into the harbour, closely followed by Bob.

The others had already gone overboard by now, including McBride, who was unable to remove his clothes because of the injury to his shoulder.

Firing at the boat slowed down momentarily as the Japanese turned their guns on the men in the sea.

Connie cringed as a maze of splashes erupted from where bullets were ploughing into the water around the swimmers. She wouldn't jump in there for all the gold in the world. Not even for Will, much as she loved him.

Her fears were confirmed as Taylor was hit. He screamed in agony. She watched in horror as he floundered in his own blood and died before her terrified eyes.

She turned away from the scene of death and went to crouch down next to the Danish captain. He moaned, and she soothed the sweat of pain from his brow. Would any of them make it to safety? Her chances were better on the boat than in the water, of that she was convinced. The Colonel had gone down below deck, leaving her to deal with the wounded. Miller was fading fast, and all she could do was comfort him. She thought about Will. Had the MTBs obeyed the order to leave? Was he on his way to Free China? It was all so terrifying, she could only hope and pray that he was.

# Chapter Twenty-Seven

In the wardroom of MTB10, Will was listening, his heart sinking with every word, as Admiral Chang Wei's ADC told his story. 'I truly believed we were setting off on a journey to certain death.' Bob's voice quaked. 'I was so sorry Connie decided to stay behind, but she was clearly terrified and with good reason. The Admiral, Cheng Jin and I sheltered behind the hull of the launch until the firing eased. Then we swam towards the nearest point of Ap Lei Chau. Cheng Jin and I tried to help our commander, who was swimming with an injured wrist and only one leg, but he told us to go on ahead. We refused, of course.' Bob shook his head. 'We reached the shore and helped the Admiral clamber up the rocks. Douglas McBride and Martin had managed to get there before us. McBride had taken a bullet and was bleeding heavily. The Admiral's wound was still bleeding as well. I ripped off my vest and wrapped it around his wrist. Fred Martin did his best to staunch the blood pouring out of Douglas McBride's shoulder.'

'What happened then?' Grainger asked, offering Bob a cigarette.

'The Japanese battery on Brick Hill began firing incendiary shells.' Bob took a Player's and leant into the naval commander's proffered match. 'The firebombs set the grass alight. Forced us to hide among the jagged rocks at the foot of a steep slope.'

'Good God,' Will exclaimed.

At first he'd been devastated Connie had stayed on the boat with the Colonel and the injured captain, but now he only felt relieved she'd done so. His mind went back to the *Carthage*, standing at the rail with her. Connie's anxious expression as she told him about the shark attacks, how a grey fin had surfaced where she was swimming, how scared she was of swimming in the sea ever again. Thank God she'd stayed put. She would have been even more frightened by what had happened afterwards. *She might even have been killed.*

'Cheng Jin and I carried the Admiral between us. Fred Martin helped McBride. We realised we needed to use the hill as protection from the Japanese and get ourselves round to the other side of the island.' Bob exhaled a puff of smoke. 'But our leader was too exhausted. He ordered us to leave him with a gun and go on without him. When we protested, he said he'd informed the Central Government that should anything untoward occur, he'd assigned me to report on his behalf.' Bob tapped ash from his cigarette. 'He made it clear that he intended to shoot himself rather than be captured. We found a small crevice in the rocks and left him hiding in there, extracted his promise not to move from that spot. We vowed we'd return for him.' Bob met Will's eye. 'I'll need your help with that.'

'Of course,' Will said. With any luck, the launch they'd been on would still be drifting nearby and he'd find Connie safe and sound at the same time.

'When we were making our way to this side of the island, we came across Owen and the young warrant officer, Tom Harris, who'd swum to a more sheltered cove. They're with McBride and Martin and should be here soon,' Bob added.

# THE FLAME TREE

After Harris, Martin, Owen and the wounded McBride had been brought from the beach by Reggie in MRB27's skiff, everyone but McBride in nothing but their underpants, stained black with oil from the sea, and McBride almost too weak to move, with the back of his coat drenched in blood, Will set off in the rowboat with Bob and Cheng Jin. Keeping as close to shore as they could, they rounded the tip of the island into the enemy's field of fire. But the Japanese guns had fallen silent, thank God. Will wiped sweat from his brow and kept his eyes peeled for the drifting launch. *Nowhere to be seen.*

Soon, they'd beached the skiff and were picking their way between the rocks. Bob went on ahead. 'The crevice is up here.'

Will caught up with him and peered into the small space. Empty. *Damn!*

'We begged the bugger not to move,' Bob grumbled.

Keeping their heads down, Will and his companions searched the area, the residue of gunpowder smoke stinging their eyes. The Admiral appeared to have disappeared off the face of the earth. It was getting dark, but they dared not use their torches or call out. Had Chang Wei been captured? Will's heart sank.

Then Bob hit upon the idea that they should whistle loudly, in the hope that the Admiral might be within earshot. Just as they despaired of ever finding him, a small stone came rolling past them down the hill. They climbed the steep slope to investigate.

Will called out softly, 'Merry Christmas'.

From above their heads came an answering 'Merry Christmas', spoken in the Admiral's unmistakable accent. *Meh Kissmas.*

Will and Bob gave each other a thumbs-up.

They found Chang Wei perched almost at the top. How he'd managed to heave himself up there was anyone's guess. He must have suffered agonies.

Cheng Jin covered Will and Bob with his Tommy gun while they took it in turn to carry the Admiral down to the boat.

He sat in the stern and crossed himself. Bob smiled and said, 'I'm glad you did not forget your vow of earlier, Uncle.'

Will scratched at his head. *What was that all about?*

Bob bent his mouth to Will's ear. 'The Admiral made a pledge to convert to Christianity if he lived through this.'

'Ah,' Will said.

Back on MTB 10, Grainger led the men in a rousing ovation, 'Hip hip hooray,' as the Admiral was lifted aboard in triumph and carried down to the wardroom. Propped up on the settee berth, he was given his regulation tot of rum and some leftover Christmas turkey.

Grainger examined the Admiral's wound. 'It's only a graze.' Chang Wei brushed him off.

'I'm sorry, Sir, but you're wrong. There's a bullet embedded in your wrist. Would you like us to remove it?'

The Admiral shrugged. 'I no mind. You take out, good. You leave in, good. I ok.'

'Best to leave it in for now,' Grainger said. 'My medical orderly can dress and bandage it. I've already decided on the same course of action for Douglas McBride's shoulder.'

Before too long, Chang Wei's arm was resting in a clean white sling, and he was wearing the uniform of a lieutenant commander of the Royal Navy. It had been made for Grainger, who was much taller. But Bob had pinned up the left trouser leg to cover the Admiral's stump and he appeared happy enough for the right one to be shortened in the same manner. His face was bright and alert and he seemed surprisingly cheerful, given the circumstances.

Will went up on deck for a cigarette and took a lingering look at the familiar hills, now darkening in the wake of a glorious sunset, one of the most beautiful evenings he had ever seen in Hong Kong. To the west a purplish afterglow lit the steely sky and the first stars had started to twinkle. Was Connie looking at the sun going down too? Where was she? How was she? Was she even still alive? His heart felt as if it had been ripped to pieces. How he yearned for her warm touch. Her delightful scent. What he would give for her to be with him right now, sharing this beautiful moment. It was hard to believe a war was raging beneath the wonders of the firmament.

He exhaled a long sigh. What a bloody awful day it had been. Although he'd been expecting the inevitable result of the historic, demoralising events which had taken place, the full significance of defeat now sank in. His chest panged painfully with despair and apprehension for Hong Kong—which now lay open to the vagaries of a cruel, unscrupulous enemy—and for his darling Connie. *God, I hope and pray that she's safe.*

Reggie came to stand by him. Will offered him a cigarette. 'Where's George?' Their boss had been on the boat sent to fetch the others from Telegraph Bay and now all five MTBs had come together.

'He's up on the bridge with Grainger and the Admiral.' Reggie waved a hand towards the three men, who were poring over maps spread out in front of them. 'Probably discussing where to go.' He shot Will a look. 'I'm sorry Connie got left behind, by the way...'

'I'm torn, to be honest. If she'd jumped overboard she might not have made it. She's with the Colonel and that man's a survivor. I only hope he keeps an eye on her and she'll be alright.'

'She has an excellent chance, Will. Try not to worry.'

'Easier said than done...'

They smoked in silence, lost in their separate thoughts until George interrupted them. 'Let me fill you in on what's been decided,' he said. 'We'll set off immediately and find somewhere that's Jap-free on the other side of Mirs Bay within our fuel range, ditch the MTBs and proceed on foot. I told the Admiral I was still hoping to link up with the groups of communist partisans near the border at Sha Tau Kok, but he knows of other guerrilla forces on the Tai Pang peninsula about forty-five miles away from where we are now. It's a wild and mountainous area and he thinks it unlikely that there would be any Japanese troops based there... particularly with the danger of being shot in the back by the group he has in mind. He suggested that we put in first at a small island, Ping Chau, just opposite the coast, where he knows the village headman.'

The Admiral radiated confidence, Will thought, and imparted it to others. There was no doubt that he was the paramount leader of the expedition, his superior rank and natural air of authority reinforced by his extensive local knowledge and connections. 'Chang Wei is certainly indomitable...'

'Indeed.' George chuckled. 'But he's finally admitted he needs to rest and has accepted to do so in Grainger's cabin.' He gave Will a sympathetic look. 'As soon as we're settled in China, I plan on getting Jean out of Hong Kong. Now Connie is stuck there too, I'll do all I can to get her out as well.'

'Thanks.' The word choked in Will's throat. He swallowed hard.

# Chapter Twenty-Eight

Will stayed up on deck after George and Reggie had returned to their separate boats. The Admiral, his bodyguard, and Bob remained in the wardroom on MTB10. The rest of the newcomers—Douglas McBride, Fred Martin, Marcus Owen, Hans Vestergaard and Tom Harris spread out between the other boats. The men were packed into the small ships to the gunwales, but it wouldn't be for long. By tomorrow, they'd be on dry land, all going according to plan.

With a deafening blast, the aircraft engines powering the five MTBs roared into life and then settled into a steady drone as they threaded their way in single file out of the bay. The moon, in its first quarter, shone over the nearby islands and lit glittering paths behind the darkened ships, sending ripples of sparkles over the calm, silent waters. With a clear sky and a gentle wind, it seemed like a perfect night for a sail, Will thought, but it was far from ideal for the task at hand. The breaking waves from the bows of the vessels, the white pluming wakes from the sterns and the silhouetted black figures standing motionless behind their guns would be easily seen from the shadowy and no longer friendly shores of Hong Kong Island, just a few hundred yards away.

Will's heart thudded. Bright streams of light from a coastal battery searchlight were trying to pick them out. But then they were too far away, leaving the sullen shoreline behind and picking up speed to crash through the sea, full throttle at forty knots. The throb of the engines beneath Will's feet felt reassuringly strong and steady but also disconcertingly loud. "Fish thunder boats" the Chinese called the MTBs, and with good reason. He gazed back at the disappearing hills, thinking of Connie left behind. How he longed for her. He stared ahead into the deepening night and wondered what lay ahead. What were his chances of making it through Japanese lines? Even more important, would Connie be able to follow him? If George didn't manage to get her out, he'd do so himself, he resolved. *Come hell or high water...*

Night had fallen, and it had become difficult to discern the boats in front, apart from their phosphorescent trails. Before too long, they'd reached deep water, and Will went to help throw overboard the locked heavy iron chests containing the flotilla's secret signal books. After passing the remote, south-eastern fringe of Hong Kong territory, the gunboats turned north and sped in the direction of the wide mouth of Mirs Bay.

Suddenly, out to sea on the starboard bow, the bright beam of a powerful searchlight swept across the heavens. Will's veins turned to ice. A Japanese warship. A cruiser or destroyer—they were too distant to tell which. It must have heard the roar of the boats and mistaken them for aircraft.

The searchlight kept probing the sky, before coming down to the water and reaching out towards them. Will held his breath. A red flare had been fired. It lit up the horizon, faded into tiny specks that came dripping down into the sea like spent fireworks. Should the boats cut their engines? Apart from the racket they were making, the wash from an MTB going at speed

# THE FLAME TREE

made it easy to spot from far away, even at night. Will heaved a sigh of relief. There was no need to do anything. Having either failed to see them or decided they might be more trouble than they were worth, the warship continued its course and soon the MTBs were out of range.

They sailed on into Mirs Bay. It was now midnight and the moon had disappeared. Ping Chau lay in the bay's northeast corner, a low, crescent-shaped island about two miles long. Although the island and the waters of Mirs Bay were part of the colony, the white sands and dark mountains on the mainland belonged to China. But as far as the Japanese were concerned, Will remembered, there was no longer any difference—their troops now controlled both sides of the border and were likely to turn up anywhere.

In the "Ping Chau Roads"—the narrow channel at the eastern end of the island, facing the peninsula—the British boats now cut their engines. They tied up alongside each other at anchor. After the noise and speed of the past two hours, the sudden silence seemed overwhelming. Someone closed a hatch. A stifled curse echoed. The two sounds rang out in quick succession across the still water.

George and Reggie came over. 'The Admiral wants us to go ashore with Bob to make enquiries,' George said.

Despite the late hour, Will leapt at the chance. It would take his mind off worrying about Connie.

Will and his companions rowed ashore under the cover of manned Lewis guns on the MTBs. Within minutes they'd landed on the island's flat, strangely coloured siltstones. Will remembered how, on sailing weekends to Ping Chau during the hot summer months, he would look down from the deck of

Deborah's father's yacht through a sea of peacock blues and greens to the rich pinks and oranges of the stones below. He used to enjoy walking along the narrow beach of smooth white sand, littered with washed-up starfish and spiky sea urchins. Now, peering into the eerie blackness and shivering in the cool night breeze, it was hard to believe he was in the same place.

Will and his companions crept up the beach onto a concrete path, which they followed through small trees and clumps of bushes, cacti and tall grasses. They passed a line of old family tombs, where joss sticks smouldered next to red brick ancestral shrines, and eventually reached the edge of a small village. The path doubled as the main street. They stopped. Listened. The squat grey houses sat silently within their thick limestone walls, their tiny windows shuttered and doors barred.

A dog launched into a frenzy of barking. Then silence again. 'Anyone there? Come out, we're friends,' Bob shouted in the local dialect, Hakka.

No answer.

'What'll we do next?' George muttered.

Bob shifted his weight from one foot to the other. 'We'll carry on searching.'

Will almost jumped out of his skin as two men came out of the shadows, holding up their hands to show they were unarmed. One was middle-aged; the other had a pronounced limp. They greeted Bob in Cantonese and said that when the villagers heard the boats arrive they'd hidden, fearing the Japanese had returned. When they'd heard Bob call out in Hakka, they thought the intruders might be thieves or bandits. 'But when we heard you speak English, we guessed you were harmless,' the older of the two men said, before going on to explain that he was the village headman and the man with the limp a member of a guerrilla band based across the bay in China.

# THE FLAME TREE

Further discussion revealed that the middle-aged man oversaw "local operations" on the island, which Will surmised meant smuggling and light piracy. Since the fall of Canton three years ago, they'd turned their hands increasingly to fighting the Japanese but now the bay was clear of them. The village leader said that he'd helped the Admiral in the past to get supplies to Free China through the Japanese blockade. When Bob informed him that the Admiral himself was on one of the gunboats, he asked if he could go and pay his respects.

So, they all returned to the beach and rowed out to MTB10, where the Admiral was roused from his bed. In typical "can do" fashion, he greeted the islanders warmly. After a rapid-fire discussion in Hakka, he announced they would take the MTBs over to the Chinese mainland and make direct contact with the guerrilla chief there. They would find him, the headman said, at Namo, a small fishing village lying just across the narrow channel from the island, halfway along the Tai Pang Peninsula. If he agreed to help them and all looked well, they would sink the gunboats and make their way on foot across the mountains to the Nationalist-held town of Waichow. After that, who could say? There'd still be a thousand miles of mountains, rivers and jungle to cross before they reached the Kuomintang government's capital Chungking, but they should at least be relatively safe from capture by the Japanese.

The crews of the MTBs murmured in dismay. For a sailor, sinking your own boat must be worse than burning your own home, Will thought. And then they would have to abandon the sea, their lifeblood, to face the perils of dry land—a strange and most likely wildly inhospitable land, across which they will be expected to walk or march for hundreds of miles.

In his inimitable English, the Admiral insisted they had no choice. It was because they were so valuable that the MTBs couldn't be allowed to fall into enemy hands. China, sadly, no longer had a navy that could use them. But more important now was the need to remove all signs that the boats ever existed. The Japanese would soon realise, if they hadn't already, that a group of senior Chinese and British officers was missing. Between them, they held a lot of valuable military and political information that the enemy would surely love to obtain. It would also soon be discovered that the motor torpedo boats had disappeared. By sunrise there would be naval and air patrols scouring the coast for them. If they caught even a glimpse of an abandoned MTB, they would be in hot pursuit. The boats must be destroyed and everyone transported inland under cover before the light of dawn could reveal their trail.

Accompanied by fishermen from the island, the five boats moved off at a slow pace, keeping close together. This time, Will stayed on board while Bob went ahead with Reggie and George to contact the guerrillas. His nerves on edge, Will waited with the Admiral until a dinghy returned with the message "Admiral Chang Wei's loyal follower, Leung Wing Yuen, is waiting to receive him".

'Come with me, Lieutenant Burton,' the Admiral commanded.

And so Will did, honoured to sit between Chang Wei and his bodyguard while they were rowed ashore through a phalanx of motorised junks.

The Admiral's bodyguard carried him piggy-back up the beach to where a group of men had congregated.

Will went to stand by Reggie and George.

A tough-looking fellow stepped forward to bow respectfully before the Admiral, who stretched out his good arm and embraced him like a long-lost friend.

# THE FLAME TREE

'That's Leung Wing Yuen,' Reggie whispered. 'The guerrillas' leader.'

The Admiral and Leung began a lengthy discussion, the gist of which, from what Will could understand, involved Leung escorting the escape party through Japanese lines to Free China. In return, the guerrillas could have everything on the boats that the British didn't need.

Events then moved at a rapid pace. Will was sent to inform Grainger of developments. In a flurry of activity, junks and sampans glided alongside the MTBs. Nimble, black-clad figures slipped on board. They gave cheery Chinese greetings to the Royal Navy crews. The British sailors helped dismantle gun mountings, then take ashore wireless transmitters and receivers, crates of tinned beef and sausages, cans of oil and petrol, and a jumbled assortment of blankets, sweaters and oilskins. They put the heavier items, the Lewis guns and radio sets, in separate piles to show they weren't needed on the journey. George and a group of ratings went to hide them, saying arrangements would be made to return and retrieve them later. Will went with the British to help interpret into Chinese and sort out what went where. Also to stop the insurgents from grabbing the guns which the escape party would take with them.

Finally, at 4.45 am, it was time to execute the cheerless task of scuttling the MTBs. The villagers assisted by bringing baskets of big stones to weigh the fragile craft down. Some joined the British sailors in hacking away at the decks with picks and axes. Will, George and Reggie also helped, driving holes with hatchets through the bottoms of the boats, slashing the buoyant cushions, and opening the seawater intakes.

At last the vessels began to settle as they filled with water and the weight of their engines started to take them down. Their bows tilted at an angle, slowly as if reluctant to give up the struggle, and only when their decks were awash did Will and the others leave them. The flotilla was no more.

Everyone mustered on the beach in the cold pre-dawn darkness. In a fever of activity, they groped about among the mass of stores that had been landed from the gunboats. Soon, each man had equipped himself with a rifle, revolver, blanket, oilskin, and as much ammunition, food, spare clothing and personal kit as he could carry.

In the meantime, Bob had arranged a makeshift sedan chair to be prepared for the Admiral. Two of Leung's men were assigned to carry it, and two more to take over when they got tired.

Will lined up with George and Reggie, casting an apprehensive eye at the dim shapes of the hills that rose behind the village. Further inland, a forbidding-looking range of mountains stretched across the neck of the peninsula. He'd been reassured when George had said they wouldn't be walking that far straight away. The priority was to get under cover before they were seen. But they had little time to spare. Dawn in this part of the world came quickly. It was now a quarter to six and still pitch dark. By a quarter past it would be broad daylight.

Will shouldered his rucksack, thankful that he'd managed to salvage the jade flame tree ornament Connie had given him for Christmas last year. It felt like he was holding a part of her with him. After what he'd been through yesterday, the first rays of morning light on Chinese soil gave him some hope that all would be well in the end, and that soon he would be reunited with her.

The Admiral's chair had been surrounded by cheering villagers. As southern president of the Kuomintang, he was clearly an influential and popular figure. Then, escorted on both sides by the most fearsome-looking bunch of cut-throat rogues Will had ever seen, he was carried at the head of the procession towards the edge of the village.

## THE FLAME TREE

'What a grand tableau for the Lord Mayor's Show,' Reggie joked.

'More like Ali Baba and his forty thieves,' Will muttered as they set off in a long, straggling line up the valley.

Feet plodding, he focussed on the positives. He was alive. There was every chance Connie was alive too. He wouldn't let himself believe otherwise. She was with the Colonel, and he would help her. Perhaps they'd even find a better boat in Aberdeen that would get them to China? Hope took root in Will's heart, and he kept it there as he headed towards the distant mountains of China.

# CHAPTER TWENTY-NINE

Connie held a canteen of water to Captain Sorensen's lips in the cabin of the launch.

'What time is it?' he groaned.

She gazed through the porthole. 'Nearly morning, I think.' The ominous pitch-black sea had turned a steely grey.

'Where are we?'

'I don't know.'

'I'll go up and take a look.' Colonel Yiu's voice came from the other side of the cabin.

Connie thanked him and soothed the brow of the wounded captain. It had been the worst night of her life. Cold terror had made her almost faint as she'd crouched below deck while the Japanese guns had strafed the water around the small ship. Had anyone survived the maelstrom? She'd fully expected to die at any moment, alternating between holding her breath and gulping down air as the explosions had ricocheted above.

When the shells had finally ceased ricocheting, the colonel said that the tide was taking them out of the harbour. Connie had listened out for the thunder of the MTB engines, but the only sound had been the distant boom of the big guns. How she'd prayed for a miracle that the Admiral and his party had managed to escape and that Will and his friends had got away.

# THE FLAME TREE

All through the night she'd huddled with the colonel and the captain in the confined space, while the launch had been tossed about on the waves. Her heart had wept that she and Will hadn't been reunited like they'd both planned. It had all gone horribly wrong and all she could do now was cling to the hope that, somehow, she would find the road back to him.

Colonel Yiu came down the ladder. 'The tide has turned. At the current rate, we'll be taken to shore within fifteen or twenty minutes.'

'Where to exactly?' Connie asked.

'Telegraph Bay, I think. Which is good as we might just get away with being unnoticed.'

'We'd better have something to eat,' Connie suggested. Her stomach was growling—she hadn't eaten since yesterday lunchtime, a rushed snack before setting off for Aberdeen.

'As long as we make it fast,' the colonel said.

Connie found some bread and ham. She made them each a sandwich, which they ate quickly.

'What are your plans?' she asked him.

'I'll disguise myself as a coolie and make my way to Free China.'

Should she request to tag along? Yiu hadn't offered, and Connie disliked the man intensely—he was sinister and she didn't trust him. She turned her gaze to Captain Sorensen. His lower legs had been pierced by shrapnel and he desperately needed medical attention. 'I'd like to try and get the captain up to the Queen Mary Hospital, if possible,' Connie said. 'It isn't far from here...'

Yiu smiled. 'I'll see what I can do.'

The Dane had gone back to sleep so, her chest tightening with nerves, Connie went up on deck. She avoided looking at Miller's dead body, still lying where he'd collapsed by the railing. Waves were nudging the boat ever closer to the Dairy Farm

Jetty. Would there be any Japs about? She squinted into the semi-darkness. Several sampans lay beached on the shore, and fishermen were loading last night's catch onto carts. No Japs, as far as she could tell.

With a sudden lurch, the launch grounded itself on the rocky beach, then slowly began to list to one side.

Connie returned to the cabin. She and the colonel managed to lift Sorensen from the bunk and up the ladder. With a grunt, the colonel picked up the Admiral's wooden leg and extracted a wad of cash. 'Wait here, Connie. I'll go and pay those fishermen to take you and the Dane to the Queen Mary. You'll be safe from the Japanese there. As far as I'm aware, they honour the medical profession.'

She wasn't sure that what he'd said was true. From what she'd heard, Jap soldiers had done unspeakable things to a group of nurses in Happy Valley before the surrender, brutalising and raping them. But she wasn't about to contradict the colonel. If the hospital had been taken over by the Japanese, she would run back to Telegraph Bay or try and made her way up the Peak.

Two hours later, dressed as a fisherwoman and carrying her basket with the books Will had given her inside, Connie made her way up Sassoon Road towards the Queen Mary with two coolies, pushing the Danish captain in a cart. They'd hidden him under sacks of freshly caught snapper and, if anyone were to stop them, they would say they were taking supplies to the kitchens. The colonel had paid the men handsomely for the subterfuge. He'd also lent Connie enough cash to tide her over until she found Jean. Yiu had seemed eager to be rid of her—no doubt believing she would only have hindered his progress had

# THE FLAME TREE

she begged to go with him. Good riddance, she thought. She wouldn't have gone with him for a big gold watch.

It was a steep climb and she kept her eyes glued to the bare, cone-like peak of Mount Davis rising into the clear blue sky. At the gate to the hospital grounds, the sound of footfalls made her startle. Her heart set up a fearful beat. Two Japanese military men were approaching. The shorter man was wearing the green tunic and trousers of a private. The other sported a sword. An officer.

'Oy!' the private called out.

Connie lowered her gaze, pretending not to hear.

'Oy!' the Jap yelled louder, his tone angry.

Connie stopped dead, her pulse pounding.

The coolies set down the cart containing the captain and ran off as if the hounds of hell were at their heels.

The officer grinned, his teeth like battered tombstones. With a smirk, he turned and walked away, leaving the private to stare at her with hungry eyes.

Connie took a step back and the sweat of fear beaded her brow.

The private grabbed her, rubbed himself against her, speaking words in Japanese she couldn't understand. She felt his hardness push against her belly and bit back a scream. The stench of the man—a mixture of garlic, pickled radish and stale sweat—made her want to throw up.

The Jap groped between her legs with rough fingers. Nausea rose in her throat. He stopped momentarily to unbutton his flies. Lust flashed in his dark eyes.

Without warning, vomit spewed from Connie's mouth. Half-digested bread and ham splattered the private's chin and the top of his tunic.

'[1] *Busu!*' He landed a slap across Connie's face and she fell to the ground.

More blows rained down on her, followed by kicks to her stomach.

Screaming, she curled herself into a ball.

With a snarl, the private scrubbed at the vomit on his chin. He shot her a disgusted look, spat at her, then turned and marched off.

Connie pushed herself to her feet. Her face stung and her tummy hurt, but her knees buckled with relief. She'd been lucky to have escaped being raped, or even killed. Her sensitive stomach had saved her.

'I'll go and fetch help,' she whispered to the captain.

She hurried up the steps to the hospital entrance. Inside, she found the reception area filled with wounded British troops. Medical staff were dealing with them and there wasn't a Japanese in sight. She walked through to the wards. No one stopped her. It was as if she were invisible. Everyone was focused on treating the injured. How would she find someone to help her with the Dane? She approached a white-coated doctor. Before she could say anything, he barked, 'What are you doing here?'

'My name is Constance Han. I'm a friend of Margaret and Harry Wyn-Jones.' It was the only thing she could think of to say. 'There's an injured man outside. I need help with him.'

'There are injured men in here too. We've got our hands full.' The harassed doctor's tone softened. 'Margaret is working on the next ward. Perhaps you should go and find her?'

Connie did as he'd suggested. Again no one stopped her. She pushed open the door to a wide room filled with women and children, a stark contrast to where she'd just been.

---

1. Ugly woman

'Connie,' Margaret said, coming up to her. 'What a surprise.'

Connie's legs wobbled. Hot tears stung her eyes. 'Thank God I've found you.'

'My dear, whatever's happened?'

'It's a long story,' Connie said, sobbing with delayed shock.

Margaret led her to her office, sat her down and arranged for a cup of tea. When Connie told her about the Danish captain, she sent a porter to fetch him. Then she listened while Connie recounted the events of the past twenty-four hours.

'You need to rest, dear girl.' Margaret gave her a hug.

'What about the Japanese?'

'They're leaving us alone for now. I remember you took a first-aid course in London. We need all the help we can get here. When you're up to it, of course.'

'Of course.' Connie looked her in the eye. 'I wish I knew if Will and the others have managed to make it to China.'

'I'll ask Harry if there's a way he can find out.'

'If it's not too much trouble, do you think he can discover where Jean is as well?'

'No harm in asking.' Margaret patted her hand. 'Now let me find you a bed in the nurses' quarters.'

Connie smiled wanly. 'Thank you.'


A month or so later, on a cold January morning, dressed as a coolie, Connie was making her way stealthily up to the Peak via the Pokfulam Reservoir Trail. She carried her wicker basket and, while she walked, she thought about how she'd spent the past four weeks.

Soon after recovering from her ordeal, she'd put on the nurse's uniform Margaret had found for her. Connie's days then became occupied with emptying bed pans and holding the hands of dying soldiers. How her heart had wept for them as she'd comforted them and listened to their final words. It was the young Canadians who'd saddened her most. They'd been cannon fodder. Raw, untrained and thousands of miles from their homes. It had all been so terribly heart-breaking.

She'd been devastated when she'd learnt that all the colony's troops who weren't killed or wounded had been rounded up and put into temporary camps while the Japanese authorities make up their minds what to do with them. Where her brothers-in-law among them? Or had they been killed? At least Will wasn't with them. Oh, how she longed for him, to just see his handsome face once more. She chided herself every waking minute that she hadn't risked all and jumped into the sea with the Admiral. If she'd done so, she could have been with Will now instead of darting for cover every time she heard a noise as she climbed the steep trail to the Peak.

With a sigh, she remembered how, in the new year, word had reached the hospital that the Japanese had put up signs in town ordering all Dutch, American, Belgian, and British nationals to report at the Murray Parade Ground near the Supreme Court Building. The Japs hadn't given any explanation. When a great crowd of people reported at the big open space, they'd apparently been surprised that their sign had been taken literally. "British nationals", they'd said. But everyone born in Hong Kong was a British national... something the Japanese obviously didn't know. They'd assumed that only the haughty whites were British. Throughout the day, they'd interned all comers, sending them off in batches to squalid Chinese hotels along the waterfront. And throughout the day people had kept coming until at last the Japs gave up. They sent the rest of the "enemy nationals" away, to await their future decision. It had been Harry who had told Connie and Margaret about this when he'd come to the hospital with patients from the over-crowded hotels. 'It was a battle to persuade the Japs to let those needing medical attention come out,' he'd said.

Connie had hoped he'd have been able to find out if the Admiral's party had made it to Free China and if he knew Jean's whereabouts. But all the British intelligence officers had escaped or had been locked up. If any of their spies were still in Hong Kong, they had yet to reveal themselves. And now the Admiral and his team had left, their agents too had gone to ground.

The day after Harry's visit, Japanese guards were posted at the Queen Mary, and all the British in the building found that they'd been interned within the grounds of the hospital. A large party of uniformed Japanese, wearing medical insignia, were shown around by a couple of British doctors. The Japs asked a lot of questions about the hospital equipment. 'I found out they're preparing a civilian internment camp at Stanley,' Margaret had said to Connie afterwards.

Connie had debated with herself whether she should leave the hospital, dye her hair black, and pretend to be full-blooded Chinese to avoid internment. It was cold and dark and sad in the Queen Mary and they were all terribly hungry. Their food, already insufficient, was being stolen, little by little, as it came up from the kitchens to the wards. Sometimes none of it was left at all.

The hospital amahs and the cleaning boys had begun to run away, one by one, stealing blankets as they escaped. Everyone was worrying about blankets and clothing and such, in preparation for being sent to the internment camp. Did she want to go to Stanley? Connie asked herself. She'd be safer there than on her own in Hong Kong. But she didn't want to stay in Hong Kong. She wanted to go to China and find Will.

On the twenty-first of January the axe fell. The Japanese ordered the British staff to leave the Queen Mary immediately. Patients were carried out by the dozen—Captain Sorensen among them—loaded onto trucks and taken away to other hospitals. Margaret, who'd been frantic with worry since she'd first known about Stanley, now appeared much more cheerful. The Japanese colonel who'd taken over the Medical Department had said that she could stay out of the internment camp with Harry and the rest of the expatriate doctors to work for the community and safeguard public health.

Margaret invited Connie to stay in a flat half way up the Peak the Japanese said she and Harry could occupy. But Connie had been worried close contact with the Japs would reveal her identity. They might torture her for information about the Admiral's secret service, so she'd declined. She still had the money Colonel Yiu had given her, and she hoped there would be more cash at home to make a tidy sum she could use to travel to Free China.

Connie's calves were aching now. Would she ever get to the top of the path? Eventually, she emerged from the thick tree cover to the far more exposed road in front of the Peak Tram terminus. Her eyes widened with shock. Many of the Victorian mansions before her had been bombed. Charred walls. Holes in their roofs. Rubble strewn gardens. *How terrible!*

The roar of an engine sent Connie scuttling to hide behind a banyan tree. A lorry sped past, filled with Japanese troops. She began to regret coming up to the Peak. Although she was dressed as a coolie, she was clearly a woman. She'd narrowly escaped being raped once. Chances were, she wouldn't be so lucky a second time.

Keeping to the side of the road with her ear alerted for the sound of any approaching traffic, she made her way in the direction of the Han Fung estate. It seemed to take for ever as she had to crouch down and turn her back on any Jap vehicle that passed. She was only grateful there weren't any foot soldiers to contend with.

# THE FLAME TREE

At last the dragon-crested gateway loomed before her. She went through the portal and then froze. *Oh, no, her car was a complete wreck and Father's mansion must have received a direct hit.* Gaping holes marred the jade green tiles sloping downwards to the red brick walls. The wide stone steps leading to the colonnaded porticoed entrance had been blown to bits. The ornately carved teak front door hung loosely on its hinges. Connie shaded her eyes and glanced around. *Where were the servants?*

Suddenly, strong arms grabbed her and yanked her backwards. A hand covered her mouth. 'Who are you?' a voice growled. A voice she recognised. *Fah Wong, the gardener.*

'I'm Number Five Miss,' she said.

He whirled her around, stared at her. 'I'm sorry. I didn't recognise you.'

'Where is everyone?'

'I'll tell you in a minute. First, we must get out of the open.'

Connie allowed herself to be led to the stone cottage where Fah Wong lived with his family.

Inside, it was empty. 'I sent my wife and children to China,' he explained. 'The rest of the staff have all gone there too.'

'Thank you for staying and keeping an eye on things.'

'I was unable to stop the looters, I'm afraid. They have stolen all your father's jade ornaments and any cash they could find. And they've ripped up the wooden floors for firewood.'

'Maybe you should go to China too?'

'No. Someone needs to be here. I can grow enough food to add to what I've managed to hide.' He went to a cupboard and retrieved a bag of rice. 'I'll make us something to eat, but first I must tell you something.'

'Oh?'

'A man came looking for you three weeks ago.'

Connie's breath stuttered. 'Who?'

'A Chinese fellow. He said he worked for a white man called George.' Fah Wong smiled. 'And, if you were to appear, I was to give you a piece of paper with an address on it that he made me bury in a bottle in the garden.'

'That's wonderful news!' Connie's heart leapt. 'Thank you.'

'I just hope this man is someone you can trust, Number Five Miss.'

'I'll be careful.'

And she would be. It wouldn't be easy. But if she found Jean, then surely the two of them would be able to get out of Hong Kong together? She couldn't imagine any other alternative.

*Oh, dearest Will, where are you? How are you? How I yearn for you to hold me in your arms.*

# CHAPTER THIRTY

Connie spent the night on the divan in the living area of Fah Wong's cottage. After preparing a breakfast of noodles for them both, he dug the glass bottle up from where he'd buried it under a rose bush, extracted the slip of paper and handed it to her. 'The man who gave this to me also gave me directions how to get there, so I'll go with you,' he said. 'In any case, you wouldn't be safe walking on your own. We should wait until nightfall. It won't be as dangerous under cover of darkness.'

She was grateful for Fah Wong's offer and thanked him. He wasn't a fighter though, and she regretted that she'd left the pistol the colonel had given her behind on the launch. She passed the time resting. After an early supper of rice and vegetables, she had a quick wash, braided her hair in a long plait, and put on baggy black trousers and a tunic. She repacked her wicker basket, adding a few essentials she'd managed to retrieve from her old bedroom. Her fingers brushed against the covers of Will's books and her heart longed for him. Would she be reunited with him soon? She hoped and prayed that she would.

When night had fallen, Fah Wong said they should leave. Lit by the moon, Connie set off with him. Fragments of spent shrapnel and bullets crunched under their feet and, at the top of Magazine Gap, they came across a grisly sight. The bodies of numerous soldiers had been left unburied by the side of the road. British soldiers, judging by their uniforms. Their faces, bloated and half-eaten by insects, were unrecognisable, and the stench made Connie retch. 'Don't look, Miss.' Fah Wong grabbed her arm and pulled her along with him.

The sudden rumble of an engine set Connie's heart racing. Fah Wong tugged her down the bank at the side of the road. The noise came closer. Headlights beamed. Connie held her breath. A lorry loaded with Japanese infantry, armed with rifles and machine guns, chugged past.

It was five minutes before they dared move off again and head down towards Happy Valley. Connie stifled a gasp. The figure of a Jap soldier was looming in the shadows. But then, she realised it was only a rock. *Get a grip!* Her eyes were playing tricks on her.

She focussed on the distant sight of moonlight reflecting in the sea. After walking with Fah Wong for hours and hours, eventually she'd arrived at the far end of the island. The Lye Mun entrance to the harbour lay before her.

Fah Wong took Connie to a small bungalow on a grassy hill overlooking the bay. It was surrounded by barbed wire and seemed deserted. They found a gap in the wire and crept up to the door. 'I'll go inside to check,' Fah Wong said. 'You wait here, Miss.'

Connie hid behind a bush until he'd returned. 'It's empty,' he confirmed. 'Maybe that man gave up waiting for you and left.'

Disappointment welled in Connie's chest. It had been three weeks since the address had been given to Fah Wong. A lot could have happened in the interim.

Dawn light was glimmering in the eastern sky. They needed to take cover. 'Let's stay here until tonight,' she suggested. 'If no one comes looking for me, then I'll try and find a way to get to China myself.'

# THE FLAME TREE

Fah Wong led her inside the bungalow and shot the bolts of the door behind them before they went through to the front room. They'd packed some biscuits, so they had a snack and took sips of water from their canteens. 'You must be exhausted, Miss,' the gardener said. 'I'll take first watch while you get some sleep.'

They settled on stacks of empty old sandbags and newspapers in separate corners. Dog tired, Connie dropped off quickly, sleeping deeply until Fah Wong woke her. 'I can't stay awake any longer, Miss,' he said.

'That's okay. You rest now and I'll stand guard.'

Soon, he was snoring softly. Connie went to the window. Two vultures were wheeling through the clear blue sky. They flew down and perched on the posts supporting the barbed wire. Connie shuddered, but they would almost certainly warn of anyone approaching. Sampans were anchored in the cove below, and a Chinese man clambered onto one of them. She smiled as he was rowed across to Kowloon. *So that way was open!*

Her heart jumped. The vultures had taken off. The blood drained from her veins. Three Jap soldiers were making their way up the hill. They kicked at stones while they chatted and smoked. Connie's hands trembled as she went to shake Fah Wong awake. She put a finger to her lips and pointed through the window.

The soldiers began to bang on the door and call out, '*Anoni! Anoni!*' which probably meant "hello".

Fah Wong cowered in his corner and Connie crouched down in hers. The dust from the sandbags got into her nose and she wanted to sneeze. She pinched her nostrils to stop herself. Her pulse stuttered. The soldiers were peering into the bungalow through the dusty windows. Surely she and Fah Wong would be discovered?

But no. Shouts echoed from below. The soldiers muttered to each other, then there was silence. 'What'll we do now?' Connie whispered.

'Let's go to the village and ask if someone can help you.'

Connie shook her head doubtfully. 'Why should they do that?'

'You are the daughter of the well-respected Sir Albert Han Fung. Of course they will agree.'

Connie and Fah Wong waited until dusk. The two vultures dropped out of the darkening sky and settled on their fence posts again. A good omen, Connie thought as she and the gardener gathered their things and made their way down the hill.

She breathed in the heady smell of fish drying on rattan mats under the portals of the grey-walled buildings. In the gloom, sampans clustered along the foreshore. A dog ran forward, barking, then sat and scratched at its fleas. Washing hung from bamboo poles and the spicy aroma of food cooking wafted in the air. An old man was sitting in a doorway, smoking his long pipe. They approached him, and Fah Wong gave a brief explanation of why they were there.

The old man shook his head. 'There were strangers staying in that bungalow.' The old man indicated the hillside. 'But they left a couple of weeks ago.'

Connie's heart sank. 'Do you know where they went?'

He pointed towards a beached junk. 'You could ask the junk master.'

Connie and Fah Wong thanked the old man. The tide had turned and was flowing in. Soon the flat-bottomed boat would be afloat and they wouldn't be able to board it. 'We'd better hurry,' Connie said.

# THE FLAME TREE

They made haste across the corrugated sand and crept around the high stern of the junk. Fah Wong called out. But a voice yelled at them to clear off.

Two small boys came out onto the poop deck and stood staring. Fah Wong was still arguing with the junk master, who had stayed below and seemed to be getting angrier and angrier.

Connie joined in the argument, pleading for help. She put a sob into her voice and said she was the daughter of Sir Albert Han Fung.

The curtain over the rear portholes was tossed aside, and the junk master poked his face out. 'I arranged for a man and a woman to be taken to a secret location a couple of weeks ago. They said you might turn up...'

The two boys put out a plank. Connie and Fah Wong went aboard and followed them into the main cabin, feebly lit by an oil lamp. The junk master passed a thermos flask of hot tea to Connie. While she drank, she told the junk master about how she'd escaped from the Japanese.

The junk master nodded knowingly. 'My son and a nephew were forced to act as coolies for the Japs. When they asked for payment, the Japanese beat them. I'm more than happy to help anyone who's against them. I'll arrange a sampan for you.'

'I could pay,' Connie offered.

'No need. Save your money for later.' He told her that the fisher-folk didn't like the Japs, who wouldn't let their boats go beyond certain limits. They hadn't notified the fish, however, who stayed outside those boundaries and refused to be caught.

Fah Wong talked with the junk master at length, stressing the need to keep Connie safe. 'I can't come with her. My duty lies in Hong Kong.'

Connie touched her hand to the faithful servant's shoulder. 'My family will forever be grateful to you.'

Not long afterwards, Connie was back up on deck, hugging Fah Wong goodbye, and thanking him for all he'd done to help her. She handed him a fistful of the dollars the colonel had given her. He tried to refuse, but she insisted. 'I have more than enough,' she said.

'Take care, Miss. I will see you when the Japs are defeated.'

'I hope so.'

Her stomach churning with nerves, she climbed down to a sampan which was now bumping against the side of the floating junk and, clutching her wicker basket, made her way to crawl under the bamboo hood at the stern.

Two young men took it in turns to row. They turned out to be the junk master's son and nephew. Soon they were well out to sea, in the middle of what appeared to be a wide channel. Connie moved out from under the matting and sat on the gunwale. Water rippled against the bow, and she dipped her fingers down, smiling with rare delight as the phosphorescent drops fell from their tips.

She thought about Will. Had the Admiral's party managed to reach their destination? Or had they been taken by the Japanese? Would she find Jean safe and sound? The delight fell from her heart. It was awful having no news of any of them.

Presently, the dark loom of land grew more distinct, and the white outline of a sandy beach shone in the moonlight. The junk master's son and nephew said the area was held by the Japs but dominated by anti-Japanese insurgents and that she might find her friend with them. Connie couldn't help feeling concerned. What if Jean had been captured? But the young men indicated towards the top of a nearby hill, hazy in the darkness, and told her she must hike up there right away and hunker down where the Japs wouldn't find her. There was a village in the next valley where the guerrillas had their base.

The sampan nudged against the shingle. Connie thanked the young men and offered to pay them. At first they refused, but then accepted twenty-five dollars, which was little enough for the risk they'd taken.

The climb up the bare, rocky hill took all her strength. At the summit, she stopped to rest. It was a beautiful night, stars twinkling in the inky blackness of the sky. A fishing sampan was dropping and hauling in its nets in the calm phosphorescent sea below, rising and diving like a distant whale.

Tiredness washed through Connie, and she decided to make a temporary camp for the rest of the night. She would go down to the insurgents' village in the morning. She extracted a blanket from her wicker basket and curled herself up in it. With her basket for a pillow and the friendly stars above her, she fell asleep to dream of Will.

The sun was high when she woke. She hurriedly drank some water, munched a dry biscuit, and rolled up her belongings. Her chest tightened with nerves. Up here, she was more than a little exposed. The slope was covered with short grass and bare grey rocks. But the beach where she'd landed the night before was still deserted, thank God. Only a few fishing sampans, far out at sea. Even so, a Japanese plane might come over. She needed to get off the hill as fast as she could.

She made her way down the other side and struck inland. Wildflowers bloomed amid the mosses, and a bubbling stream flowed beside the pathway. She sniffed the fresh air and couldn't help rejoicing. Come what may, she'd set off to find Will and hopefully would be reunited with him before too long. Holding onto that thought, she kept going.

Presently, she came across an ancient temple, surrounded by old trees. A Chinese woman was standing by the doorway, wearing a dark-blue cotton coat and trousers, with a triangle of black cloth tied over her head. Connie approached and asked if she might enter the temple to rest.

With the typical charming politeness of a country person, the woman said that Connie was welcome and ushered her through to a grey stone-paved courtyard where blackbirds flitted through the overhanging trees. In the dimly lit main room, the huge, gold-lacquered figure of the Buddha sat in holy ease, with the smoke of incense sticks set in a big bronze urn rising slowly before him. Connie brought her palms together and bowed at his feet, then followed the woman through to a smaller courtyard and the apartment where she lived with her husband, the temple keeper.

They offered Connie jasmine tea and peanut toffee, which she accepted gratefully. After she'd told them something about herself and where she was heading, the temple keeper offered to consult the gods on her behalf. Connie felt a little sick, knowing that any news he delivered could be bad. He went to fetch a holder filled with bamboo sticks. Closing his eyes, he gave the holder a shake, then tipped out a few sticks. He picked them up one at a time and considered the characters inked on them before finally addressing Connie. 'You have been in grave danger but it seems you will soon be in safe hands,' he said. 'I will guide you to the partisan village and take you to their leader.'

Connie's hopes suddenly soared. She saw herself in Will's safe hands, dancing, laughing. Praise be to the gods, she thought.

And once again, Connie found herself thanking someone for their help as she waved the temple keeper's wife goodbye.

# THE FLAME TREE

Villagers were usually nervous of strangers, so she was glad the temple keeper had offered to go with her.

About an hour or so later, they were strolling along a narrow, murky street between tall, oddly shaped houses. The musk of wood smoke, the bitter stench of the communal latrines, and the fragrance of myriad joss sticks wafted around them. They walked past stalls selling eggs, bean sprouts, cuts of meat, cabbages, long green lettuce, peanuts, Rat and Pirate and My Dear cigarettes, and a dozen types of candy and sweet rice cakes. Just seeing all the food so freely available, Connie felt her spirits lifting. After the deprivations of Hong Kong Island, it was almost like a miracle. She found she was smiling; the promise of safe hands feeling ever closer.

They rounded a curve and stopped before a building, the door of which was partly open. Connie followed the temple keeper into a big, mud-floored room. On the sides perched straw-covered bales and bundles of bedding rolled in matting. In the centre stood a wooden table and several stools.

A Chinese woman came out of the shadows.

'Connie!' the woman exclaimed in a familiar voice. 'You got here at last.'

'Jean!' Connie rushed forward and embraced her friend. 'I'm so happy to see you.' She kissed Jean's cheek. 'Have you any news of George, Will, and the rest of the Admiral's party?'

'Yes.' Jean smiled and kissed Connie in return. 'They made it to Waichow, I heard. I will send a message that you are here and, as soon as they can, I'm sure they will come for us.'

Connie could have fainted. She caught her breath and grabbed Jean's arm at the same time. 'Thank you so much for waiting for me, Jean.'

'Oh, I couldn't ever have gone without you, honey.'

Connie's eyes welled. Tears of relief trickled down her face. She would be with Will soon.

## SIOBHAN DAIKO

Dancing.
Laughing.
*Loving.*
Safe hands.
It all felt so surreal.

# Chapter Thirty-One

In the staff quarters of the Wai On Hospital, part of an American Seventh Day Adventist Mission in Waichow, Will placed Connie's flame of the forest tree ornament next to the pistol in his kit bag.

'Ready?' George asked, shouldering his haversack.

'More than ready,' Will said with a smile.

It was early morning, and he hadn't stopped smiling since news had arrived last night that Connie had managed to join Jean. 'Thanks again for holding on for her.'

George could have set off to fetch his wife weeks ago and Will had been perplexed that he hadn't done so. When George had heard via his agents that Connie had made it off the launch, a message had been left for her on the Peak. Then information had come through that she was at the Queen Mary. Although the hospital was still being run by the British, it had soon been surrounded by the Japs—too dangerous for any of George's contacts to infiltrate. Will had been distraught while he'd waited for further news. Despite his perplexity that George hadn't gone to Jean sooner, Will was grateful his commander had offered to hang on until the end of the month. That deadline was only days away. *Thank God Connie had got out in time.*

'Let's go!' George clapped him on the back.

Will matched his stride and soon they'd left the hospital grounds. Overlooking the East River and the mountains beyond, it had been a haven of tranquillity for Will, George and Reggie, who'd stayed on to await instructions for Z Force operations after the Admiral and the rest of the party had boarded riverboats to head north on New Year's Eve. The British had travelled on to Burma subsequently, Will had heard. But the Admiral, his bodyguard, and Bob had gone to Chungking.

After leaving the hospital grounds, Will walked with George along a cobbled road thronging with people, dogs, chickens, pigs and even rats. It had been the same scene when they'd arrived at the town nearly a month ago following a gruelling hike with the long line of men from the MTBs. Word had gone ahead, and a group of Chinese civic officials and army officers had met them at a nearby military rest house, then escorted them on to the ancient gate in the town's massive stone defensive walls.

A small force of soldiers had drawn up to attention and saluted them. But then there'd been an air raid, and while they'd waited for the all-clear they were treated to tea—accompanied by peanut, lotus and sesame buns, which had been steamed and wrapped in green banana leaves. How Will had wished that Connie had been with him to enjoy the treats.

For the next hour, his heart breaking for her, he'd watched column after column of Chinese soldiers march by—part of the army that would have relieved Hong Kong if it had held out for just two more days.

Now, taking the opposite route to the one they'd taken on their arrival in Waichow, Will remembered how he and the rest of the British had tried to smarten up and march in time as they'd paraded before the populace, who'd lined the narrow, cobbled roads to greet them. Unshaven, unkempt, with no two men dressed alike, they'd formed up three abreast, shouldered

## THE FLAME TREE

their weapons, and marched past the chief magistrate who, together with other local luminaries had led them in ceremonial style, dodging rubble and craters in the bombed streets, at a low-geared pace which the Europeans had found difficult to keep in step with. But the spirit was there, and it was a fond memory.

When they'd arrived at the hospital, there'd been whoops of joy as the men had discovered they could wash in hot water and sleep in proper beds with real sprung mattresses. Professionally trained nurses had pampered them, treating their blisters and making them feel so welcome.

Washed, refreshed and with appetites duly whetted, they'd been escorted to dine at Chinese Army Headquarters at the invitation of the two senior commanders. In the cool of the early evening, they'd strolled along the grassy bank of the East River, past venerable banyan trees and clumps of giant bamboo to a grand, elaborate mansion with an ancestral hall at the centre. The Admiral—who'd been billeted with his staff in a house in the middle of the city—had been the guest of honour and the banquet attended by hundreds of people.

The meal had started at six thirty in the evening and finished at nine, each of the twenty courses of delicious food toasted with rice wine. None of the MTB crews had been able to use chopsticks, a fact Will had found a tad embarrassing as he'd watched them resort to using their fingers. But their hosts had graciously helped them out by placing morsels of roasted suckling pig, pigeon eggs, bamboo shoots and other delicacies into the sailors' bowls. The British soon learnt to respond to the toast master's "yum sing"—*cheers*—with the required cry of "ganbei"—*dry cup*. Will smiled to himself as he remembered how the MTB ratings had gone on to teach their new Chinese friends the English response, "bottoms up".

Another good memory to have. If only Connie could have been there with them, she'd have loved being one of the stars of the show.

With a spring in his step and his heart lifting with joy that he'd soon be reunited with the girl he loved, Will left Waichow behind and made his way with George towards the coast, relatively undaunted by the fact they were heading back into Japanese territory. They'd made it through Jap lines once before and he trusted they'd do so again. But he couldn't help remembering how the first sight of the greenish-yellow cotton uniforms and padded jackets of the regular troops of Free China had cheered his spirits when they'd arrived in unoccupied lands.

They'd been given a warm welcome. The Admiral had sat in the small courtyard of the nationalist garrison. Next to a dry fountain, he'd exchanged courtesies with the official reception committee—village elders and the captain of the stronghold. The villagers had prepared them a meal of rice and pork with boiled turnip tops, water chestnuts and other vegetables. The mention of the Admiral's name had ensured their smooth progress from then onwards.

Dinner for the group had been hosted by the Chinese Military, the rice wine going down a treat. George, the Admiral and his men, and the Kuomintang generals had continued eating and playing drinking games late into the night, but Will and Reggie had been too exhausted and had bunked down on bales of straw with the others instead.

Will remembered how he'd listened to the snores of the men and had struggled to fall asleep. Connie had been left behind in Hong Kong and his heart had been crushed with worry that he might never see her again. How relieved he'd been when the news had come through yesterday that she'd managed to escape. Soon she'd be in his safe hands, and so help him God he would never, ever let her slip away from him again.

And so Will and George marched on towards the coast. Will got very little sleep at night when he and George rolled up in their sleeping bags under the stars. Images of Connie played in his head, of her falling into his arms, her warmth, her sweet jasmine perfume. Her perfume that he could almost smell as he and George headed off in the mornings with their weapons at the ready.

On the third day, they walked along a narrow gorge cupped in the hills. After a steep climb, which made Will's legs ache so badly he thought they might seize up, they found a series of wide stone steps concealed under a canopy of overhanging trees and shrubs. George said that this was the key section of a route used by smugglers to convey merchandise unloaded from junks into the interior. Badly needed supplies still came this way through the Japanese blockade.

'Should we rest for a bit?' George suggested.

Thoughts of seeing Connie were a balm to Will's tired legs. 'Let's keep going,' he said.

They climbed to the top of the second peak, where they finally sat and rested. Below, in the distance, lay the craggy islets and crystal coves of Mirs Bay—Hong Kong territory. Will's chest filled with pain at the realisation it was no longer British, but Japanese. Thank God, Connie had got away. His heart pounded with anticipation. He'd hold her in his arms soon. He'd press his nose to her hair and inhale her divine scent. He'd make love to her so passionately they would both be breathless.

Will's spirits remained high as they marched along the ubiquitous raised paths through paddy field after paddy field. He drank in the beauty of the surrounding hillsides dotted with clumps of bamboo alongside the streams, lychee orchards, pink and red clusters of oleander and hibiscus. A shiny blue-black water buffalo stood rock still, a small boy in a pointed hat perched on its massive neck.

The barking of village dogs alerted them that they'd come upon a human settlement. 'We've arrived,' George said, consulting his map.

Buffalo boy approached, having left his beast in the field. 'What do you want?' he asked in Hakka. George spoke the language fluently, but Will didn't, so George translated and then, from what Will could understand, went on to ask the boy to take them to the village headman.

The boy turned out to be a runner for the guerrillas. He took them down a narrow, dark cobblestoned street between tall higgledy-piggledy houses. The road curved and the boy stopped in front of a dwelling with a wooden door. He rapped at it. Will's heart set up a jubilant beat that Connie would be on the other side. Just moments and she would be falling into his arms.

The door opened, and Jean stepped forward.

Will eyed the space behind her.

Empty.

'I'm so sorry,' Jean sobbed as George took her into his arms. 'But Connie is being held by the reds and they won't release her unless you meet their demands.'

Will felt the blood drain from his face.

## Chapter Thirty-Two

Connie walked up and down the small room where she was being held, the heat of anger flushing through her. She'd been brought here yesterday afternoon after she'd blurted she was the daughter of Sir Albert Han Fung. How naïve! But it was the communists who'd provoked her. It was their fault China had been overrun by the Japs. If the reds hadn't been trying to take over the country, Chiang Kai Shek's army wouldn't be fighting them when they should have been fighting the Japanese.

Connie gritted her teeth. It had all gone wrong when she'd been invited along with Jean to attend a political meeting. It would have been rude to refuse—the meeting was being held in the house where she and Jean shared a room at the top of a flight of rickety wooden stairs.

An earnest, bespectacled young man had stood in front of the villagers, indoctrinating them. Indoctrination was the only word that could describe it, Connie thought. They were simple, countryfolk who listened avidly and believed everything they were told. That the tax collectors were "blood-sucking devils", that their landlords were "capitalist running dogs" and "fat cats" living off the toil of ordinary people. It was all too much for Connie. She'd worked for the Admiral and knew the facts. Without thinking, she'd got to her feet and lectured the young man about where his loyalties should lie. 'China had been invaded by Japan. The Japanese are the enemy and the Chinese need to unite against them,' she'd spat.

The bespectacled youth asked her who she was, and she'd pulled herself up to her full height and introduced herself. 'I'm Constance Han Sun. The daughter of Sir Albert and sister of Matthew, a commander in Chiang Kai Shek's army.' Put that in your pipe and smoke it, she'd wanted to say in English, any Chinese equivalent not coming to mind. But Jean had grabbed her arm, a horrified expression on her face. 'Connie,' she'd hissed, 'hold your tongue!'

In the blink of an eye, two guerrillas came up. Without a word, they'd tied Connie's hands behind her back and marched her out of the room. She'd struggled and had tried to kick them away. But they were too strong for her. She'd screamed. No one had come to her aid. Why hadn't anyone warned her that these partisans were reds? With hindsight, she should have realised. Hadn't Will once mentioned that Z Force had been trying to contact communist guerrillas beyond Sha Tau Kok and run guns to them to fight the Japanese? The Admiral had been reluctant to help them on that score, and with good reason now Connie thought about it. They would have used them to attack the nationalists.

Bunching her fists as she paced the small room, she remembered her first meeting with the guerrillas soon after she'd arrived. Womenfolk had appeared with sweet cakes and tea and they'd all sat around the table listening to Connie recount how she'd escaped. The guerrillas had seemed friendly and she'd assumed they were nationalists. Uncle Wei had contacts with Leung Wing Yuen, a partisan leader who supported the Kuomintang, and Connie had believed the group were his followers.

One of the insurgents, a short fat young man with a round face, had boasted, 'I often go to Hong Kong to kill Japanese.

# THE FLAME TREE

There are crowds. I hide in them. A Jap officer comes along. I pull my gun from my sleeve. Bang! Bang! The officer falls dead. I disappear into the crowd...' He'd illustrated the whole scene in pantomime—his gunplay, the officer crumpling to the ground. The entire room had erupted into laughter. Eyeing the guerrillas' cartridge belts and rifles, Connie had given a shiver of apprehension. But she'd put it to one side, believing herself to be under their protection.

That night, she and Jean had slept in a big bed with a mosquito net over it. They'd talked about their excitement to be seeing George and Will soon. How much they were looking forward to supporting their work against the Japanese in Free China. Jean had shared that she and George were planning to start a family when the war was over. And Connie had told her of her intention to introduce Will to her father and ask for his blessing. The next morning, Connie had gone downstairs to be greeted by the ubiquitous stench of animal ordure. As was the custom in rural China, the household's pigs, ducks and hens had spent the night inside with their humans. At breakfast Jean said she had matters to attend to and would Connie be alright on her own. She'd assured her that she would be fine and had decided to go for a walk. After wandering down the village main street, she'd gone through the gate and on towards some trees and a grassy mound. She'd sat on a rock and gazed at the distant mountains, etched against the misty skyline. Will would be crossing those ridges to find her any day now. Her heart ached with yearning. She wouldn't feel entirely safe until she was with him...

Connie's thoughts had then turned to her family. Father, Mother and Mamma would be worried about her and she'd hoped that, as soon as she reached Waichow, she'd be able to get word to them that she was safe. She'd wished she knew what had happened to her brothers-in-law. Had they been captured or, the gods forbid, killed? A heavy lump of sorrow had formed in her chest. Would she have news of her brother Matthew when she arrived in Waichow? Perhaps she would even see him in Free China? How she'd prayed that would be the case.

Connie's foot now kicked against her chamber pot in the small room. She'd been cooped up here for the past two days with only cold rice and water to eat and drink. At least her hands were no longer tied behind her back. Those horrible men had taken the last of her money, which she'd kept in the pockets of her trousers. For the umpteenth time she wondered where she was. It hadn't taken long for her to be frogmarched here, so she must still be in the village. She strained her ears and her heart gave a sudden leap. A voice echoed from somewhere outside. Will's voice. 'Will!' she cried out. 'I'm here!' But only silence greeted her and hot tears of dismay spilled down her cheeks.

A bucket of rice arrived, but she left it uneaten. Dusk came, followed by darkness, and Connie prepared herself to spend another sleepless night on the cold, stone floor. There'd been no sign of Will and she was starting to think she'd imagined hearing him.

She jumped to her feet when a loud bang came from the other side of the door.

A pistol shot.

Connie's heart began a terrified beat.

The door flew open and a Chinese man in a bamboo hat appeared.

He grabbed her.

She struggled and aimed a kick at his shin.

'It's me. Will.'

'Will?'

The Chinese man had blue eyes. Will's beautiful, vivid blue eyes. He was dressed as a peasant in baggy black trousers and a

## THE FLAME TREE

padded jacket. His powerful arms enveloped her and he kissed her. 'We need to run, darling. Can you manage that?'

'Yes. Oh yes.'

He took her hand and pulled her with him.

She ran. Oh, how she ran. She ran with Will until they'd left the village behind. They stopped to catch their breath. Will shushed her questions. 'I'll tell you everything soon, sweetheart, I promise. But first we must get out of here.'

Under the moonlight, they walked briskly along raised paths through endless paddy fields, then climbed to the summit of a mountain ridge, listening out for the sounds of pursuit. Every time a stone tumbled or a stick cracked, Connie's heart nearly beat out of her chest.

Eventually, dawn light lit the sky and they took shelter in a crevice. 'We need to hide during the day, my love,' Will said. 'Are you hungry?'

'Just thirsty.'

He passed her his water canteen. 'I've a sleeping bag in my haversack. We can squash in together if that's alright with you?'

She gave him a sad smile. 'I left your books behind, my dearest. And a change of clothes. I haven't had a wash in days so I won't smell nice.'

'Ha,' he laughed. 'And there was me longing for your beautiful jasmine scent.'

'I didn't bring any perfume with me, Will,' she said seriously as he laid out the bed roll.

'I was only teasing, Connie. Come, I just want to hold you, my darling.' And he did just that, tucking her into him.

She relished being in his arms. 'Where are George and Jean?' she asked a short time later.

'Ah. That's a sorry tale, I'm afraid.' He gave a sigh. 'I'd had my suspicions for a while, and they've now been confirmed. I believe George and Jean are both on the side of the reds.'

'What?!?' Her jaw dropped. *No, it couldn't be true...*

'When those buggers who locked you up made their demands, George was more than willing to take them to a hiding place near the fishing village where we'd landed with the MTBs. It was where we'd scuttled them. George and a group of ratings had hidden our Lewis guns and radio sets in a secret cave. He agreed to hand them over to the communists without batting an eyelid.'

'But that doesn't make him a communist sympathiser, surely?'

'No, but he discouraged me from going with him last night. This morning, Jean started asking me a lot of questions about Chinese army positions. I thought her curiosity a tad excessive. Then, George came back this afternoon with the guerrillas, very pally with them. He told me he'd decided to stay and help them fight the Japs for a while. It was only then that he'd thought to mention he'd received a telegram from the British Ambassador in Chungking before we set off to get you that Z Force were about to be disbanded.'

'I'm so sorry, Will. I know how much you care about that group of men.' Connie laced her fingers with his, sorrow welling in her eyes for what had come to pass.

'Reggie has gone north to meet up with our old house mate, Nigel Bridges. He and the others managed to make it to Kukong through Japanese lines. No doubt I'll learn soon enough what the plans are for how we'll spend the rest of the war.' He kissed her on the lips. 'Whatever happens, I'm keeping you with me, my love. I don't ever want us to be parted again.'

'And I don't ever want to be parted from you, my dearest Will.' She snuggled into him. 'How did you find me?'

'The guerrillas were reticent about fulfilling their part of the bargain. Their leader said you would be released tomorrow. But I didn't believe him. I went on at George and he told me not to worry. That everything was in hand. But I couldn't wait. The fact that you're Sir Albert's daughter, and your connections with the Admiral and your brother, made you a valuable hostage. I knew I had to get you out of there. So, when George and Jean went to bed, I hid in a doorway. One of the partisans came out of the house where we were staying, carrying a bucket of rice. I followed him to the place on the edge of the village where you were being held. Waited till he'd gone, then fired my pistol at the lock to break you out.'

'I can't believe our closest friends put our lives in danger,' she said with heaviness in her heart.

'Me neither. I hope we'll get a proper explanation one day. But I didn't want to risk putting you in further danger by hanging about.'

She lifted her face to be kissed. 'I heard your voice earlier and I called out.'

'Oh, my darling. I'm sorry I didn't hear you. I was walking around trying to find you.'

'Well, you found me in the end. Thank the gods.' She raised his hand, kissed his wrist. 'How long until we're safely in unoccupied China?'

'We'll need to cross another mountain ridge tomorrow night, sleep through the next day and walk through another night before we make it, my love. It will be very tiring for you, but I'll carry you piggy-back if necessary.'

She smiled. 'I'll do my best to keep up.' And she would. She was with the man she loved and nothing would separate her from him ever again.

Connie's feet ached from several blisters, but she made herself soldier on. Whenever she felt pain, she chanted a Buddhist mantra in her head and remembered the saying "mind over matter". Simply being with Will was more than enough to distract her from discomfort, although subsisting on a diet of the tinned meat he'd stashed in his rucksack was proving to be somewhat of a challenge. During their night-time trek they maintained silence, but the following day, hiding in the countryside, wrapped up in Will's bedroll, they talked about anything and everything until sleep claimed them. Connie found herself falling more and more in love with him as he told her stories about his past, his childhood in Bristol, his time at university, and how he'd always wanted to go to China.

'Don't you miss your brother and your parents?' she asked, wrapping her arms around Will's waist in the confined space of his sleeping bag.

'Of course. But they're avid letter-writers and we've maintained contact despite how long it takes mail to get through. I managed to send a message to them via the Embassy in Chungking that I've escaped from Hong Kong. They'll have been worried about me.'

'I hope to find out what has happened to my brothers-in-law once we get to Waichow. Also get in touch with Matthew.' Will had already told her about the hospital where he'd been billeted and about the Chinese Army Headquarters. Waichow was the command centre of a nationalist front line division, he'd also said.

'You'll be made so welcome, my darling.' He looked deep into her eyes. 'Remember when I asked you to marry me before the Japanese invaded and you said we needed to talk to your father first?'

She nodded. 'It all seems like a lifetime ago...'

'Darling, I'd like to marry you when we arrive in Waichow. I want us to live together as man and wife.'

# THE FLAME TREE

Connie pulled her brows inwards. She wanted that too. Wanted Will to make love to her as her husband. They'd only kissed and cuddled since their reunion, both seemingly holding back for a more appropriate time and place.

'Yes, Will. I'll marry you. I love you with all my heart. I love my father and my family too, but you are my family, my new family, and I want to be your wife.'

He kissed her deeply, then said, 'You've just made me the happiest man alive.'

'And I'm the happiest woman.' She held his hands. Safe hands. She felt truly loved and protected. Burying herself in his chest she released a contented sigh and then let sleep claim her.

# Chapter Thirty-Three

On the morning of her wedding day, Connie was dressing in the white silk gown she'd borrowed from the pastor's wife at the Seventh Day Adventist Mission house in the hospital grounds.

She thought back to her arrival in Waichow a month ago, smiling as she remembered Will borrowing a bicycle for the final few miles and how she'd perched on the pillion seat—a threadbare cushion on an iron frame over the mudguard—with her blistered feet sticking out on each side. They'd almost fallen into a tank trap, but Will had managed to skirt it at the last second. A patrolling Japanese aircraft had come into sight, and they'd taken cover, dismounting from the bicycle and hiding in a field until it had passed over.

Eventually they'd cycled through the gates of the town. She'd been horrified to see that most of the buildings were in ruins and that the bridges over East River had also been bombed and were in various states of disrepair. Japanese bombers staged regular raids on Waichow, Will had told her beforehand. The townspeople spent their days sheltering in the countryside, only returning shortly before dark to do their shopping and conduct their business.

When she and Will had arrived at the hospital, Connie's heart had rejoiced at the sight of the unscathed compound overlooking the river and the mountains beyond. The main building boasted a tiled roof, white wooden shutters and meshed windows that kept out the flies. There was a well at the front with a windmill pump, and a line of flame of the forest trees screened three attractive staff houses from a small church set in the middle of an open grassy space.

It was in that church where she and Will were about to be married. Connie had accepted to be baptised into the Christian faith soon after her arrival, for the sake of expediency. God was God, whatever the religion, she'd decided. And she would say as much to her Buddhist mother when she saw her again. She'd sent word to her parents that she was safe but had yet to receive a reply from them.

The pastor's young wife, Yan, came into the room. 'You're looking beautiful, Connie,' she said. 'Will won't be able to take his eyes off you.'

'Thank you again for lending me this dress. It's gorgeous.'

'You're so welcome.' Yan smiled. 'Come along. I need to get you to the church.'

It was only a short walk across the peaceful garden where the flame trees had only just burst into flower and where Matthew was waiting to give her away. He'd arrived yesterday, having heard she was here. After learning how Will had rescued her from the communists, he'd given his blessing to their marriage. 'Father will come around,' Matthew had said. 'He didn't approve of me marrying Esther because she's American. But once we'd provided him with another grandson he accepted the inevitable.'

Connie hadn't reminded him that Esther had Chinese blood. Getting Father to accept Will would be an entirely different matter. But she resolved not to worry about that now. She stepped towards her brother and linked arms with him.

'You look stunning, little sis,' Matthew said, leading her into the church.

Butterflies fluttered in Connie's stomach while they walked down the aisle, but as soon as Matthew placed her hand in Will's her nerves disappeared. This was where her destiny lay. With Will, the man she loved.

Standing next to Reggie, his best man, Will swept his blue eyes over her face. 'I'm the luckiest chap in the world, to be marrying you.' His voice choked with emotion. 'My beautiful, brave Connie.'

She gazed at him, so incredibly handsome in his new suit and tie. He was about to become her husband; she almost pinched herself.

The ceremony passed in a blur. Soon they'd arrived at the point where they were expected to make their vows. Will said his first, and then it was her turn. Her heartbeats skittered.

She repeated after the pastor, 'In the name of God, I, Constance, take you, William, to be my husband, to have and to hold from this day forward, for better, for worse, for richer, for poorer, in sickness and health, to love and to cherish, until we are parted by death. This is my solemn vow.'

Will caught her eye, pride reflected in his gaze.

*'Ngo Oi Nei,'* he whispered the words *I love you* in Cantonese.

'Love you too,' she said, softly.

They exchanged the rings they'd managed to buy downtown with pay that had come through for Will from the British Army representative in China.

Will kissed her, deep and possessively, then led her out of the church.

# THE FLAME TREE

After myriad toasts and delicious food in the hospital refectory, someone put a record on the gramophone, *The Way You Look Tonight*.

Will took Connie in his arms and waltzed her around the room. 'Happy, Mrs Burton?'

'Constance Burton is very happy.' She smiled. 'I remember dancing with you to this on the *Carthage*.'

'I'll never forget it, my darling.' He inhaled through his nose. 'Ah, your sweet perfume. I need to write a poem about it as soon as I can.'

Will had been hard at it these past weeks with no time for writing, Connie reflected. A unit had been established to help prisoners of war escape from Hong Kong. The Japs had incarcerated them in horrific disease-ridden camps, starving them and making them work on building an airport runway. A field doctor with the Volunteers, an Australian, had succeeded in escaping from the camp at Sham Shui Po and had established the British Army Aid Group, the BAAG, recruiting Will, Reggie, Nigel and other ex-members of Z Force to set up a network of agents in the colony. Mike Middleton had also made a bid for escape and had arrived a few days ago from the civilian internment camp in Stanley, providing a list of the internees and reporting on how badly they, too, were being treated. He'd joined the BAAG as had Connie, who'd volunteered to assist with administrative tasks. She hoped she would soon learn if her brothers-in-law were in one of the camps. Plans were afoot for her, Will and the others to move from Waichow and establish a headquarters in Kweilin near the American air force base. A new life beckoned for them all.

Will was holding her close and she basked in the love shining from his eyes and in the warmth of his smile. 'It's time for us to go to our room, my dearest wife,' he said proudly.

Her tummy fluttered and she returned his smile. 'I'm ready.'

He took her hand and led her from the canteen, across the lawn, to the staff house where a suite had been prepared for them. He undressed her reverently, then undressed himself.

She feasted her eyes on him. He was truly divine. All hard muscle. Every inch of him perfect. She went to stand in front of him, stretching herself upwards.

He bent his head to kiss his way down her face to her neck, making her tingle all over. Then he lifted her and carried her to the bed.

She laid back and parted her thighs, keeping her eyes glued to his.

He lowered himself, his flesh meeting her heated skin. He took her hand and kissed her wrist. 'God, how I love you, Connie.'

She cupped his face and pressed her lips to his. They kissed slowly, passionately, hungrily as he slid into her, covering her with his body. 'I love you too, Will. I love you so much.'

Afterwards, they fell back on the bed, panting. The musky scent of their lovemaking filled the air and their bodies glistened. They ran their hands up and down each other's sides, stilling their gasping breaths.

Her heart thudded as he kissed her. 'We'll be together for the rest of our lives. You and me, Connie. For ever and ever.'

She nestled against him. 'You and me,' she repeated, 'for ever and ever.'

# CHAPTER THIRTY-FOUR

## CANTON, CHINA, 17TH JANUARY 1946

Will held Connie's hand as they stood in the teak-panelled banquet room at the Canton town hall on the Bund overlooking the Pearl River. They were sandwiched between her two brothers, Matthew and Jonathan, and surrounded by a group of about thirty local grandees. Admiral Chang Wei, who'd assumed the role of Mayor the previous September, was hosting a farewell reception in honour of Will and Connie on the evening before they were due to leave for Macau, and he was about to launch into a speech with Bob standing next to him.

The Mayor held a glass of champagne in one hand, and a piece of paper in the other, from which he read, 'I would like to pay tribute to the work of William Burton and his fellow officers in the British Army Aid Group. From the time the unit was formed in early 1942 until the Japanese capitulated last August, they rendered assistance to 33 British and Allied services escapers; to over 400 Indians—140 of whom were in the forces and whose escapes they organised—and to 40 American evaders, who were brought to safety through the BAAG network. They passed into the prison camps medicines, messages, information and escape aids, giving comfort and hope to those who'd been forced to endure the horrors of interment. They provided relatives with news of prisoners. They gave assistance to almost 1,000 Chinese members and civil employees of the British services and supported them, and in many cases their families also, in China. They helped get 120 Europeans and over 550 Chinese civilians out of enemy territory. They planned and supervised the spending of over three million Chinese dollars of British funds for refugee relief. Their food and hospital services saved the lives of thousands suffering famine, epidemics and air raids. They set up an intelligence service when information from Hong Kong was lacking and provided data vital to air and naval operations in the China Theatre. I would like us to raise our glasses to William Burton and his brave fellow officers, who have now returned to Hong Kong.'

Everyone did as he'd requested before drinking and bursting into loud applause.

Will took a step forward. 'I would like to thank Mayor Chang Wei for this splendid party and for his kindness to my wife and me during our time in Canton. Please raise your glasses to the Mayor!'

More raising of glasses followed by cheering and clapping.

Connie gave Will a nudge. 'We should go home soon and finish packing.'

He bent to her ear. 'How are those nerves?'

She held out her trembling hand and smiled. 'Steady.'

He lifted her hand and brushed a kiss to her wrist. Her perfume was as enticing as ever and she looked so beautiful in her elegant silk brocade cheongsam. 'We have our whole lives in front of us and can look forward to the future with confidence,' he said. They would be seeing her father tomorrow. 'It will be fine, my darling,' he added. 'I'm an honorary Chinese, remember?'

It was how his staff thought of him and how he'd come to think of himself these past three and a half years. And what turbulent years they'd been. Not long after he and Connie were married, George and Jean had reappeared in Waichow. Will had asked George the reason for his arranging for Connie to be taken to a communist stronghold. Shamefaced, George had apologised and said they weren't meant to find out who she was. It had been Connie herself who'd let the cat out of the bag and then matters had got out of hand. But it had always been his intention for the reds to take possession of the Lewis guns. 'They're making a better job of fighting the Japanese than the bloody nationalists,' George had muttered.

Subsequently, Will learnt that Z Force had been disbanded because the Chinese wouldn't give them permission to operate with arms and explosives in the communist guerrilla-held areas. The nationalists feared that the reds would obtain money, arms, equipment or training from the SOE group, which would ultimately be used against them. Not long after he'd returned to Waichow, George Robinson was ordered to leave China. No doubt the nationalists had found out where his sympathies lay. At least Jean and Connie had taken the opportunity to reconcile and promise to keep in touch. Last Will had heard, they were in India, where George was teaching commando tactics at the Force 136 Eastern Warfare School in Poona.

An unexpected arrival not long after the Robinsons had left, was Colonel Yiu, who'd managed to escape from Hong Kong and make his way north. But he hadn't stayed long. Will heard later that he'd fallen out with the Admiral over the money left behind in his wooden leg. Chang Wei had arranged for him to be jailed, but the Colonel had friends in high places and was subsequently released.

Two-gun Cohen had also made it out of Hong Kong, and could be found propping up various bars in Chungking, regaling anyone who would listen with stories about his adventurous life.

Will, Reggie, Mike and Nigel had been allowed to remain in Waichow, but only on the stringent proviso they would restrict themselves to carrying out escape and evasion work. They were directed to give the nationalists maximum credit in all operations and to take Chiang Kai Shek's miliary authorities into their complete confidence.

Will took a sip of champagne now and stole a glance at his nationalist brother-in-law, Matthew. From him, he'd learnt that the Kuomintang would have preferred that the BAAG had nothing to do with the communists, but they recognised that some contact between the two was necessary and inevitable if the aid group was to achieve its purpose. Whenever British co-operation with the reds was raised officially in Chungking it touched a raw nerve, by all accounts. Each time an escaper or evader arrived in Free China and whenever the BAAG wished to send missions into Hong Kong, the same problems and the same threats of expulsion were brought up anew.

Soon after the Robinsons had left the country, Will and Connie were transferred to Kweilin, their new headquarters. Will would never forget the beauty of the landscape, the jade waters and bamboo-lined banks of the Li River, where he and Connie lived on a houseboat in newly wedded bliss. Every evening they would watch the sun go down behind the cone-shaped karst hills and marvel at the glorious sight. Several hundred refugees were under their care, mostly Hong Kong Chinese, housed in barracks where they were fed and cared for. Connie worked tirelessly helping them while Will was out in the field.

Will glanced at her brothers, both tall handsome men who fought for their beliefs. Jonathan had become a BAAG agent soon after Will had managed to contact him when he'd taken charge of his own field operation group in Samfou, south-west of Canton, to oversee the escape route via Macau and Kwangsi province. There'd been no warning of the atom bomb on Hiroshima last year, but it was clear from news reports following the event that capitulation by Japan was imminent. The end toward which the BAAG had worked since its inception had been at hand. Will received a wireless message from the British Embassy in Chungking to pass a message to the senior Hong Kong Government official interned in the civilian camp, that he was to assume authority for the colony when the Japanese surrendered. Will got one of his agents to take the message to Jonathan in Macau, who arranged for one of his runners to convey it to Stanley. On 27$^{th}$ August, Rear-Admiral Harcourt received the official surrender of the Japanese Forces and a powerful British naval task force sailed into Hong Kong harbour three days later.

At the end of September, all BAAG posts were withdrawn from China and disbanded. Reggie flew home to the UK, where Deborah and her father had made it to safety. Reggie and Deborah were due to be married in the spring and planned to return to Hong Kong for Reggie to resume his job in the Department of Education. Will was looking forward to seeing him again. His other chums had also gone back to the UK on leave, including Harry and Margaret—who'd ended up interned in the Stanley Camp along with all the other British civilians. Will, too, would go home to see his family, taking Connie with him next month. But their plans for afterwards were still in abeyance.

Will sighed to himself. He'd yet to decide if he would go back to his old job. It would depend on how he got on at the meeting with Sir Albert. He led Connie across the room to bid farewell to the Admiral. They'd remained in Canton after Chang Wei, on a new false leg, had marched at the head of the Chinese Army's triumphant re-entry procession into the city last autumn. Because the British Embassy had not yet had time to send a Consul-General, Will had been asked to handle temporarily all consular duties in the area. It took nearly two months for a permanent consular official to arrive, and then Will had agreed to stay on as provisional Liaison Officer. His and Connie's close relations with Mayor Chang Wei had helped cement British-Chinese relations.

But finally, the time had come for them to focus on their own family relations. Jonathan had assured Will and Connie that Sir Albert's attitude had softened after Will had helped arrange for Connie's brothers-in-law to escape from Hong Kong. He hoped fervently that Jonathan wasn't mistaken. Connie had given up so much for him, but Will knew she wouldn't be entirely happy until she'd made peace with her father.

It was raining when they arrived in Macau late the next morning. Will eyed the sampans and junks clustered along the foreshore as Jonathan's driver took them towards the southern tip of the peninsula on which the Portuguese enclave was situated. Many of the buildings in the beautiful old terraces were crumbling into decay, and the whole place had a neglected air about it. Will had been here before the Japanese had arrived and not much had changed—except for the fact there were more beggars lining the avenues than he'd remembered.

Connie squeezed his hand nervously. 'Don't worry,' he said with more confidence than he felt. 'Your father loves you as you love him. How can he not accept your decision to marry me?'

'I hope you are right, my dearest,' she said.

Jonathan, who was riding shotgun, chipped in. 'I'll drop you both off, then I need to attend to business in my casino. Things are only just starting to get back to some normality...'

Will thanked him. Macau, although neutral in the war, had been inundated with Japs, who'd put a blockade around the territory and paraded their soldiers and the *Kempetai*, their secret police, openly in the streets. But at least the British Consulate had remained open, and Sir Albert and his family had managed to survive.

Jonathan's Rolls Royce was taking them along a boulevard lined with banyan trees and up a small hill. Soon they'd arrived in front of a white, elegant nineteenth century three-storey building of neo-classical architecture with a black-tiled roof. The rain had stopped and a rainbow spread across the pale blue sky. Quite fitting, Will thought as the car rolled to a halt.

A short flight of steps led to a big wooden door that suddenly burst open, and a group of women came rushing out. Connie's mothers and her sisters, her father's concubine and the omnipresent Gloria, who hadn't been able to return to the UK as planned.

Connie jumped out of the car and raced into their arms, hugging and kissing them.

Will followed and strode forward, smiling.

'Will.' She turned and reached out for him. 'Come and meet my family.'

He'd seen the Han Fungs before at the races, but up close the women were even more lovely. They shook his hand and smiled warmly. The first hurdle overcome. *Phew!* Now for the hardest. Sir Albert.

'Father is waiting for you both in his study,' Mary, Connie's eldest sister, said. 'Oh, and thank you, Will, for your help with getting my husband out of Hong Kong. My sisters will also thank you personally.'

'You're more than welcome,' he said. Chinese and Eurasian members of the Volunteers were released from the POW camps in September 1942 on condition they would stay in the colony and not talk about their experiences. It had been quite a feat to arrange for Connie's in-laws' escape and it was one of Will's proudest achievements.

Connie took his hand and led him across the porcelain tiled hall. She knocked at a teak panelled door. 'Come in,' a voice said in Cantonese.

Will walked across a deep piled carpet with her to where Sir Albert was sitting in a plush armchair, smoking. He glanced up at them. 'So, you've finally decided to visit me, daughter.' His dark eyes raked over Will. 'And this is your husband, I presume?'

Connie squeezed Will's fingers, and he felt her tremble. 'Yes, Father.'

Sir Albert indicated the sofa in front of him. 'Sit. Both of you.'

The soft cushions gave way beneath them.

Will cleared his throat. 'I'm truly honoured to meet you,' he said. The Cantonese words tripped easily off his tongue.

'Humph. I heard you speak our language like a native. And that you've fully immersed yourself in our culture, unlike most of your countrymen.'

Will carried on speaking Chinese. 'I love your daughter, Sir. With all my heart.'

'As I love Will,' Connie said. 'We've come to ask for your blessing.'

Sir Albert huffed again. 'You should have asked for that before you married a foreigner. But I do understand how impossible that was in the circumstances.' His steely gaze swept over Will again. 'I heard you rescued Connie from the communists?'

Will nodded, his throat suddenly dry.

'He's such a brave man, Father. He helped a lot of people escape from Hong Kong during the Japanese occupation.'

'Don't speak about your husband as if he wasn't here, daughter. I'm sure he can speak for himself.'

Will leant forward. 'Connie worked with me, Sir Albert. She gave tirelessly of herself, helping the refugees.'

# THE FLAME TREE

Connie's father laughed. 'And now you speak for her. What a pair you are!' His eyes twinkled. 'So, William. What are you planning to do now that you are no longer with the BAAG?'

'I'm due some leave, so I'd like to take Connie to England to meet my family. But Hong Kong is home to us both, so we'll return in due course.'

'And what will you do then?'

'I'm in two minds. Either I'll take up my old job with the colonial service or I'll set up an import-export business...'

'Hmm. If you decide on the latter, I'd be more than willing to invest in a new venture.'

'Oh, Father, that would be wonderful,' Connie said.

'Well, I've helped your brothers-in-law in their businesses. It would be unfair if I didn't lend your husband a hand getting started.' He pulled a wry face. 'Even if he is a foreigner.'

Warmth spread through Will. 'I'd be extremely grateful, Sir. If that's what I decide to do...'

'I think you probably should,' Sir Albert said. 'All the bomb damage in Hong Kong is being repaired. We'll return as soon as my houses have been renovated. I've promoted Fah Wong to be the site supervisor, by the way. In recognition for his services to the family while we were away. There will be many opportunities for us all as the colony recovers.' He chuckled. 'But we can iron out the details later.' He pushed himself to his feet. 'Let us go and join your mothers and sisters,' he said. 'They're waiting in the dining room and I, for one, am ravenous.'


After lunch, Connie and Will retired to her old bedroom for a rest. 'That went so much better than I dared hope it would,' she said.

He sat on a chair and pulled her onto his lap. 'What did I tell you? Your father loves you and would never do anything to upset you.'

'I know. He's spoilt me since I was little. But I couldn't help being worried. I mean, he wanted to arrange a marriage for me...'

Will kissed her on the forehead, then tucked a strand of hair behind her ear. 'I think the war has changed a lot of things, my darling. Your father's attitude especially.'

She gazed into his eyes. 'I suppose so. I wonder if attitudes in Hong Kong will be any different towards mixed marriages?'

'Ah, that might take some time...'

'Well, I hope it doesn't take too long. I mean, I'd like our baby to grow up in a world without prejudice.'

'Connie?! You're not...' They'd only stopped using contraception recently.

Her eyes shone with happiness. 'Yes, Will. I'm pregnant. I was waiting to tell you until after we'd seen Father. Baby will arrive in about seven months from now.'

He wrapped his arms around her, then stroked her back, her arms, her head. God, she was beautiful. Her skin so smooth. Her hair so silky. 'I love you, my darling. I'm so proud of you and I can't wait to meet our daughter.'

'So, you believe we'll have a girl first?'

'Just a feeling. Of course, I'll love our son too.'

'How many children do you think we'll have?' She giggled.

'At least two, Connie. More if you want them.'

She nestled into him, yawning. 'I'm so sleepy.' She sighed. 'I think our baby would like a snooze.'

Tenderly, he lifted her, carried her over to the double bed and joined her, cuddling up behind her.

'Thank you, Will,' she said as he smoothed her hair.

'For what?' he asked.

'For... loving me. I've never felt so happy.'

# THE FLAME TREE

'Me too, sweetheart.'

He kissed her head and held her close, savouring her scent, her warmth. Soon she fell asleep, but Will's mind was too alert to do the same. Quietly, he went over to his suitcase, unbuckled the straps and retrieved his writing case. Then went over to the desk. The latest draft of a poem he was writing only needed a few finishing touches. He picked up his pen with a contented smile.

## SIOBHAN DAIKO

*That day I first saw you*
*You brushed past*
*And your scent lingered*
*With your enchanting smile*
*Your intoxicating aroma*
*Filled my heart with desire*
*Driving me mad with longing*
*For you.*
*Your perfume*
*So delicate and sweet*
*In summer reminding me of garden flowers*
*In winter the warmth of jasmine*
*But always uniquely yours*
*So you.*
*When I catch your scent, my dearest love*
*I feel as if I've come home*
*And your perfume becomes*
*My refuge*
*Your delightful aroma*
*My only abode.*

# THE FLAME TREE

I hope you have enjoyed reading *The Flame Tree* as much as I loved writing it and, if you did, I'd be hugely grateful if you'd take the time to rate it and even write a short review. I'd love to hear what you think, and it will help new readers decide to take the plunge and discover one of my books for the first time.

The first standalone book in the collection, *The Orchid Tree*, is available from your favourite online store and the next story in the series, *The Jacaranda Tree*, will release in the summer of 2024. In the meantime, a new Siobhan Daiko Italian World War II historical novel will be published by Boldwood Books in November 2023.

Turn over a few pages to read an extract from *The Orchid Tree*.

# AUTHOR'S NOTE

*The Flame Tree* is inspired by a true story, the real-life Chinese Admiral Chan Chak's Christmas Day dash from Hong Kong in 1941. He is such an inspiring character, and I couldn't help basing my fictional admiral on him. The events described in Tim Luard's fascinating book, "Escape from Hong Kong", formed the framework for my tale. I also read the diary of Colin McEwan, made available by his daughter on the Gwulo website, which informed me of the actions carried out by Z Force.

Although *The Flame Tree* is based on historical events, all my characters are fictional—except for those in the public domain.

With respect to the spelling of Chinese names and cities, I've used the orthography that was current in the 1940s.

The following books have provided me with inspiration and information:

Alan Birch & Martin Cole, *Captive Christmas*
Vicky Lee, *Being Eurasian*
Tim Luard, *Escape from Hong Kong*
Gwen Priestwood, *Through Japanese Barbed Wire*
Han Suyin, *A Many Splendoured Thing*

# EXTRACT FROM THE ORCHID TREE

*Hong Kong 1941 and the streets are filled with Japanese soldiers. Two young people are brought together then separated by terrible cruelty.*
*Fifteen-year-old Kate lives a rarefied life of wealth and privilege in the pre-war Hong Kong expatriate community, but when the Japanese invade she's interned in squalid Stanley Camp with her parents.*
*Enduring cramped conditions, humiliation, disease, and starvation, Kate befriends seventeen-year-old Charles, who is half Chinese, and they give their hearts to each other under the orchid tree.*
*Meanwhile, forty miles away in Portuguese Macau, thirteen-year-old Sofia's suspicions are aroused when her father invites a Japanese family to dinner, an event which leads to a breach between Sofia and her controlling half-brother, Leo.*
*In December 1948, adult Kate returns to Hong Kong, determined to put the past behind her. Sofia dreams of leaving Macau and starting a new life, and she won't let anyone, not even Leo, stop her. A young Englishman, James, becomes the link between Kate and Sofia. The communist-nationalist struggle in China spills over into the colony, catapulting the protagonists into the turmoil with disastrous consequences.*

# SIOBHAN DAIKO

*Kate, Hong Kong, December 1941*

Bamboo by the side of the path rustles in the breeze, and a waterfall gurgles into a natural pond. My pony bends his head to crop the grass. I let go of the reins and slip off my riding hat. It's time for a rest now. Papa and I set out from the stables at Jardine's Lookout an hour ago and have ridden right round Happy Valley.

After dismounting, I run my hands over the smooth leather of my saddle. It's too small since my recent growth spurt; I'm such a beanpole.

I glance at my father. 'Papa, do you think I can have a new one for Christmas?' I give him my best smile.

'We'll see.' He winks and reaches into his pocket for his pipe. Papa is tall with wavy dark-brown hair, amber-coloured eyes and a high forehead. I adore him, of course, but hate taking after him. I wish I'd been born blonde and blue-eyed like my beautiful mama.

Rubbing Merry's dusty chestnut neck, I breathe in the sweet scent of equine sweat, one of my favourite smells. Of course, Papa will get me the saddle. Mama says I'm spoilt rotten and it's true. Only Papa does the spoiling, though . . .

'Come on, Kate,' he says. 'I need to change my breath.' Papa says that every week and it's become a joke between us. All he really wants is a change of scene. We remount and trot back to the stables, then stop off at the Yacht Club on the way home.

Papa goes to the bar, but I'm not allowed in there as I'm not sixteen yet. So I wait outside the clubhouse, soaking up the winter sunshine and watching the junks in the harbour, their sails open like giant butterfly wings. The creak of an oar echoes as the boatwoman selling orchids from her sampan sculls across the water. She ties up at the jetty and steps ashore with

# THE FLAME TREE

a bouquet in her hands. I smile at the baby, head lolling but fast asleep, in a sling on her back. Then I pay the woman and clutch the purple flowers. I'll give them to Mama, like I do every Sunday. And Mama will nod, smile, and hand them to one of the servants as usual. Far be it for her to put them in a vase herself.

The scrunch of foot falls on gravel come from the path behind, and Papa arrives. 'All the chaps have been called up for manoeuvres,' he says in a false jaunty tone. 'I was practically the only one in there.'

A prickle of anxiety creeps up my spine. With a sharp intake of breath, I grasp his hand.

'Nothing to worry about, dear girl.'

I relax my shoulders and walk with him towards the pier.

The next morning air-raid sirens wail from Victoria City far below. I stifle a yawn, thinking it's only another drill. I pull at my maroon school jumper and lean back at the breakfast table opposite Mama and Papa. There's a geography test in this afternoon's class and I wonder if I've done enough revision.

A pang of disquiet disturbs my equilibrium. Something's different. The sirens are wailing longer than usual and a droning sound echoes. The door bursts open and my amah erupts into the room.

I eye the chopping knife in my old nanny's hand. Ah Ho has been a constant presence for as long as I can remember, yet never have I seen her take a knife from the kitchen.

Rocking from one foot to the other, Ah Ho drops the blade onto the table and wraps her arms around her starched white tunic. 'Too much air-plane,' she says in a shrill tone of voice. 'Too much air-plane.'

Leaping up, I send my chair crashing to the floor. Hong Kong only has a few aeroplanes. Are these intruders American? Or even Chinese? Not Japanese, though. That would be unthinkable. Besides, everyone knows how hopeless their pilots are . . .

I rush through the wide doors and onto the veranda skirting the front of the house. Planes soar in a V-shaped formation above the harbour almost level with my eyes. Grey planes with a red sun under their wings. Something, I'm not sure what, spills from their bellies.

The echoes of explosions ricochet off the distant hills. Papa comes up and pulls me towards him. 'Bally hell!' His grip is so firm that it hurts.

My gut twists and the orange juice I drank at breakfast comes back up my throat, the sourness stinging my tongue. A flying boat is on fire. Coils of smoke rise from the airport. I clamp my hands to my ears, a sick feeling spreading through me.

Papa's hold tightens. I push my head into his shirt; I've recently turned fifteen and haven't done that for years. Then I lift my gaze. One by one, the planes tilt their wings and peel off in the direction of China. 'Is it over?' I manage to ask.

Papa shields his eyes with a hand, his knuckles white. 'I hope so.' He leads me back into the house.

In the dining room I run to Mama. She stands at the picture window, her lower lip trembling. I squeeze her icy fingers. 'They've gone.'

Mama blinks, takes her hands away and shakes her bobbed hair. 'Why on earth did you run outside?'

'I don't know. I just had to see. Where's Ah Ho?'

'She went to find Jimmy.'

He's Ah Ho's son, one year older than me and a close friend. Breathing in short, sharp bursts, I run after my amah.

*Pray God Jimmy hasn't left for school yet!*

# Acknowledgments

I have so many people to thank for help in writing this book.

Firstly, I owe a debt of gratitude to my developmental editor, John Hudspith, truly "a doctor of words, a surgeon of writing".

Also thanks to Trenda Lundin, my content editor, for her comments on the final draft.

Huge thanks to my beta readers: Ann, Fiona, Joy, Luisa, and Nico for their helpful feedback on my chapters.

Thank you, also, to my cover designer, Jane Dixon Smith, for her fabulous design.

I'd like to thank my husband, Victor, for putting up with me spending hours at my laptop while I indulge my love of writing.

My family: my brother, Diarmuid, and my sister, Clodagh, for their encouragement. Also my son, Paul, and his wife, Lili, for their help with technology.

Last, but not least, I thank you, dear reader, for buying this book and reading it.

# ABOUT THE AUTHOR

Siobhan Daiko is a British historical fiction author. A lover of all things Italian, she lives in the Veneto region of northern Italy with her husband, a Havanese dog and a rescued cat. Siobhan was born of English parents in Hong Kong, attended boarding school in Australia, and then moved to the UK—where she taught modern foreign languages in a Welsh high school. She now spends her time writing page-turners and enjoying her life near Venice. Her novels are compelling, poignant, and deeply moving, with strong characters and evocative settings, but always with romance at their heart. You can find more about her books on her website www.siobhandaiko.org

# ALSO BY SIOBHAN DAIKO

The Girl from Bologna

The Girl from Portofino

The Girl from Venice

Lady of Venezia

Veronica Courtesan (Erotic Novella)

The Orchid Tree

Printed in Great Britain
by Amazon